Lorraine Heath's unforgettable books have thrilled her countless readers. Now, she's created her most breathtaking story of all . . .

Innocent Angela Bainbridge's dreams of a fairy-tale wedding and finding pleasure in a man's embrace can never come true. So when she's swept into the arms of—and kidnapped by—notorious renegade Lee Raven she's both righteously angry . . . and curiously captivated. This brazen outlaw awakens Angela's passions, but she realizes that a lifetime together with Lee can never be . . .

Lee Raven knows he's only two steps ahead of the law. But Angela has him longing for more than a life on the run. She's made it clear that she's determined to discover all of his secrets—but how can he let her learn what's hidden in his past? And how can he let her give him her heart today, when he can't even promise her tomorrow?

"Heath is known for her deft characterizations, attention to historical detail and mastery of small moments."

Publishers Weekly

LORRAINE HEATH

The Outlaw and The Lady

An Avon Romantic Treasure

AVON BOOKS
An Imprint of HarperCollinsPublishers

AVON BOOKS
An Imprint of HarperCollins*Publishers*
10 East 53rd Street
New York, New York 10022-5299

Copyright © 2001 by Jan Nowasky
ISBN: 0-7394-2050-X

For my granddad Jacka,
who fixed me tomato sandwiches,
took me hiking in English woods,
taught me how to protect my valuables from pickpockets,
and often remarked, "I'm ever so glad I come this way."
I'm ever so glad you did as well.

In loving memory

Chapter 1

Fortune, Texas
1891

*L*ee Raven.

For as long as he could remember, the name had swirled like a gray mist at the edge of his memories. Hauntingly familiar, but elusive. He couldn't comprehend its significance or understand why it hovered just beyond his grasp.

He only knew that it was the name he'd chosen to use the night he died.

It suited his purposes well. It did not hint at his beloved heritage, family, or roots. No one associated the name with him. Only his family knew what he looked like. As far as the world was concerned, the naïve, trusting boy he had been was long dead.

The man who had risen up from the depths of hell to take his place instilled terror within those who dared to whisper his name. Some believed he was Diablo, others thought he was a phantom. How close they all were to touching the truth. His charred soul made him hollow throughout, merely a shell of what he had once been.

Standing in the bank, surrounded by a shroud of darkness, he acknowledged once again that only fools wallowed in a past that could not be changed. He had chosen his path, fully understanding its consequences. Given the choice, he would choose to follow that road again.

Calmness settled over him as he pressed his ear against the cool metal door of the bank vault. In the dim light cast by the low flame in his lantern, he concentrated on the task at hand. His first order of business upon entering the bank had been to hang blankets over the windows so no light escaped into the night. The covering also prevented the soft glow of the street's gaslights from silhouetting any activities within the building. He found modernized towns to be a thoroughly aggravating nuisance.

He rubbed his thumb across his fingertips before flexing his fingers repeatedly. Taking a deep breath and holding it, he very slowly turned the dial with practiced ease, listening intently for the audible click. He stilled as the first set of tumblers fell into place.

He rotated the dial in the opposite direction. The tumblers immediately dropped, and he froze.

They thought they could trick him. *Estúpido*. Obviously, they didn't have a clue as to exactly how accomplished he was.

He turned the dial until he heard the final clink. Smiling with satisfaction, he unfolded his lean body, cranked down the handle, and swung open the door to the vault. He stepped aside, a gallant wave of his hand serving as an invitation to those who'd stolen into the bank with him. "*Hombres*."

"I don't know how you do that," Alejandro whispered reverently as he peered cautiously into the dark cavern.

"I am a man of many talents," Lee assured his brother with a slap on his broad back. Slightly older, Alejandro did not possess Lee's relentless resolve for revenge. Lingering within death's shadow, he had not witnessed everything that Lee had that fateful night. It was one thing to hear tell of all that had happened. It was another to have the images emblazoned on his memory, to hear forever the anguished cries and unacknowledged pleas for mercy, to always see the glistening blood. Too damned much blood. "Get the money."

"How much do we take?" Jorge asked with his typical reckless eagerness. At eighteen, he was the youngest of the group. He worshipped the scent of retribution only because he could not forget the rancid odor of defeat.

"Two thousand two hundred ninety-nine dollars and thirty-seven cents," Lee told them.

Alejandro groaned. "Can't we just make it an even twenty-three hundred?"

"No. That is not how much Shelby put in the bank," Lee explained as he did each time they visited a vault.

"Why do you think he chose this particular bank?" Roberto asked. Older than Jorge, not as old as Alejandro, he was always solemn, always inquisitive. "It is far from his ranch."

Lee shrugged, feigning disinterest. No reason to worry his brothers with the truth. The farther they were from home, the more likely Shelby's henchmen could capture them. He'd been surprised that he'd had only one man—skulking in the shadows like the vermin he was—to subdue outside the building.

Shelby tended to surround himself with minions similar to himself, rabid animals who took with no thought of giving. The other men he'd hired were no doubt sleeping the night away in the hotel, their failure to protect the money to be reckoned with, come dawn.

"The bastard is trying to find a safe haven for his money, but as long as I live, no such place exists." He jerked his head toward the vault. "*Ándale.*"

His jangling spurs disturbingly loud, he strode confidently across the bank, the only other sound the muffled hush as his brothers quickly filled their burlap sacks. When he reached the bank president's desk, he pulled the stopper off the inkwell. He retrieved a piece of paper from a nearby stack and dipped a pen into the black ink. He hastily scribbled a message similar to the dozen he had left in other banks.

*$2,299.37 has been withdrawn from the account
of Vernon Shelby compliments of . . .*

With a flourish, he scrawled his signature. *Lee
Raven.* He plucked a raven's feather from the
leather band circling his black Stetson and positioned it directly below his name. His calling
card. Arrogant, he knew, but it ensured no one
else paid the price he owed for his crimes.

Angela Bainbridge flattened her ear against the
cool glass of the saloon window. She heard her father's boisterous laughter echo into the night, the
deep rumble as telling as the cards he dealt. He'd
allowed someone to win a hand at faro. If the re-
cipient of his good humor was a smart man, he'd
take his winnings and head home. The next
round of Bucking the Tiger would not find her father so generous.

She pushed her palm against the windowsill
until the wood bit into her tender flesh. How she
longed to stand beside him and deal cards. When
she was a child, he'd promised that she could
work with him in the saloon. He was convinced
she'd inherited his gift for manipulation. At the
age of five she'd been adept at stacking a deck; at
six she'd mastered false shuffles and cuts; at
seven she'd excelled at keeping track of the cards
played and determining which ones remained
available; at eight she'd been proficient at gauging the odds of winning by analyzing the cards
that had been revealed.

When she was twelve, her father had made her

a special deck of marked cards. From that moment on, she'd known that she'd never ask him to keep his promise, understood that she'd never touch her dream of being a dealer at the Texas Lady.

She realized it was ridiculous to long for things that could never be, knew she should appreciate what she had. After recently acquiring a position as a seamstress at Damsels in Dis Dress, she had independence. She'd moved into a room at the boardinghouse. She still visited with her family frequently, and she spent every Sunday afternoon at her parents' home, listening as her two younger sisters waxed poetic about the young men seeking their favors.

Her routine was comfortable, dependable ... utterly boring. Not at all what the daughter of a woman who had struck out on a cattle drive in 1866 had envisioned for herself as she'd grown up. She wanted to make her mark on this state as her mother, her father, and their friends had done. Pioneers in farming, ranching, business enterprises, and law enforcement.

Instead she sewed fancy bodices and bell skirts. Hardly her idea of making a notable contribution to society.

Her father's laughter rang out, and she smiled at the warmth and triumph within it. He'd won that round. She knew if she asked that he'd allow her to sit beside him, but if she couldn't command the deck, she didn't want to hear the shuffle.

With a deep sigh of acceptance for the yearnings that would remain unfulfilled, she stepped onto the boardwalk and remembered the festivities that had taken place the day that the township installed the gaslights along the main street of Fortune.

Her father's friend Grayson Rhodes had held her high above his head so she could touch the glass globe. Her father would have lifted her, but an injury he'd suffered years ago had left him with a weakened hip and in constant pain. Although he never complained, the grooves on his face were deeper than the lines that added character to the faces of his friends. Admiring her father as she did, she followed his example and never grumbled about her own limitations. She understood them and dealt with them, but inwardly she resented the hell out of them.

As she walked briskly along, she briefly touched the Indian statue that stood outside the general store. The chiseled features intrigued her, and she often trailed her fingers over the intricately carved wood. Her heels clicked along the boardwalk, her skirt whispering over the worn planks. As though she had a beau calling upon her, she always donned her finest favorite green dress for her midnight strolls. She had a keen fascination with men, but they had little interest in her.

She strolled past the millinery. Perhaps tomorrow she would order a new hat with bright, colorful ribbons and an emerald bow. As the boardwalk ended, she strode onto the dirt path that led to the alley between the shop and the bank, the ground muffling her footsteps. Somewhere down the alley, a horse snorted and struck a hoof impatiently at the ground.

Strange. Most horses were tethered at the saloon this time of night if they weren't boarded at the blacksmith's.

Perhaps Mr. Sims, the bank president, was working late—although she thought it more likely that he was illicitly stuffing his pockets with money before heading to her father's gaming tables.

Her father often questioned the man's penchant for gambling, thinking it an unseemly habit for a man who was responsible for handling others' money. Yet in spite of her father's concerns, he never turned Mr. Sims away from his table.

Then she heard the door leading into the bank open with a rush of hushed movements and jangling spurs. Someone rammed into her. She teetered backward before catching her balance. "I'm sorry—"

"Goddamn it!"

That deep whiskey voice, that Mexican accent, did not belong to anyone who worked at the bank. Panic surged through her as comprehension dawned instantly. She'd inadvertently stumbled across a bank robbery. She took another quick step back, fully intending to beat a hasty retreat, but a strong hand wrapped around her arm and yanked her forward.

"No!" She bucked wildly.

Everything happened at once. Her arms were pinned to her sides, soft cotton, no doubt this vile man's bandanna, was shoved into her mouth, and her feet skipped over the boardwalk as he hauled her away.

"What are you doing?" another man with a thick Mexican accent asked.

"The street lamps, goddamn it! She saw my face. She knows what I look like."

Angela shook her head frantically and twisted her body in an attempt to gain her freedom, but the iron band of his arms only tightened as he dragged her into the alley. She heard the restless horses tamping the ground, their harsh breathing filling the air.

"Lee, you can't take her with us," the other man pointed out.

Lee? Lee Raven! Was it possible that the one who held a death grip on her was the notorious outlaw? Dear Lord, help her! She had to escape.

"I have no choice," he said.

Like a hellion, she fought to break loose of his unrelenting grasp, tried to cry out.

"Be quiet, *señorita.* I am not going to hurt you," he said in a low voice.

Not hurt her? The man was a murderer, a thief. She knew all about his harrowing reputation. Her heart pounded so hard that she was surprised her father didn't hear it.

For an insane instant, before she realized what his plans were, he released her. She quickly jabbed her elbow into his gut, finding brief satisfaction in his grunt. She managed two rapid steps, barely skimming her fingers across the cloth in her mouth before he wrenched her arms behind her back. She growled her protest against the gag while he wrapped another bandanna tightly around her wrists. Bending over, she kicked back, frustrated that she couldn't connect the heel of her shoe with this desperado's shin.

"*Señorita*, do not fight me," he ordered.

Don't fight him? She'd damn well kill him if she got the opportunity!

She didn't know how the man managed it, but he tossed her on his horse, quickly mounted behind her, formed a barrier around her with his arms, and grabbed the reins. "*Vámonos, hombres!*"

The horse burst into a gallop, the wind slapping Angela's face. The only things keeping her from falling and being crushed beneath the pounding hooves were the strong arm he'd snaked around her waist, the firm thighs she was nestled between, and the paralyzing fear that she was now at this murderer's mercy.

And from the tales she'd heard, he possessed no mercy.

Chapter 2

Dawn was just beginning to emerge as Lee brought his horse to a halt in a small clearing, hidden by an abundance of trees, far from the main road. The woman sitting before him had stopped struggling, but small tremors continued to cascade through her slender body. Slender, but ah, the soft, rounded curves. Enticing, just the way he enjoyed them. Calling for a man's hands to cradle them, knead them . . .

Swearing harshly beneath his breath, he threw his long leg back and dismounted. The last thing he needed right now was a woman. It was not in his nature to panic. What in the hell had he been thinking to haul her away with him? What did it matter that she'd seen his face? He'd known sooner or later that his identity would be revealed. He couldn't keep it hidden forever, no matter how diligently he avoided those who might recognize him. As it was, he'd had five years in the grave. But he had plans for his resurrection that did not include some woman describing him accurately to the Texas Rangers.

Damn it! His repeated successes had led him to believe he didn't need to wear a mask for a night job. Arrogant. Incredibly arrogant. He'd paid the price for it tonight.

He glanced at his brothers, who remained mounted. "What are you staring at? Prepare a meal. It will be our last before we ride like the wind. Roberto, see to the horses."

He reached up and wrapped his hands around the woman's waist. Such a tiny waist. She stiffened. "I am not going to hurt you, *señorita*. I swear to God on my mother's grave."

Gently, he brought her to the ground, her body scant inches from his, her chest—heaving with each breath that she took—coming incredibly close to skimming across his. She stared up at him with the greenest eyes he'd ever seen. Beautiful eyes. Innocent eyes. "I am sorry, *señorita*. I made a mistake but I promise I will find a way to fix it."

Carefully he pulled his red bandanna from her mouth.

"You damn well better, you worthless son of a bitch," she snapped.

He quirked a brow in surprise. Maybe not so innocent after all. Fire sparked within those emerald eyes, and he imagined them directed his way, smoldering with the flames of passion. He shook his head in an effort to clear his mind. What was he thinking?

"I'm going to untie your hands, but if you try to run, I will be forced to take drastic measures. *Comprendes*?"

In answer, she quickly spun around, presenting him with her back, impatiently jiggling her hands up and down as much as she was able in what he knew was an uncomfortable position. He unwound Alejandro's bandanna, freeing her from its restraint. She swung her hands forward and rubbed her wrists. Guilt surging through him for the discomfort he'd caused, he touched her shoulder with the intent to offer comfort, perhaps rub her wrists himself, but she twirled around, her eyes shooting daggers that would have wounded a lesser man.

"Keep your bloody hands off me!"

As though she'd slapped him, he jerked back and held out his hands. "There is no blood on them." A thousand scrubbings had washed it away. "Why do you say they are bloody?"

She rolled her eyes as though he had no more sense than a fence post. "It's an expression... like 'damned.' "

"So it is profanity?"

"Yes, British in nature. My father and his friends use it constantly. Bloody. Bloody hell. Bloody damned. Bloody damned hell." She fired each word with the precision of a well-aimed bullet.

He bore his gaze into her, a practiced look that

caused most men to flinch. She simply ignored him. "*Señorita*, I think you use too much profanity."

"I truly don't think you're the one to instruct me in the art of social graces."

Her words struck a nerve. What did he know about the finer aspects of life except that he longed for them? "Make yourself useful. Gather up some kindling for a small fire."

He was surprised when she slowly turned, stepped forward, reached down, and picked up a twig. He did not quite trust her acquiescence. She had been fighting like a wildcat outside the bank. He had a feeling she was gauging her surroundings, plotting her escape. He would have to watch her vigilantly, but that chore would be no hardship.

Roberto grabbed the reins of Lee's horse and led him away. Lee sauntered to a nearby tree. Leaning against it, he studied the woman. Her red hair had been caught up into a neat bun when he'd rammed into her in front of the bank. Now it had fallen to one side, threatening to spill free of the pins that held it in place. He was incredibly tempted to help it along, remove the pins, and watch it cascade over her shoulders, along her back.

Bending to pick up more twigs, she unwittingly gave him the pleasure of gazing at her small, rounded backside covered by the finest of materials. Perfection.

She bolted upright and glared over her shoulder at him as though she knew exactly where he'd been staring. Arching a brow, he flashed a cocky grin. She snapped her head around and dragged her feet as though she was a mutinous little girl who'd just been punished. He did not think she was afraid as much as she was angry. For some strange reason, that knowledge pleased him.

Alejandro snatched his bandanna from Lee's fingers before tilting his head toward the woman. "What are you going to do with her?"

Lee shook his head. "I don't know."

"What were you thinking to drag her off?"

He sighed heavily. "For five years no one has seen my face. I wanted to protect my identity. In retrospect, a stupid move."

"Hurry up, *puta*!" Jorge called out. "We don't have much time."

"Jorge!" Lee scolded. "Do not call her that, *hombre*. It does not make you tough. It only makes you mean."

"We are outlaws. We are supposed to be mean," Jorge retorted like a petulant child before crouching to set the branches he'd gathered into place.

"I told you not to bring him," Alejandro said.

"What choice did I have? He was shadowing our trail. I would rather have him where I can see him than find out that he is in trouble and I cannot get there in time to save him."

"You saved us once," Alejandro said quietly. "You cannot save us always."

"I can try. I owe it to the memory of our parents to always try."

"They would not expect you—"

"I expect it of myself, Alejandro. That is the way of it."

Lee returned his attention to the woman. She was incredibly slow at gathering kindling, shuffling her feet along the ground. He smiled with the knowledge that she was attempting to stall them. She lurched forward and quickly caught her balance.

"She will slow us down," Alejandro said.

"*Sí*. If we have to, we will split up."

"That is a very nice dress she is wearing," Alejandro murmured. "Perhaps she has a rich husband who will pay a ransom for her."

"She has no husband," Lee assured him—and she had far too much green material. The puffy sleeves had gotten in his way when he'd struggled to subdue her. The bodice rose to her neck, where a collar circled her throat, every button snugly secure. She only exposed the flesh of her face and hands, and yet she was a temptation he could not explain. Perhaps because she left too much to a man's imagination. Yet he had a feeling that once a man saw what was beneath all that cloth, he would work diligently to keep it uncovered. "She would have been warming his bed, not walking the streets at midnight."

"You find her attractive?" Alejandro asked.

Incredibly so. More than her petite frame, her lush coloring, and her delicate features, he was attracted by the untamed spirit he'd felt in her when he'd first grabbed her. She was no simpering female willing to follow. She would fight tooth and nail to achieve what she wanted, and right now she craved freedom. He did not trust her, but she lured him like a siren's song. "She is not so hard on the eyes."

"Her hair is too red for my taste," Alejandro said.

"I like her hair. It reminds me of . . ." Something teased his memory, a glimpse into a past he could not remember. Quickly unveiled only to be hidden once again.

"What? What does it remind you of?" Alejandro asked.

Lee shook his head. "The flames dancing in a fire."

"Then you must be careful, brother. With her, you could get burned."

A price he imagined any man without a bounty on his head would be more than willing to pay. He was damned near tempted himself as he watched the morning shafts of sunlight tease her hair and play over the delicate slope of her shoulders. She stumbled again.

"She is a clumsy one," Alejandro remarked.

Narrowing his eyes, Lee studied her more closely. She held out one hand as though to fend off an attacker, when the only thing before her was a copse of trees. She pitched forward once more.

"Damn it!" Lee barked. He shoved himself away from the tree, strode across the clearing, grabbed the woman's arm, and spun her around.

He raked his gaze over her and released a slew

of expletives designed to make Satan blush before announcing with disgust at his own stupidity, "She is not clumsy. She is blind! I had no reason to take her."

Chapter 3

"**I** am not blind!"

Denying the truth, Angela wrenched free of Lee Raven's unrelenting grasp. The derision in his voice—as though the knowledge he'd gained suddenly made her not worthy of abducting—rankled.

"It does not bother you to have a man standing before you who is not wearing a stitch of clothing?" he asked in a voice that reminded her of the manner in which whiskey burned her throat.

Bluff riddled his words; it was as worthless as a man holding nothing but daring to wager everything he possessed. She angled her chin defiantly and narrowed her eyes.

"You haven't removed your denim britches or your chambray shirt." Clothing that fit him so snugly she'd been able to feel the heat of his flesh penetrating her gown as they'd galloped away from Fortune.

"You accurately identified my clothing, *señorita*, but you do not know if I am still wearing it," he mused, and this time she heard the humor laced in his low-pitched voice and could almost envision him shaking his finger at her. "I bluff. You bluff. I bet you would make an excellent poker player."

"I'm one hell of a poker player," she snapped, having left her patience on the boardwalk outside the bank in Fortune. "And you can stop talking with that irritatingly fake Mexican accent."

"What?"

He sounded truly baffled, but she didn't think she'd read him wrong. Beneath his Mexican accent was a shadow of another, faint and distant. "I know you're not Mexican," she insisted.

"*Mi madre y mi padre* would argue otherwise. Eh, Alejandro?" Then he spewed off a tangle of Spanish that made her doubt her convictions, not that he necessarily had to be Mexican to speak so fluently.

The man he called Alejandro responded in kind. She identified his voice as belonging to the man who'd originally questioned Raven's actions outside the bank. Alejandro's voice carried no shadows, and she recognized the tone of familial love reverberating between them. Their apparent teasing banter made absolutely no sense to her, was contrary to her perception of desperadoes.

"Enough already!" she shouted, slashing her hand through the air. "You've made your point."

"Why didn't you tell me you were blind?" he demanded.

She dropped the pitiful bundle of twigs she'd gathered, planted her hands on her hips, and leaned forward slightly. "I tried, you idiot! But then you shoved that filthy piece of cloth—"

"Whoa! Whoa! Whoa, señorita. I gifted you with my favorite bandanna. I do not think you know who you are insulting."

"Lee Raven."

Silence, thick and heavy, permeated the air and she wondered if she'd been too brazen. To the disappointment of the few men who had deemed her worth courting, however briefly, docility had never been one of her character traits.

"Then you must know, señorita," he said silkily, "that it would behoove you to behave."

"It would behoove you to let me go. My father is an extremely influential man."

"Alejandro guessed that much. Perhaps your father would be willing to pay a handsome ransom to have you returned unharmed."

"What he will do," she said in a curt voice as though she were talking to someone who had nothing under his hat but hair, "is contact Captain Christian Montgomery of the Texas Rangers and have your head delivered to him on a silver platter."

"Kit Montgomery?" he asked mockingly. "Your father knows Kit Montgomery?"

"Yes. They're extremely close friends."

"Alejandro, her father knows the famous Kit Montgomery. Can you believe this?"

"Which means you've stepped into a pile of cow dung," Alejandro said.

She bit back her smile of satisfaction at the man's adequate description of the situation. Kit Montgomery's legends were indeed rooted in fact, which meant this outlaw's days of freedom were numbered.

"I don't think so," Raven said. "He is in west Texas. We are in south central Texas. We are safe."

"The hell you are. My father will send him a telegram, and Captain Montgomery won't hesitate to come."

Not only because he was her father's best friend, but because he, too, had experienced the anguish of losing a child. The grief rolled through her with the reminder, and she forced back the memory of her failure to protect his son.

She couldn't dwell on the past now. She had to focus on the present if she intended to play well this hand she'd unexpectedly been dealt. "He can track down a whisper in a strong wind."

"I'm shaking in my boots," he said caustically.

"I know. I can feel the ground trembling."

"But you cannot see me shaking," he said in a seductive voice, his breath skimming along her cheek. She resisted the urge to recoil at the intimate contact. She would not grant him the satisfaction of intimidating her.

"Your eyes are so expressive that for a moment I almost thought I was mistaken."

She wanted to slap his face, but she feared she might have already pushed her boundaries with this man to their limit. "You're right. I have ab-

solutely no earthly idea what you look like.
Therefore you have no reason to keep me."

This was a small lie. Based upon where her
head had hit his chest when he'd first grabbed
her, she knew he was an inch or so taller than her
father. Remembering the way his arms had come
around her on the horse, cradling her protec-
tively, she knew he had broad shoulders. A wash-
board stomach. Iron thighs. Gentle hands. His
hands had surprised her when he'd lifted her off
the horse as though he truly worried that he
might hurt her, and she could detect no tender
spots to indicate that he'd bruised her when he'd
fought to subdue her outside the bank.

"It is not that simple. The posse will be hours
behind us. I cannot leave you here unprotected,
and I won't wait for help to arrive and risk capture."

"I'll be perfectly fine waiting alone," she assured him.

"What happens when that rattler coiled over
there decides to move from the shade into the
sun?" he asked.

Honestly, how many times did the man think he
could bluff before she'd call? "There is no rattler."

She heard a popping sound, bones snapping as
though he'd crouched. A dull thud reverberated
as a small object hit a nearby tree, followed by a
sharp rattle, then the sickening swishing of something slithering along the ground.

An icy shiver rippled through her, and she
fought to keep her face a mask of stoicism while
her heart thudded against her ribs. "Apparently I

was mistaken about the snake, but he's gone now. I'll take my chances."

"It's not that simple," he repeated.

Anger surging through her, she latched onto the most improbable thing to say. "It *is* that simple. I'd rather take my chance with a poisonous snake than a vicious murderer!"

"Unfortunately, *señorita*, the decision is not yours to make."

Lee stared at the writhing flames of the small fire as Alejandro cooked the hare he'd managed to snare. Lee knew they would be wise to keep riding, but the horses needed to rest, and his brothers would do better with something in their stomachs. As for the woman . . .

He sighed, a useless release of breath that did nothing to assuage his concerns. He'd made many mistakes in his life, but this one was by far the stupidest. It would serve the contrary lady right if he abandoned her to her own devices. Unfortunately, his mother had raised him better than to do that to a woman. Even one who possessed a sharp tongue. He had been called the worst of names, but having her refer to him as a vicious murderer had cut deeply.

She sat on the ground nearby, her legs folded beneath her. Earlier she'd pulled a deck of cards from her skirt pocket. After shuffling with a grace that had amazed him, she had set about laying down cards, one after another, creating seven stacks. Now she flipped the cards over one at a time and rearranged them on the stacks. She looked incredibly peaceful ... yet her absolute absence of fear bothered him. A female who lacked apprehension was a dangerous thing.

He cursed harshly. They'd gotten such a good head start. She would slow them down. He had a feeling she would *deliberately* slow them down.

Alejandro removed his catch from the flames. Lee unfolded his body and sauntered to the fire. "Four ways."

Alejandro glanced up at him. "You have to eat."

His brother knew him too well. "Four ways," he insisted. He would not have his brothers take less because of his idiocy.

With a shake of his head, Alejandro began to divvy up the hare. "Could this situation get any worse?" He shot a look at the woman. "She is blind."

Lee shrugged. "She does not appear to be helpless."

"Her father is a friend of a legendary Texas Ranger."

Lee gave a brisk nod. "*That* could be a problem." He held up a hand when Alejandro opened his mouth. "But I will handle it."

"You should just leave her," Alejandro insisted. "That is what she wants, and what would be best for us."

"But it is as you say, Alejandro, she is blind." And so lovely that he found it difficult to breathe whenever he was near her. He took the tin plate Alejandro held out. "*Gracias.*"

He walked over to the woman and crouched before her.

"You need to rub some grease onto your knees," she said bluntly as she lifted the five of hearts and set it on the six of clubs.

"What?"

"Whenever you squat, your knees sound like a cork popping out of an old bottle of wine."

He glanced briefly at his bent legs. "I never noticed." He studied the cards she'd laid out. Red. Black. Red. Black. Red. Black. The ones showing were in order. Queens on top of kings. Jacks on top of queens. "How do you manage to do that when you cannot see?" he asked, mystified.

"My father marked the deck and taught me how to read it."

He raised a brow. "So your influential father is knowledgeable in the ways of cheating."

"He's a gambler. Right now, I imagine he's wagering on whether or not you'll beg for mercy before he kills you."

Anger rolled through him. "I do not beg, *señorita*. Not for any man or any thing."

She angled her chin and, with irritating calm, moved a card. "We'll see."

Her hands weren't even shaking. How could she not be terrified? She was the captive of the notorious Lee Raven, and she acted as though she were merely attending a Sunday afternoon picnic. Although he wanted only to instill terror in Shelby's heart, he thought this woman should show him a measure of respect and have a slight tremor in her voice. But no, she exhibited no signs of fear . . . but then, what did a person who lived in darkness fear? The light?

He touched her hand. With a grimace, she snatched it back. He barely acknowledged the insult because to do otherwise would force him to open himself up to hurt, and that he could not afford to do. "I have some food for you."

"I'm not hungry." She placed the four of spades on the five of hearts.

He sighed deeply with frustration. "You need to eat, *señorita*."

"I need to go home."

"I will take you home. Just not today."

She closed her eyes as though to shut out the world. He wondered why she did that when she couldn't see. She opened her eyes. Such a brilliant green. It was a sin that they could not see the beauty that surrounded them. "What were you doing walking the streets at midnight?" he asked quietly.

"None of your business."

He set the plate on her lap. "Eat. If you do not, I will. I would think you would prefer I know hunger rather than the satisfaction of a full belly."

He watched as she set the cards aside before gingerly touching her fingers to the plate, searching cautiously until she found a strip of meat. She brought it to the most luscious mouth he'd ever seen. He imagined her smile, how glorious it would look. And how she would never know.

"Stop staring at me," she ordered.

"How do you know I'm staring?"

"Because I didn't hear you leave and there's nothing else to look at."

"You are wrong, *señorita*. There are many things to gaze at: the sky, the trees, and the mockingbird in the nest with her babies."

"Three babies," she said, while a small smile played at the corner of her mouth.

Something unfamiliar tightened in his chest. "How do you know there are three?"

"Am I right?" she asked hopefully, and even if she were wrong, at that moment, he knew he would have lied.

"*Sí.*"

"Each one sounds a little different."

"They sound the same to me."

"Because your world is bigger than mine," she said without any self-pity. She slipped another strip of meat into her mouth.

"What is your name?" he asked.

She hesitated, and he could see the battle raging as, like him, she tried to determine how much she could reveal and still remain safe. "Angela Bainbridge."

"Angela," he murmured, testing it out. Something flickered in his mind. "Angel."

Her good humor fled. "Don't call me that."

"But you look like an angel."

"I'm not an angel."

"You are right. You may look like one, but you do not sound like one. You have a temper."

She scoffed. "I was abducted. I think I have a right to be angry."

"You have the right to be angry, but not stupid.

You must realize that you have no choice but to come with us."

"I can stay right here and take my chances."

He dug his elbows into his thighs and clasped his hands into an aching grip. "With us you will not be taking a chance. My brothers and I will not hurt you."

"You murdered a man," she pointed out. "In a cowardly manner from all accounts."

"A man, but I have never harmed a woman. You will be safe with us. I cannot guarantee that you will be safe if we leave you."

"I don't need nor do I want your guarantees."

"But I need them. I am a man of honor."

"You are a murderer and a thief."

"I will not argue that some aspects of my life are questionable, but not when it comes to my treatment of women."

"I don't understand why you can't circle back around and return me to the edge of town today."

"I do not know how the posse will fan out. Once I know that my brothers are safe, I will take you back. I promise."

"Why are you telling me all this?" she asked. "You could just force me as you did before."

"If I have to, I will. I would rather not have to," he said solemnly.

"If I agree to cooperate, will you promise not to stuff that filthy cloth into my mouth?" she asked.

"Sí."

"And you won't tie my hands?"

"I will not bind you in any way."

She gave a brusque nod. "All right. You'll have my full and utmost cooperation."

A slow smile eased over his face. Damn, but the woman laid out a convincing bluff. He was actually anticipating the journey.

Chapter 4

Incensed, Angela flung a thousand silent curses at the man riding behind her. At least he'd bound her wrists together in front so she could grip the saddle horn. She couldn't believe he'd actually called her bluff.

Or that he'd roughly shoved his hat onto her head once the sun had risen higher in the sky. She'd welcomed the shade it provided. With her fair complexion, she was prone to freckles, sunburn, and blisters. She'd always hated the freckles. When she was younger, she'd often wished that she didn't have to look at them. Too late, she'd learned to be careful of what she wished for.

They rode at a steady pace. A quick burst of galloping, followed by a longer stint of walking. She hadn't expected a man with Raven's reputation to take such care with his horses, although when she thought about it, she realized the only thing abusing his animals would gain him was capture and the noosed end of a hangman's rope.

Every rational bone in her body told her that she should be terrified, and for the life of her, she couldn't figure out why she wasn't. Perhaps it was the way he'd scolded Jorge for calling her a whore, or the manner in which he'd gotten after her for using profanity. An outlaw who worried about such matters . . . he was a puzzle and none of the pieces seemed to fit properly.

She wished she could say the same thing about the way her body molded into his, but the truth was that it did fit with his . . . perfectly.

She felt Raven draw back on the reins and was relieved that this bout of galloping was at an end. Although the slower pace wasn't much better, she had more success at holding her body away from his when the horse plodded along. At a gallop, Raven folded himself around her like a long-lost lover, his beard stubble catching in her hair from time to time.

"We should probably alternate the woman between horses so yours is not overly burdened," a voice she didn't recognize announced.

"Or you could just leave the *burden* right here," she snapped.

"I think you offended her, Roberto," Raven said, his warm breath skimming along the nape of her neck, causing a delicious shiver to scurry down her spine. How did he effortlessly elicit this unwanted response in her?

"Roberto is right. Your horse will not be able to

keep up with ours if he has to constantly carry the extra weight," Alejandro said.

"I am not that heavy!" she retorted, her anger growing to encompass each man, the entire intolerable situation, but most of all, Raven's damned constant breathing.

"I think she prefers to stay with me, *hombres*," Raven said, and she could envision a satisfied smile on his dark face.

"I prefer a rattlesnake," she said curtly. At least a serpent gave warning before it struck.

"Then why do you argue against moving to another horse?" he asked.

Why indeed? Because for reasons she could not fathom and did not really want to contemplate, she did feel safe within the enticing circle of his strong arms.

"I need a moment of privacy," she announced to distract herself as much as them.

"Again!" Roberto shouted. "You cannot possibly need time behind the bushes so soon."

She angled her chin defiantly. "I'm sorry, but I've always had to . . . relieve myself frequently." The words were a lie, but she knew the blush burning her face was true. She didn't want to speak of bodily functions, but it was the only excuse she'd been able to come up with to slow their progress.

"It has not even been an hour," Roberto said.

He was obviously the complainer of the group. Raven never chastised her when she indicated that she needed time alone. She'd been able to convince him to stop six times now. The man was either a fool or more considerate than she cared to give him credit for. She turned her head slightly so he could see her licking her lips as though she was embarrassed by and sorry for her request.

"I really can't wait much longer," she said in a low voice. "I'd hate to ruin your fine saddle."

He brought the horse to a halt. His spurs clinked as his boots hit the ground. Bracketing her waist with his hands, he lifted her and lowered her slowly, very slowly, her body close enough to his that she was acutely aware of the heat radiating from his chest, actually heard the fabric of her dress rasping against the material of his shirt, and felt the warmth of his breath wafting across her cheek. That damned breath again. If he meant to disconcert her, he was accomplishing his goal with remarkable deftness.

As soon as her feet were planted firmly on the ground, she stepped away, decidedly uncomfortable with the proximity of Raven's body. Too near because somehow the fact that they weren't on his horse made him that much more threatening.

Just as he had each time before, he placed his hand on her back with a surety that no doubt came from knowing an abundance of women. "This way, *señorita*."

A pang of guilt shot through her as he guided her away from the others, toward what she knew would be a secluded area. Most people took her arm and walked her as though she were a favored pet, not an independent woman. It was uncanny the way Raven would subtly press on one side of her back or the other to ensure that she side-stepped objects.

He removed his hand from her back. Halting, she lifted her bound hands. He untied the bandanna from her wrists.

"Am I hidden?" she asked in as meek a voice as she could muster.

"*Sí.*"

She listened to his retreating footsteps before quickly circling the small area. She located a tree and the nearby brush. She rustled her skirts to give the impression that she was lifting them, and then she very slowly, very quietly, eased her way to the ground. With a triumphant smile, she reached into her pocket, withdrew her beloved deck of cards, and settled in to play three games of patience.

Her goal was to slow them down until they had no choice but to leave her behind or be captured. A dangerous undertaking that carried risks . . . and a measure of unanticipated excitement.

She certainly couldn't classify the last twelve hours as dull. No, dull was sitting beside a window with only the warm sunlight for company and having her meticulous stitches earn praise from the owner of the shop where she worked.

Now, she was being challenged as she'd never been before, striving to anticipate Raven's goals and seeking ways to thwart him. Without a doubt, she wanted to be free of him, and yet a part of her welcomed the opportunity to outsmart him, to put him in his place atop the gallows. To prove to herself and the world that she didn't need anyone in order to survive. She was perfectly capable of taking care of herself.

Of course, the fact that she was in this predicament to begin with might detract from her victory, should she ever achieve it.

"*Señorita*, we don't have all day!" Roberto yelled.

"I'm trying to hurry," she sang back, laying out her last row of cards.

She heard footsteps growing louder, then fainter, as though someone was pacing a short distance behind her—no doubt Raven, waiting for her to announce she was finished. She turned over the top card.

The ultimate satisfaction would reside in capturing him herself. Although even if she somehow managed to meet that goal, she wasn't certain how she would deliver him anywhere.

More often than not, she considered her blindness a minor inconvenience, but sometimes it proved a definite disadvantage. The most she could realistically hope for was escape. The sooner the better, because the farther she traveled from home, the less likely she thought it that he would keep his promise and return her to her family.

Why would a notorious outlaw even bother to make such a promise? He obviously put his needs first; otherwise, he would never have abducted her.

As for Raven's concern about her welfare . . . she didn't trust him. He had another motive in

mind, no doubt the ransom he'd mentioned earlier. Her father *would* pay handsomely for her return, and her mortification would be complete
with the undeniable evidence that her independence was little more than an invisible thread
tethering her to family and home.

As she placed the eight of hearts on the nine of
spades, she heard a pop and froze. It couldn't be
Raven. No approaching footsteps had provided
warning of his imminent return, and she'd definitely heard his retreat. Her active imagination
was running wild. Slowly releasing her tension,
she turned over another card.

"The black jack—" Raven began.

She yelped at his irascible voice, near enough
that the air shimmied.

"Goes on the red queen," he finished.

He plucked the card from her fingers. Anger
shot through her with the intensity of a thunder-
storm. "You promised me privacy."

"You swore you were going to ruin my saddle." He snatched the deck from her hand.

"Give those back to me! They're mine!"

"I think you have played enough, *señorita*, with
the cards *and* with me."

For the first time, she actually heard rage slithering through his voice as though he'd spoken
with his teeth clenched.

"Get up!" he ordered in a voice that announced
he'd brook no argument.

Still, she licked her lips and decided to try to
squirm her way out of his bad favor. "I can explain. You see, I have to relax before I can—"

She shrieked as he unexpectedly grabbed her arm and jerked her to her feet. "You will have the remainder of the day to relax."

The fury shimmering off him was palpable as he marched her away from her sanctuary, his hold on her arm firm but not bruising. She felt his gun brush against her leg. He was left-handed. Another tidbit of information to store away and share with Kit Montgomery, who she was certain would welcome anything she could add to his knowledge regarding this outlaw. She swept her free hand across her stomach, closer to his hip. If she could just grab his gun . . . she knew she wouldn't have much time, but if she caught him unawares—

"Hey, Lee, what is that cloud of dust rising up behind us?" Jorge asked.

She was jarred as Raven turned, no doubt to look over his shoulder, and provided her with an unexpected opportunity to fall, seemingly innocently, against him. She curled her fingers around the smooth handle, twisted her body to block any attempt he made to stop her, and managed to draw the revolver from his holster. He swore harshly as she broke free of his grasp and backed up quickly, gripping the handle with both hands as she pointed the barrel toward the last place where she knew he'd stood.

"I know how to use this, so nobody move." She heard saddles creak and footsteps. She waved the gun wildly in a circle. "Nobody move!"

"Be still!" Raven yelled.

She zeroed in on the location of his voice and

steadied the gun. "My father taught me how to handle a gun effectively, and I'm not afraid to pull the trigger. You can well imagine that the bright red hue of blood will not make me squeamish." She swallowed hard, trying to calm her own breathing as she listened intently for any signs of movement. "I don't want to shoot anyone. I just want to be left here. Is that cloud of dust riders?"

"*Sí.*"

Raven. He was still directly in front of her. "It's probably men that my father sent to find me," she hastily explained. "So get on your horses and ride. Just leave me."

"The posse's nearness is an illusion, *señorita,*" he said quietly, as though she could see the cloud of dust his brother had mentioned.

She wished she could hold them all—or at least keep Raven here—but she wasn't foolish enough to believe she could avoid them overtaking her for long. If they had any intelligence, they'd soon realize that by creating noisy distractions, they could force her to shoot at phantoms until she'd exhausted the small supply of bullets.

Although she wasn't certain Raven would risk his brothers in that dangerous endeavor. When he spoke to them, his voice carried an undercurrent of affection, completely at odds with what she knew of the outlaw. Inwardly, she shook off the fleeting thought. She didn't need anything to distract her. She had to ensure that he didn't send his brothers on and then play the game with her.

Why hadn't she heard him approach her while

she was waiting in the bushes? Could he move that stealthily, or had she been concentrating too much on her wayward thoughts that had continually drifted to him? Was he walking toward her now? It was far too quiet. She waved the gun in a wide circle. "Don't move!" she ordered.

"I'm not moving, *señorita*," Raven replied.

"Keep talking so I know exactly where you are."

"So you can shoot me?"

She nodded jerkily. "I swear you'll be the first one. Now talk."

"What do you want me to say? You tell me to get on my horse and ride away, then you tell me not to move. I cannot do both. Which do you want?"

He was talking too loudly, using too many words. "I want to know where everyone is."

"My brothers are on their horses."

"Not all of them. I heard at least one dismount." He and Alejandro seemed closer. Jorge and Roberto simply followed orders. "Alejandro. Alejandro got off his horse."

"Now, why would he do that?"

She tightened her hold on the gun. "I swear to God that I will shoot if each man does not call out his name."

"No one speaks!" he ordered. "No one but me. I will not allow them to become targets. If you want to shoot, *señorita*, shoot, but I warn you now that it is not a good thing to aggravate me. I am a man of limited patience, and when that patience—"

Someone grabbed the gun. Reflexively, she

squeezed the trigger and an explosion ripped through the air as the weapon was torn from her hands.

"Good work, Alejandro," Raven said as he snared her arm, his voice exuding controlled rage.

She tried to fight him off, but again his strength put her at a disadvantage. He caged her within the circle of his arms while he wrapped the hated bandanna around her wrists. "Please—"

"No!" he barked.

When she was secured, he shoved her away and she teetered backward, nearly losing her balance. Hearing metal glide against leather, she realized Alejandro had returned Raven's gun to him. Panic seized her with the thought of losing what might be her sole chance for rescue. "Don't you see that the longer you keep me, the more I'll discover about you? I know you're left-handed."

"No, he's—"

"Jorge!" Raven yelled. "Let her think what she will."

She backed up a step as the fight drained out of her. "Or you wear two guns."

"Very wise, señorita, but not wise enough. My other gun was aimed at you the entire time. Endanger my brothers again with your childish games, and you will feel the bite of my bullet."

She was astonished that he hadn't automatically fired his weapon when her gun's retort had ripped through the air. The man appeared to be a master of restraint, and yet he had killed a man and abducted her. "Why do you insist on keeping me?"

"Because I do not know the men who follow. Mount up," Raven ordered.

"But, Lee—" Alejandro began.

"Mount up," Raven repeated. He put his hands on her waist—just as he had every time before—with a gentleness that astounded her. He lifted her, and with a sinking heart, she grabbed the pommel as he placed her on the saddle. It shifted while he took his place behind her.

Raven urged the horse into a gallop. Angela heard the pounding hooves of his brothers' horses beating unmercifully at the ground. She wanted to beg Raven to stop, to leave her to the safety of the men who followed.

Surely, once she gained her freedom, Raven and his brothers would be left to escape in peace. She was certain her father had hired the men who were following them, and he would hire men who would not stop until she was returned home.

But she understood with an uncanny certainty that Raven wasn't in the mood to listen to her pleas. Her botched escape stung her pride. She should have killed him while she had the chance, and for the life of her, she couldn't understand why she hadn't.

Standing within Fortune's only bank, Harrison Bainbridge had taken an immediate dislike to Vernon Shelby when the man had strutted into the building like a bloody peacock. In small ways that he couldn't quite put his finger on, the stout fellow reminded Harrison of the jawhawker, his wife's former lover, who had crippled him years before.

"What in the hell did Raven look like?" Shelby demanded of Howard Sims, the bank president, who sat behind his desk, cracking his knuckles one at a time. Harrison recognized the balding man's telling habit. He was holding nothing of importance.

"They were already in the shadows of the alley by the time I spotted them." Sims gave Harrison a beseeching look from behind his thick spectacles. "I knew that they had a woman with them, but I thought they were just a group of cowboys looking for a little innocent sport. I didn't hear the woman hollering, so I figured she was willing. It never occurred to me that she might be Angela, not until you reported her missing early this morning. And I had no idea whatsoever who they were until I found this damned note when I opened the bank for business."

"You didn't notice anything amiss last night when you came here?" Harrison asked.

Forlornly, he shook his head. "The vault door was closed and locked. I just came in to get some money to take to your tables, but they didn't steal enough for me to notice. I didn't even glance at my desk."

"And you're certain that the note has Raven's signature on it?" Harrison asked Shelby.

Shelby glared at him. "Do I look like I'm prone to wading into a river so I can drink standing up? Of course I'm certain. He even left the damned black feather, the conceited bastard."

Gripping his cane until his knuckles turned white, Harrison glanced at his wife, standing at the window, gazing out. It constantly amazed him to discover that when he awoke each morning, he loved her more than he had the day before. He wished to God that he could spare her this anguish.

"Based upon this discussion, I suppose we can accurately deduce that the man was Raven and the woman was Angela." *Woman.* To him she still was, and would always be, his little girl.

Jessye slowly nodded. "Why would he take my baby?"

"Raven does whatever the hell he damn well wants to," Shelby said. "Takes whatever he damn well wants: my son's life, my money. Why not a woman?"

Harrison rubbed his thumb over the golden lion's head that adorned his cane. "How does he know where you deposit your money?"

"I haven't a clue, but he'll tell me once the men I sent out have captured him," Shelby said in a voice that sent cold chills traveling along Harrison's spine.

"You've already sent men after him?"

"The best bounty hunters money can buy."

"How do you suppose they'll react when they find our daughter with him?"

Shelby had the grace to blush. "They'll probably think she's his whore."

"Well, then, we'd better hope the men I send out find her first and quickly. Jessye, shall we go?"

As she moved away from the window, Sims

stood. "I'm sorry. If I'd realized the woman was Angela—"

Jessye placed her hand on his shoulder. "It's not your fault. Angela was simply in the wrong place at the wrong time. She's been there before."

She slipped her arm around Harrison's, and he escorted her outside.

"That Shelby strikes me as a man who thinks the sun comes up specifically to hear him crow," she said as soon as they were on the boardwalk.

"I couldn't agree more."

"His trap for capturing Raven wasn't very well thought out."

"I think it was extremely well thought out if he never intended to capture him here. He lured him in, allowed him to escape, and sent ruffians after him." He glanced around the town that had long ago become home. "I don't trust the man, Jessye, and I trust his minions even less."

"You'd better send for Kit."

"I already have, love. He should be here by nightfall."

Chapter 5

Angela was well aware that they were moving farther away from Fortune. As the day wore on, they galloped for longer periods of time, slowing the horses only when absolutely necessary. Raven refused all her requests to stretch her legs with a short stroll. She supposed she couldn't blame him. She'd abused his trust with her attempt to slow them down. But did he honestly expect her to idly accept her abduction and do nothing to thwart his escape?

The sun's heat vanished over the horizon, and on they rode, not stopping for food or rest. She was certain that hours passed—an eternity, it seemed. The night air began to cool as it wrapped itself snugly around her, working its way through her to her very core. Last night, she had welcomed the coolness after a hot day. Tonight she was exhausted, starving, aching in every conceivable place.

At last Raven slowed the horse to a walk, and she wanted to weep with relief. He removed his hat from her head. She didn't care what he did as long as he didn't let her fall from the horse. She was aware of his subtle movements, heard leather slap against leather. Cloth fell around her shoulders, the warm folds of material draping her body. A poncho.

Tears burned her eyes. He was a murderer. She didn't want him to be kind. She'd been raised in a family that believed in justice. She wanted him to hang. She wanted to go home.

She ran her fingers over the soft wool. A heaviness settled over her limbs, and she was afraid she might drift off to sleep, might slip from the horse.

"What color is it?" she asked, the first civil words she'd uttered since her escape attempt that afternoon.

Silence stretched between them, and she thought he intended to ignore her question.

"My poncho?" he finally asked.

She nodded jerkily.

"You know colors?"

Again she nodded, almost smiling at his obvious bafflement. "I wasn't always blind."

His arm tightened around her. "How did you lose your sight?"

"Sickness, high fever."

"How old were you?" he asked, and she would have sworn she heard compassion reflected in his voice.

"Twelve."

"Blue," he said quietly. "The poncho is striped, different shades of blue."

"My favorite color," she said slowly, forcing the words out in spite of her incredible weariness.

"Here, eat this." He shoved some jerky into her hand.

She gnawed on the toughened meat, glad for anything to fill the emptiness in her stomach. Her feeling of gratitude taking her off-guard, she wondered if, deprived of freedom, she was becoming thankful for every scrap of kindness so that she'd stopped viewing him as the enemy and instead saw him as her savior.

Well, she wouldn't be grateful. She'd accept his offerings because they were due her, but she would not become obligated to him for anything. When another chance came to escape—or to kill him—she wouldn't hesitate to take advantage of the opportunity. But the next time, she swore to herself, she would succeed.

She didn't know how much time passed before he drew the horse to a halt. He dismounted, wrapped his hands around her waist, and brought her to the ground. With her knees wobbly, she started to sink to the ground, but he snaked his arm around her. To her utter mortification, she sagged against him.

"Why are we stopping?" Jorge asked.

"To rest the horses," Raven said. "We'll sleep for two hours and then start off again."

Saddles creaked as his brothers dismounted.

She heard the heavy tread of one advancing toward them.

"Is it because of her?" Alejandro asked harshly. "You think she needs to sleep."

"The horses need to rest."

"She is going to get us caught," Alejandro spat.

"Jorge, Roberto, see to the horses," Raven ordered.

"Damn it, Lee—"

"The horses are tired. They need to eat. They need to be watered. They need to rest before we drive them harder."

"Listen to me," Alejandro said quietly. "You are the only one with a bounty on his head. I can take her back to Fortune."

"And if someone sees you?"

"No one knows I ride with you. I will be in no danger."

Raven sighed heavily. "You don't understand, Alejandro. She is white. Do you honestly think the *gringos* will ask if you touched her before they string you up?"

The way he spat "*gringos*"—as though the word left a bitter taste in his mouth—erased any doubts she'd harbored that he might not actually be Mexican. A hand clapped against a back or shoulder.

"I appreciate your concern, Alejandro, but this mistake was mine. I will make it right or pay the price for it."

She heard footsteps retreat, and with them, her chance for freedom. "I wouldn't let them hang him."

"You wouldn't be able to stop them, *señorita.* Once *gringos* have it in their mind to hang a Mexican, nothing will deter them."

His vocabulary surprised her. There were moments when she almost suspected him of being an educated man, but no educated man would turn to a life of crime. She heard someone approach.

"Lee, I made her a place to sleep." She recognized Roberto's young, cautious voice.

"*Gracias, hombre.*" Raven started to lead her away.

"Lee?"

He stopped at Roberto's inquiry. "*Sí?*"

"I was thinking . . . I do not have a bounty on my head. I could take the woman home. I'd make a wide circle, avoid riders—"

Flesh slapped against flesh, a hand patting someone's neck or cheek.

"Alejandro and I have already discussed this," Raven said, understanding laced through his voice. "It is not a wise plan."

"But if they catch you—"

"They are not going to capture me. Now, get some sleep. Two hours is all we can spare."

He tightened his hold on her waist and led her through the darkness that she knew surrounded them. Night somehow carried a different feel to it than day, and the sun had yet to send its tendrils of warmth over her. Raven stopped walking. His fingers grazed the back of her hands before he worked to untie the binding. "You may have a few moments of privacy here. Do not do anything to aggravate me."

She heard his retreating footsteps and set about taking care of business. When she was finished, she briefly considered heading away from the camp but she was too tired to exert the effort that would be needed to make good an escape. With a sigh, she walked back in the direction from which she'd come. Three steps later, she bumped into Raven. Obviously, he didn't trust her any farther than he could hear her.

"You will sleep here," he ordered and guided her onto a mound of blankets.

Gratefully, she dropped down and tucked her legs beneath her. The familiar pop of his knees signaled that he'd crouched beside her. A twig snapped as someone came near.

"Lee, I have a magnificent plan—"

"The woman stays with us, Jorge," Raven cut in.

"But you can trust me—"

"It is not a matter of trust, but a matter of what is best for all of us. We stay together. Now sleep."

She listened to the departing footsteps. "They love you," she said in awe, surprised she'd spoken aloud.

"What is there not to love?" he asked.

"Offhand, I could think of a thousand things."

"Name one," he dared her.

"You murdered a man."

"That, *señorita*, is the reason they love me most of all," he said in a chilling voice that sent icy shivers cascading down her spine. "Now, lie down."

Cautiously, she stretched out on her side, listening intently, prepared to bolt if a need arose. She heard the unmistakable sounds of a gun belt being removed and the blankets rustling. He wrapped his arm around her. She tried to get up, but he pressed her firmly against his hard body.

"Relax, *señorita*. Since we cannot have a fire, you will have to settle for my warmth."

Terror gripped her. "What are you going to do?"

"Hold you until you stop shivering."

She didn't think having him this close was going to make her stop quivering. She'd never in her life known such exhaustion. Nor had she ever been so incredibly aware of a man, the way her backside fit snugly within his lap, the breadth of his chest as his shoulders curled around her. The hard edge of his chin as it rested against the top of her head. The arm he'd somehow managed to work beneath her so she now had a pillow. His rugged scent mixed with the smell of horses and leather.

A few men had courted her, a couple had even dared to kiss her, but they seemed astonishingly tame when compared to this unsettling outlaw. He emanated incredible confidence, seemed sure of his course, but she couldn't label him as haughty or arrogant. He was simply a man with a purpose, an errant purpose to be sure, but one he was determined to pursue.

She eased out of her reverie as she became increasingly cognizant of something moist and warm dampening her side. "What in the world is that?"

Raven grunted as she shoved him away and sat up. She touched her fingers to the stickiness that now coated a small section of her bodice. She sniffed her fingertips and a rustic odor assailed her nostrils. "It's blood."

"I started bleeding again," he said calmly, as though he was commenting on the sun coming up.

Stunned, she twisted around. "You're wounded?"

He chuckled low. "You shot me in the arm."

Her stomach roiling, she pressed her unbloodied fingers against her mouth. She hadn't noticed the wound as they'd ridden because he'd used his other arm to hold her. "Why didn't you tell me?"

"What did you want me to say? That I learned you do not make idle threats?"

He thought she'd shot him on purpose, when in fact it had happened by chance. But his misconception might at some point put her at an advantage if she did not challenge his perception of the event. "You have to tend the wound. Is the bullet still lodged in there?"

"It went clean through. I will stop bleeding in a little while."

"In a little while? I can't have you bleeding on me all night," she snapped, hoping he wouldn't detect any measure of concern in her sharp words. She'd never actually shot anyone, and the mere idea made her ill. "You have to do something."

He sighed heavily. "I have already told you that I cannot risk a fire so I cannot cauterize it."

"You could sew it. I always carry needle and thread," she said.

"Neither I nor my brothers can sew in the dark."

"I can."

He released a low, soft chuckle that somehow carried a threat with it. "I think not, *señorita*. A needle in your hand would cause more harm than good."

She didn't want to acknowledge how his words stung. True, he was an outlaw with a bounty on his head—wanted, dead or alive. She should let him take his chances . . . if only he would treat her badly so she could justify shooting him. She twisted around until she thought she was facing him squarely. "I give you my word that I'll tend your wound properly."

"Your word? This afternoon you were going to ruin my saddle, and yet you sat and played with your cards as though we had all afternoon to while away the hours."

With a huff, she flopped onto her side. "Fine. Bleed to death. I don't care." How she wished that was true. But she did care. She didn't want to be responsible for his death, only his capture. Maybe when he fell asleep, she could determine the severity of his wound. Based on the way he'd been holding her, she could ascertain its location, prod gently . . . and awaken him, but perhaps in a drowsy state he might accept her ministrations.

"You have experience sewing?" he asked cautiously.

A small thrill of victory speared her. She didn't want this outlaw to see her as inadequate. "Yes, as a matter of fact, I'm a seamstress. I use my fingers to determine the shape of the seam and sew incredibly neat, meticulous stitches," she assured him.

"I'll probably regret this, but . . ." He growled low, and she imagined him narrowing his dark eyes at her in warning. "You can stitch me up."

She rolled into a sitting position, reached into her pocket, and removed the small sewing case that her parents had given to her shortly after she'd announced that she'd acquired a position as a seamstress. She skimmed her thumb over her initials carved within the gold lid. She heard the whisper of movement and the brush of air ripple across her face. "What are you doing?"

"Taking off my shirt."

"Can't you just roll up your sleeve?"

"The bullet went through near my shoulder."

"Oh." She hadn't considered that he'd sit before her shirtless. Unsettled, she decided to finish the task as quickly as possible. "I need your canteen."

He handed it to her. She opened it and poured water into her cupped palm. He snatched the canteen from her.

"You're wasting my water!"

"I'm trying to clean my hands so you don't get an infection."

"No more water. Just do the best you can. I'll deal with infection later."

"I know a man who died from an infected little toe," she said as she spread the little bit of water she'd managed to obtain over her hands. Drying them on her skirt probably would undo what she'd tried to accomplish. She flicked them in the air until the droplets were gone. She opened her sewing kit, pulled out a small spool, broke off a long piece of thread, and deftly inserted it through the eye of the needle. All by touch. She'd pricked herself a hundred times when she'd first decided that she would learn to sew. Her father had said she was stubborn. Her mother had called her "determined."

Now, she was going to prick Lee Raven. She tore off a section of her petticoat. "I'll need you to lead me to the wound."

He wrapped his fingers around her hand and slowly rubbed his thumb across her knuckles before placing her hand on his arm. The heat of his flesh nearly scorched her fingertips, and she imagined that his entire body felt this smooth, this taut, this muscled, this hot. With the strip of her petticoat, she wiped at the wound. "Keep your arm straight and try not to twitch when I poke you."

"I do not twitch."

"And you do not beg," she said caustically.

But he did intake a sharp breath when she trailed her fingers over the ragged edges of mutilated flesh. "I'm just going to . . ." She swallowed in an attempt to stop the tingling in her jaw. "I'm going to prod around just to make sure there's no bits of cloth . . ." Oh, God. A bullet created such an ugly mess.

When she was certain she'd done her best to clean the wound, she jabbed the needle into his skin. She thought she might have preferred something from him other than stoicism. "I'm sorry. I know it must hurt." Her voice quivered but at least her hands were steady.

What sort of man was Lee Raven? She knew he'd been put out with her for taking his gun and holding it on him, but he'd never hinted that she'd shot him. He'd never raised his voice or his hand to her. If someone had shot her . . . he would have faced her unmerciful wrath. The man was a contradiction to all she knew about him, all she believed.

Leaning close, she bit off the end of the thread and then proceeded to tie it off. She heard him exhale slowly. She stuck the needle into her waistband before reaching for the end of her skirt.

"Here, use my shirt," he ordered, and thrust the chambray garment into her hands.

When she'd lost her sight, her fingertips had become her eyes. She'd wanted to again know all that she'd once seen. She'd learned to identify all sorts of textures and shapes, making her family crazy as she requested item after item, hungry for the feel of everything, desperate to rebuild a world that she'd lost—the only thing that now eluded her was color. She missed it with a passion.

She handed his shirt back to him. She opened her kit, removed more thread, retrieved her needle, and proceeded to thread it. "I'll do the other side now." She took a deep breath. "I don't suppose you have any whiskey."

"You drink?"

"My father owns a saloon. Of course I drink."

He released a quick burst of laughter. "I think your father should have had a son."

She smiled warmly. "But my mother wanted daughters, and he usually gives her what she wants. Whiskey?"

"No."

Her smile faded as she touched his arm and located the other side of his wound where the bullet had torn a larger hole going out. "I suppose you're going to try and tell me that the notorious Lee Raven doesn't drink," she chided.

"I don't."

She paused in disbelief. "You've never been drunk."

"No."

Incredible. She'd never met a man who hadn't indulged in too much liquor on at least one occasion. She touched his arm.

"Have you?" he asked.

She halted, her fingers resting against his flesh. "Been drunk?"

"*Sí.*"

She smiled at the memory. "In celebration of my sixteenth birthday, my two younger sisters and I snuck a bottle of whiskey out of the saloon and proceeded to gulp down the contents. Then abruptly brought it all back up. Since then, I drink a little more cautiously."

Once again, he hissed through his teeth as she began working. When she was finished stitching, she tore off another section of her petticoat and wrapped it around his arm, tying it to protect the wound. "There. All done."

She pushed the needle into her waistband and reached for her skirt. Raven stopped her, taking her hands in one of his and holding them out. She heard the swishing of water and then felt the warm trickle as he washed the blood from her hands.

"Your precious water," she murmured.

"We'll find more tomorrow."

He again used his shirt to dry her hands, gently, as though her hands were fragile and he feared breaking them. She felt tears sting her eyes. It had been such a grueling day and she was incredibly weary. She did not want him to treat her kindly.

When he moved away, she slid her needle into her sewing kit before lying down on the blankets. Hearing his movements as he slipped on his shirt, she rolled onto her side and brought her knees up. She still couldn't fathom that she'd actually shot him or understand why he hadn't taken her to task for it.

He stretched out beside her and placed his arm around her. He tucked something beneath her hand. She couldn't stop herself from smiling as some of the loneliness receded. Closing her fingers around her deck of cards, she pressed them against her chest. "Why didn't you get mad when I shot you?" she dared to ask.

"I was furious, but I understand your desire to escape. Besides, a man does not take his anger out on a woman."

The night enveloped them in the intimacy of darkness, bringing him into a world she'd inhabited for too many years. Tonight the moon was but a sliver in the sky. She knew because each evening she took a mental note of its phase. She might be blind, but she refused to be ignorant of the world around her. She'd have an advantage tonight if she decided to slip away after Raven fell asleep.

"This friend of your father's," he said quietly, startling her from her reverie. "This Christian Montgomery. Have you ever met him?"

"Of course," she replied, wondering why he would bring up this subject now.

"I know this man. Not personally, of course, but I read his story. *The Texas Ranger Who Didn't Wear a Gun.* He is amazing."

"Yes, he is."

"Did you know that at one time he was a marshal? Many, many years ago, they wrote a book about him called *The Marshal Who Didn't Wear a Gun.* I could never find it."

Angela opened her mouth slightly. The notorious Lee Raven sought out books?

"Is there someone in Fortune besides your father who will be worried about you?" he asked after several long moments of silence.

"My mother, my sisters."

His chest rumbled against her back as he chuckled.

"I meant a man."

Her father's friend Grayson Rhodes would be livid. He'd probably come in search of her, but she didn't think he was referring to him. He was asking if she had a beau. She contemplated lying, but saw no advantage to it. "No."

"Good."

Within that one word, he'd managed to wrap an undeniable sense of possession. She didn't know why the realization made forbidden sensations swirl through her.

Or why, when she finally managed to drift off to sleep, she dreamt of him. He stood within a thick mist. She couldn't see his face, and yet, she knew him so well that it was frightening.

Chapter 6

Lee's left arm ached unmercifully, while his right arm felt nothing at all, not even the heavenly softness of the woman whose head had managed to make his arm numb while she used it as a pillow. An incredible shame, he thought, as he cautiously, slowly, pulled what he hoped was the last pin from her hair. He tossed it into the darkness, to join the others he'd painstakingly located and removed. Her hair was incredibly thick, amazingly silky, and very abundant. Long. He was certain it would reach past the small dip in her lower back.

She snuggled closer against him. He suppressed a groan and balled his hand into a fist to stop it from cradling her face. He did not want to wake her because the moment she became aware of the way she'd burrowed into him as she slept, she would move away from him with the speed of a bullet fired from a gun.

She looked peaceful, her soft features limned by the pale, forgiving light of the moon and a million stars. While she was blissfully unaware of the way her body betrayed her, he relished the gentle swells flattened against the planes of his hard chest. He'd barely breathed when she'd first turned into him, fearful of disturbing her, of losing this moment of holding a woman close.

Five years ago, he'd made the decision to travel a lonely path in the name of retribution, but until now, the loneliness had never seemed so deep, the sacrifice so great. During all the long, solitary nights of imagining, he'd never dreamed that embracing a woman while she slept would bring with it such a measure of completeness.

Despite his reputation, in spite of her wariness, she had to trust him a little or her breathing would have never evened out, grown shallow, and become as lyrical as a lullaby. It lulled him into a serenity he wasn't certain he'd ever experienced, made him long for a life that he knew he could never possess.

"Lee?" Alejandro whispered harshly.

"Shh. She's sleeping," he murmured, skimming his fingers over the magnificent tresses. He wanted to see the morning sunlight turn them into flames.

"It's been two hours," Alejandro pointed out unnecessarily.

She sighed, stretched, and turned away from him. If Alejandro were not crouched nearby, Lee might have followed and wrapped himself around her, anything to retain the false peace a little longer. Instead, he rolled into a sitting position and pushed himself to his feet. The sun was barely beginning to ease over the horizon. Rubbing his arm, he glanced at the woman. How did she measure the day?

"What's wrong with that arm?" Alejandro asked. "I thought she shot the other one."

"She slept on it. It's just numb . . . and keep your voice down." He walked to the edge of the clearing, ignored the prickling in his right arm, and watched as sunlight began to bathe the sky in various hues of orange, pink, and blue, Angela's favorite color. He couldn't remember the last time he'd taken pleasure in the arrival of dawn.

"How is the wound?"

He clenched his left fist and twisted his arm slightly. "Tender, but I'll survive."

"You should have let me treat it yesterday."

He remembered Alejandro voicing his objection when Lee had first ordered them to ride out. "You worry like an ancient woman, Alejandro."

"Because you do not. Take off your shirt and I'll tend to it now."

"Angela already did. She sewed it up last night." With a gentle touch that he would remember long after they slipped a noose around his neck.

"You trusted her with a needle in her hand?"

"*Loco*, I know, but I thought she felt guilty." An emotion he knew only too well, but understood not at all. "I wanted her to be able to sleep."

"Unlike you, who can never sleep. I don't know whose nightmares are worse, yours or Juanita's."

"Juanita's," he murmured without hesitation. His dear, sweet, little sister's cries in the night tore at his soul.

"Yet the dreams are the same, aren't they?"

"No, they are very different and I don't want to talk about them." Crouching, he rested his elbows on his thighs.

"What do you think you are doing? We need to ride," Alejandro said, his voice edged with impatience.

"Angela is sleeping well. A few more moments won't make a difference."

Kneeling beside him, Alejandro extended his hat. "Your face is burned. Use my sombrero today."

Lee shook his head. "She is a smart one. She has already guessed too much. I do not need to confirm what she suspects."

"Another day without the protection of some shade, and you are going to blister. You do not have Juanita's salve to ease the pain of a burn."

A natural healer, Juanita wasn't gifted enough to heal herself.

"Be cautious, and she will never know you are wearing my hat," Alejandro continued.

Reluctantly acknowledging the truth of Alejandro's words, Lee took his brother's offering and settled it into place. "*Gracias*."

"Don't thank me. She is causing you to take chances that will get your neck stretched."

"I killed a man, Alejandro. Perhaps I *deserve* to get my neck stretched." He pulled a blade of grass from the earth and slipped it between his teeth. "She called me a vicious murderer."

"Juanita calls you a savior."

"I am not a savior. I got there too late to save her." Lee knew that night haunted her, would always haunt her more than it did the others. She was not the child she had once been or the young woman she should have become. He unfolded his body. "I am going to find us something to eat. When the sun is a little higher, we'll risk a small fire."

"Because you don't want our captive to go hungry?" Alejandro ground out at his retreating back.

Lee neither broke his stride nor answered because the truth was that he was simply growing weary of battling the demons that plagued him.

Angela awoke to the tantalizing aroma of cooking fish. Her mouth watered and her stomach rumbled. She sat up and her hair tumbled around her. With a tiny gasp, she thrust her hands into her hair, searching for her pins. Not a single one remained. She began patting the area of the blanket where her head had been resting—

"You won't find them," Raven said quietly.

With a little shriek, she twisted around. "You removed the pins from my hair?"

"*Sí.*"

"Why did you do that?"

His answer was silence, as though she should know the reason and was dense for asking.

"Do you have a comb?"

"No."

"I should have expected that outlaws are not overly concerned with hygiene."

"Outlaws do not have hair as long as yours. We can just use our fingers to keep it in place. Would you like me to comb your hair?"

"With your fingers?"

"*Sí.*"

His voice had suddenly grown thick, tight. Her breathing became erratic with the thought of him raking his fingers through her hair, long fingers that had pressed against her stomach before she'd fallen asleep. "No, that's not necessary. Do you at least have something with which I can tie it back?"

"My filthy bandanna."

She held out her hand. "I suppose I can make do with that." He laid the cloth on her palm. It was still warm, and she realized it had been resting against his throat. It didn't seem quite so filthy, now that it wasn't going into her mouth. Besides, with it around her hair, it couldn't be around her wrists. He wasn't such a smart outlaw after all, she thought smugly.

"If I wanted to bind you, *señorita*, I could use one of my brothers' bandannas."

She jerked the soft cloth into a knot. "What are you? A mind reader?"

"It is as I said, you have very expressive eyes."

The bandanna in place, her hair out of her face, she folded her hands on her lap. "Does this mean you don't intend to keep me tied up today?"

"As long as you behave."

She nodded. "How is your wound?"

"Much better, thanks to your tender ministrations."

She didn't want to think about touching him, about how hot he had been, how smooth, how firm. "Is that breakfast I smell?"

"So I do not have to convince you to eat this morning? That is good."

He set a plate on her lap. She plucked a bit of meat free with her fingers and popped it into her mouth. She'd never tasted anything so delicious in her life. Amazing, how being starved could change one's perception of things. In truth, the fish was dry, overcooked. She could feel his gaze honing in on her. She despised the way it unsettled her. "So you took me because you thought I'd seen your face?"

"*Sí.*"

"Your likeness isn't on a wanted poster?"

"No, until last night I was clever at hiding my identity, not only for my protection, but for the protection of others. There are men who would do anything to discover what I look like. You need to eat more quickly so we can leave."

"And if I don't?"

"I will bind you."

She began shoveling the food into her mouth, hoping that she'd at least managed to delay him enough that today, at some point, he would be willing to leave her behind.

Lee brought his horse to a halt. Nestled snugly between his thighs, Angela eased forward slightly.

She apparently welcomed every opportunity to move away from him. He searched for any chance to hold her close, an incredibly dangerous preoccupation. He had more pressing matters to worry about. Such as the posse that was getting ominously closer.

At least today Angela was not asking to stop every twenty minutes for a moment of privacy. As a matter of fact, she had not asked once. He could only assume that she was experiencing a measure of guilt for shooting him and might behave for the duration of the journey. Inwardly he chuckled. He was no fool: if she thought she could gain her freedom, she would do whatever she needed to obtain it.

He studied the rugged terrain surrounding him. This place was as good as any. "*Hombres*, we are going to split up."

"But you said we would stay together," Jorge pointed out.

"I changed my mind. Those men either are after me, or they want to rescue the woman—"

"The *woman* has a name," she cut in.

He really needed to put the fear of God into her, or, failing that, at least the fear of himself. "It is rude to interrupt, *señorita*."

"You think it's polite to drag me where I don't want to be?" she asked sarcastically.

"You are getting much too bold." And she had been ever since she'd awakened from her four-hour sleep. When she'd sat up, just as he'd anticipated, her hair had tumbled around her. Glorious. His gut had clenched with desire, and it had yet to loosen.

"Then leave me," she threw out.

"We have discussed this matter. I am not leaving you." She shifted in the saddle, causing the ache in his groin to intensify. It was all he could do not to groan aloud.

"How close are they?" she asked.

"They are hours behind us." He slid his gaze from her delicate profile to his brothers, circled around him. He did not like the speculative look on Alejandro's face. "We separate here. You three ride together. *The woman* and I will travel in the opposite direction until I think it is safe to circle back around."

"Have you considered that those might be Shelby's men?" Alejandro asked.

He had not only considered it, but he thought it highly likely—the reason for selecting a bank far from the Mexico border. He'd heard that Shelby assumed they sought refuge on the other side of the Rio Grande. This bank had given them days in unfamiliar territory, and only one man had been standing watch at the bank because they hadn't wanted to capture him there. They wanted to catch him out in the open, away from witnesses.

"They will be unmerciful," Alejandro said, as though he understood the conclusion Lee had reached.

"First, they must take me prisoner . . . alive . . . and that will not happen. Once they have lost the scent, I will return *the woman*"—he smiled as within his arms she stiffened with righteous indignation—"to Fortune. If you do not see me within a month, you know what to do."

Alejandro hesitated before nodding briskly. "I give you my word that I will see that all is done as we planned."

Lee lifted the reins. "Then I will see you at home. *Vaya con dios.*"

He nudged his horse into a gallop. The woman settled back against him. His horse was the strongest of the lot, but even he could not continue at a gallop indefinitely. A shame.

Home. Angela had expected Raven to tell his brothers that he'd meet them at a hideout. She'd never expected him to talk about home as though it was a place of fond memories and love.

She'd heard his brothers' horses gallop away shortly after Raven had urged his own into a dust-rising pace. They hadn't traveled long before she noticed the horse straining to work its way up. She couldn't be certain if they were ascending a rise, a hill, or a small mountain. She only knew that the terrain forced her to sink into Raven. She wished he weren't so tantalizing . . . that he could make her want to recoil instead of immerse herself more deeply into the sturdiness he offered.

The horse gained its footing at the top of the climb. Raven dismounted and helped her down. She no longer stiffened at his touch.

"Walk around, *señorita.* We will be on the horse for a long time."

She heard ground shift, rocks pop from beneath the tread of his feet. Silence. Then the crack of his knees. She followed the sound and knelt beside him. "What are you doing?" she asked.

"I want to make sure the men pick up our trail and not my brothers'."

"What will you do if they follow your brothers?"

"I will have to go back and kill them," he said in a distracted voice, and she could imagine him scanning the horizon, searching for a sign of the riders.

"How many men are there?"

"Eight."

Would her father send that many? He'd probably send the entire male population of Texas. "You honestly think you could kill them all?" She snapped her fingers. "Just like that."

"I am very skilled with weapons."

"If you're so skilled, then why don't you kill them now?"

"Because they have yet to aggravate me. You, however, *señorita*, are coming very close to aggravating me."

"Are you threatening to shoot me?"

He released a deep sigh. "Perhaps I will just gag you."

"You promised—"

"Shh. They have reached the spot where we split up. One is dismounting."

"Are they close enough to hear us?"

"No, but we do not need to take a chance on drawing their attention."

"I thought you wanted them to follow us."

"To follow us, *sí*, to know exactly where we are, no. Now, he is kneeling to study the ground. It is a shame you do not weigh more."

Her mouth dropped open at his audacity. "I beg your pardon?"

"Not so loud."

"You prefer rotund women?"

"I like all women, but a heavier woman would cause the horse to leave deeper tracks, and it would not be so difficult for them to decide which ones to follow."

"Then you think they're looking for me?"

"No. I think they are lazy fools and the clearer markings would appeal to them."

"If they are near enough for you to see, then you could leave—"

"No!"

"Why not?" she asked, exasperated.

"I do not know these men. Me, I know."

"I'm sure my father sent them."

"How can you be sure?"

She loathed admitting the truth because it made her seem like a little girl who needed to be tucked into bed each night. "Because he always looked in on me at the boardinghouse after he closed the saloon. He tried to do it on the sly because I always hated it when he was overprotective after I lost my sight, but he's not the quietest of men." Although she had to admit that he was the most loving because she knew climbing stairs was agony for him, and yet he opened the door to her room every night, peered inside . . . and now he would endure the torment of having a lost child. "Anyway, he would have known before the bank opened that I was gone. So it stands to reason that the first men to follow us would be men my father hired."

"Do you know a man who wears a feather in his hat?" he asked.

"They're close enough that you can see a feather?"

"It is a fancy feather that sticks up, waving in the wind. More of a plume, I guess."

"I suppose my father might know a man who wears a hat like that, but he's not in the habit of discussing men's clothing with me." And she was going to lose her chance for freedom if she wasn't careful. "Yes, yes, as a matter of fact, I remember him mentioning that a dear friend of his had won a garish hat in a poker game."

She held her breath, waiting for his acquiescence. Her entire body ached, and she was so incredibly fatigued. As a rule, she was not a complainer, but right now she would sell her soul for a hot bath, a warm meal, and a soft bed.

"You're bluffing," he said quietly.

"What if I am? I'm damned tired of being protected. First my father and now you! I'm not a child."

"That fact is extremely obvious, *señorita*."

Surely she had not heard appreciation reflected in his voice. She'd always attributed her lack of gentlemen callers on her stubbornness. They wanted to coddle her, and she wanted to be an equal, a daunting expectation in the world of darkness she now inhabited. Even moving into the boardinghouse had not provided her with the independence she craved. The owner, Mrs. Gurney, cooked all the meals and cleaned the rooms. Angela felt as though she'd only braved a tiny step when she longed to take a flying leap.

"They might be Shelby's men," he murmured. "There was one waiting outside the bank."

"Did you kill him for *aggravating* you?"

"I only knocked him out. When he came to, he would have gone for the others. It is unlikely Shelby would only send one."

"I wouldn't be surprised if he sent a hundred. After all, you killed his son."

"You are remarkably informed."

"I'm blind, not ignorant."

She heard his knees pop as he stood. "They've picked up our trail. Let's go."

She held her ground as he walked away.

"If you cause me to lose any more time I am going to bind your hands and stuff a gag into your mouth," he threatened.

"*Now* who's bluffing?" she muttered, rising to her feet, not willing to test his words. It was bad enough to be shackled by the darkness. She hated having her hands bound. If only she had a stronger power of persuasion. "Were you able to identify anything else about them?"

"No."

The horse snorted and slapped his hoof at the ground.

"How far behind us are they?" she asked as she stopped beside him. He had such a palpable presence that it unsettled her. She was drawn to him like metal to a magnet, always knew when he was near, didn't have to reach out to know that she stood within his shadow.

He hoisted her onto the saddle. "About three hours."

"How can you see them if they're that far away?"

"Because my sight is as the crow flies, and they must travel a serpentine path." He mounted behind her, and her rebellious body eased into the familiar contours of his.

"Still, to be visible, they had to start out before the bank opened," she argued.

"I thought we'd already established that."

Beneath her, the horse began to walk.

"I'm just trying to reinforce my theory that they won't harm me."

"You think you could survive three hours by yourself, waiting for them?"

"Yes," she blurted, without hesitation, hope swelling within her that freedom was at hand.

"Too bad I am not ready to give you up."

Lee studied the tiny lights glittering in the black sky. The light of the quarter moon guided his way as much as the stars. He gauged his location in comparison to his destination. If it were not for the woman, he would not be worried. He had always known he was living on borrowed time, had always known that sooner or later, he would have to pay the price for his actions that long ago night.

Although he often felt that he'd been paying

the price for five years. Hoping to avoid capture, he kept himself isolated. No woman warmed his bed. No woman smiled when she caught sight of him.

He never had the delicate scent of a woman wafting around him as he did now. Her fragrance reminded him of his mother's flower garden in late spring. Did he keep this woman nestled within his arms for her protection or his salvation?

Her silence was almost as torturous as her nearness. "Three hours," he said quietly.

She stiffened and turned slightly. "What?"

"It has been three hours since we left the ridge. It seems like a long time to wait alone."

She slumped against him. "They would have found me by now."

"If you were still alive. If no snake or wildcat had crossed your path. You prefer a wild animal to me, though, eh?"

"Definitely."

He smiled in the darkness. She had such spunk, this small woman he held tightly, more tightly than he *needed* to, not nearly as tightly as he *wanted* to. After so many hours of travel, she still carried her unique faint fragrance.

His bristly chin continually caught on her tangled hair. Her lovely dress of soft material that he did not know the name for was smeared with dirt, sweat, and his blood, and probably ruined beyond repair. Her eyes were red and swollen from lack of sleep. The corners of her mouth remained turned down. How he would like to see her smile, hear her laughter, have her whisper his name in a moment of passion.

The intensity with which he longed to make her his was ludicrous. His mind knew it, but his body always listened to his heart, and his heart had never felt this incredible yearning to possess a woman.

She had every reason to complain, to protest. Yet she remained stoic and brave. She had not shed a single tear, when most women would have succumbed to a fit of hysterics.

He did not think it was her blindness that made her different. There were moments, many moments, when he forgot that she could not see him. Her eyes had a way of resting on him until he felt that perhaps she *could* see him. Not the outer shell, but the inner core. The part of him that was terrified of the hangman's noose, of kicking in the wind, as his father and brother had done, of fighting desperately to draw in air that would not come—

"What's wrong?" she asked, breaking into his thoughts.

"Nothing."

"You grew tense."

He wanted to turn her around, wind her arms around his neck, and bury his face within the silky curve of her throat. "Bad memories."

"Were you thinking of the man you murdered?"

"No." He removed his hand from her waist and bunched his fingers around her hair. Even

with the tangles, it was incredibly soft. It had
been too long since there had been any softness in
his life. She grew so still that he was not even certain that she breathed.

"What are you doing?" she whispered in a
voice that carried an undercurrent of fear.

In the beginning, he had wanted her to be wary
of him so he could manipulate her. Now, he desperately longed for her trust. He fisted his hand
more tightly around her red strands. They reminded him of molten flames. He wondered if
they could burn away his doubts, his disappoint-
ments.

"You have such beautiful hair. Why is no man
waiting for you in Fortune?"

"That's none of your business."

"You tell me that you are none of my business—"

"Because I'm not, and keeping me will not
change anything. You're just going to make the
situation worse for yourself," she snapped.

Ah, her anger excited him. She had so much
passion quivering along her body. He wanted to
bury himself in her and forget his past, his future.
For just a short time, he wanted to feel normal, to
recapture the dreams he'd once possessed of having a woman who loved him, children who
adored him, and years before him that consisted
of nothing more than days of laborious work and
nights of hard loving.

"There is nothing worse than knowing that a
hangman's noose awaits you, *señorita*. You have

nothing with which to threaten me, nothing that will make me release you—until I decide it is time."

"You know so little. The worst thing in the world is losing someone you love."

Within her hair, his fingers spasmed as he recognized the resounding emotion in her voice. Love, deep and binding. "You lost someone you loved?" he asked cautiously.

"Not *loved*. *Love*. I still love him. I'll always love him."

The reason no man waited for her. Her heart was closed. Unexpected envy, hot and blinding, toward the man she loved seared his soul while disappointment reeled through him. He unclenched his fingers and took his hand away from her hair.

He was a fool. What had he been thinking? Where she was concerned, he seemed to have misplaced his common sense. Even if her heart belonged to no one, he could still never possess her. He had nothing to offer any woman except the pain of a heart shattered while she was still young because the path he now trod guaranteed him a short life.

"Tell me of this man."

"He's none of your business."

Neither was she, but that knowledge didn't stop his yearning to know everything about her. "Please. I am bored, we have many miles to travel, and I like the gentleness of your voice."

She shook her head slightly and he thought she would say nothing, but then she spoke with a fondness riddled with sadness. "He wasn't a man. He was a boy."

A boy. Unwarranted relief coursed through him. "Did you lose him long ago?"

"Yes, but it seems like yesterday. Since I was older, I'd watch him whenever we visited his family. I have sisters, but he was special."

"What happened?"

She released a deep, shuddering sigh. "We were playing hide and seek. He went to hide and I counted to a hundred. I heard horses. Then his cry. Just one cry. Renegades took him. I saw them . . . and then I hid, afraid they'd see me and take me, too."

"It is good that you hid."

She sat up straighter. "You don't you understand. I did nothing to stop them, nothing to save him. Three days later Uncle Kit found the remains of his bloodied clothes."

He furrowed his brow. "Kit Montgomery?"

She nodded. "His son. I lost his son."

The deep anguish in her voice cut into his heart like the rusty blade of a knife. "You did not lose him."

"Yes, I did," she insisted. "I was supposed to watch him."

"You were a child—"

"I was nine. Old enough to take care of him. Three years later, when I became ill and lost my sight, I thought . . ." Her voice trailed off as though the thoughts were too unbearable to say aloud.

"Thought what?" he prodded.

"That God was punishing me for losing him."

He tightened his hold on her. "No one was punishing you."

"But if I'd been watching him more closely—"

"It was a horrible thing, but you were not responsible."

She scoffed. "How could you possibly understand? You don't know the meaning of responsibility. I don't even know why I told you so much. Maybe because I'm extremely tired."

He cradled her face and pressed it into the nook of his shoulder. "Then sleep, *señorita.*"

"Now, you know why Kit Montgomery will be relentless in his pursuit," she mumbled. "He completely understands the pain my parents now face."

In all his readings on Montgomery, he'd never read of a lost son, although the man revealed nothing of his family. No doubt the Ranger was cautious and understood that he might endanger those he loved if he gave away too much information.

Long minutes passed before Lee felt Angela grow limp against him and drift into an indulgence he no longer had the luxury of experiencing. He could not remember the last time he had slept soundly . . . if he ever had.

His dreams had been riddled with demons long before the night Shelby had attacked his family. Although the nightmares had worsened since the assault, they had always shadowed his dreams. He'd never been able to determine what had provoked them. He only knew that he dreaded their arrival because he was powerless against the images they evoked ... and always after they'd passed and he had awoken, to his shame, he'd discovered his face damp with tears.

"Damn it!" Raven spat.

Angela sat up straighter in the saddle. He'd brought the horse to a halt at what she felt certain was the summit of a rise. In the past few days, he seemed to be stopping more frequently, glancing over his shoulder, growing increasingly tense with each mile they covered. "What is it?" she asked.

"One has broken away from the pack, and he has a very fast horse."

"His horse only has the burden of one rider," she pointed out unnecessarily. "Yours has two. You can't possibly stay ahead. Leave me—"

"No!"

"How close is he?"

"An hour, perhaps less," he bit out.

"Then leave me. For God's sake, leave me. I'll be all right for that short bit of time."

"I don't know this man who follows us."

"Neither do I." She fought back the tears of anger and frustration. She would not cry. God help her, she would not cry. "But I don't want to be here! I don't want to be near you. *I want to go home.* I'll take my chances with the other man."

He dismounted. She expected his hands to come around her waist. Instead she heard his boots thundering over the ground and his spurs jangling as he paced, his anger evident with every stride.

Carefully, she swung her leg over the horse and worked her way to the ground. Never had she despised the darkness more because she could not judge his mood. Intense, angry, she knew. But was his anger directed at her or himself? She didn't know how to play the hand. How to win what she so dearly wanted.

"Please," she pleaded softly. "Please leave me here."

The pacing came to an abrupt halt, the silence almost deafening.

"If I give you one of my guns, will you shoot at this man the way you shot at me?" he asked quietly, no emotion reflected in his voice.

Hope spiraled through her that freedom was imminent. "Yes, if he threatens me in any way, I won't hesitate to squeeze the trigger."

She heard the haunting hiss as his gun cleared the leather holster. When he took her hand, she realized that she was trembling. He folded her fingers around the handle of his gun.

"Aren't you afraid I'll shoot you again?" she joked pitifully, so afraid she'd lose this opportunity if he realized how terrified she was to be left alone.

"I prefer a bullet to a hangman's noose."

"I won't shoot you."

"I know. Once was enough. Keep the gun hidden within the folds of your skirt until you know you can trust him. If you think you can't, raise the

gun quickly . . . this high." He lifted her hand.
"And shoot. You'll hit him in the chest. He is not a
tall man."

She nodded, her mouth suddenly as dry as the
air in west Texas where Kit Montgomery lived.
Raven slowly released her hand. She dropped the
gun to her side, hiding it within the material of
her skirt.

"If he tries to harm you, I will be too far away
to hear your scream." Regret laced his voice.

Until this moment, she hadn't fully realized
that it truly was concern for her welfare that had
prevented him from leaving her behind earlier.
She knew only the outer man and very little of the
inner one. She was intimately familiar with his
chest, his stomach, the inside of his thighs, and
the arm that held her as she slept. She didn't
know what to make of this outlaw whose reputation seemed so inconsistent with his behavior.
"He won't hurt me. I'm sure of it."

"Then remember me, *querida.*"

His mouth captured hers. Snaking one arm
around her waist, he drew her up against his firm
body while he plowed his other hand through the
tangled mess of her hair, angling her head to better accommodate his desires. And she had no
doubt that he desired her or that she should be
afraid, afraid of all the incredible sensations and
misgivings he stirred to life within her.

Never had she been kissed with such rapacious
hunger. Never had a man's mouth possessed hers
as though he owned it. Never had a man poured
so much molten passion into a kiss that she

thought she might melt at his feet. He plunged his tongue deeply, exploring intimately as though it was his undeniable right to do so.

Her mouth betraying her, she returned his kiss with a fervor that frightened her. She could blame it on the intimate moments when she'd slept within his arms or the long hours of riding when their bodies were pressed so close as to be almost one. But her yearning for his kiss went beyond the physical, to a heart as lonely as hers, to a soul as battered and bruised.

Abruptly, he drew away. She staggered backward, breathless and trembling. She heard his footsteps as he stomped to the horse, the creaking of the saddle as he mounted, the horse's hooves pounding the earth as he rode off . . .

The silent echo of her heart calling him back . . .

Chapter 7

Still trembling with the lingering passion of Raven's departure, Angela heard the horse and rider arrive. Had an hour passed already?

During that time, she had relived Raven's bold, demanding kiss a thousand times, contemplating all the things she should have done: stomped on his foot, jerked her knee up and caught him in the groin, pleaded with him not to leave her.

How could she possibly harbor this intense longing for an outlaw, for a man who had abducted her in the dead of night? She blamed her unfathomable desire on hours of riding within his embrace, feeling the sting of his anger, the warmth of his concern, the hint of his teasing. As preposterous as it was, she wished she had known him before he'd turned to a life of crime.

"Where's Raven?" a masculine voice demanded.

She heard the man dismount, and his horse snort.

"He . . . he left. Rode away. Hours ago."

"He left you here alone?"

She nodded at his cautious inquiry. "Yes, so you can take me—"

"Did he grow tired of you warming his bed?"

She released a startled scream, the gun flying from her hand as he knocked her to the ground unmercifully. A sharp pain ricocheted through her skull, bright stars bursting through the darkness.

The man's heaviness pressed down on her, threatening to crush her ribs. She bucked ineffectually, distantly aware of his hand creeping beneath her skirt, his thick fingers digging into her thigh as oblivion and blessed escape claimed her.

Her head thrumming with a dull ache, Angela awoke slowly, vaguely conscious of the tendrils of warmth sent out by the nearby crackling fire, acutely aware of the soft, damp cloth outlining slowly, ever so slowly, the curve of her cheek. She somehow knew with an undeniable certainty who was touching her with a gentleness that made her throat grow tight with emotions. "Lee?"

"*Sí*. I am here."

She started to rise up on her elbows, only to have him press her down. "Lie still," he ordered. "You hit your head on a rock."

She settled back against the hard ground, an astonishing thought swirling through her hazy mind. "You came back."

"I never left, *querida*." With incredible tenderness, he trailed the cloth across her chin and along her throat. Then he gave the same exquisite attention to the other side of her face.

Her body ached in every conceivable place except the one where she had expected the most pain. "You never left," she repeated softly.

"I did not expect him to move so quickly." He traced his finger along her exposed collarbone. "He ripped your dress, but he accomplished nothing more."

A wretched, dry sob escaped her as he assuaged her fears, terror at the thought of what the man might have done after oblivion had descended, events that mercifully she could not remember. Lee slid his hand beneath her head, lifted her slightly, and pressed her face into the crook of his shoulder, murmuring gently in Spanish, words she couldn't comprehend, though they provided solace. She let the tears fall and curled her fingers around the opening to his shirt. "You knew he would attack me," she said.

"I only knew he broke away from the pack of wolves. An avaricious man who wanted to share the bounty with no one. A man such as this is often greedy for other things."

She squeezed her eyes shut to stay the tears. Dreading the answer, she dared to ask, "Did you kill him?"

"No, I crept up behind him and knocked him out with the butt of my gun. When we left, he was still breathing."

She thought she detected disappointment in his voice, not so much because the man still lived, but because her question had wounded him. What did he expect her to think when he was wanted for murder? Gently he laid her down.

"When we left?" she repeated.

"We rode for a while, but when you would not wake up, I got worried."

Worried? In his concern for her welfare, he'd made her a pallet, used his poncho for a pillow, built a fire ... a fire ... crickets chirped. "It's night! They'll spot this fire."

"Probably," he answered, resignation laced through his voice. "But your hands were like ice. I was afraid you were dying. I did not want you to die cold."

"Put out the fire."

"You surprise me. I assumed you would welcome my capture."

Until a few hours ago she would have, but now she was astonishingly aware of the difference between the men who followed and Raven. She had expected the outlaw to be uncouth, immoral, without a fiber of decency woven through the tapestry of his character. Instead, she was discovering that he was a labyrinth of contradictions. A man who failed to heed the law but still managed to appear chivalrous. "Now, I owe you."

"Is that all there is to it, *querida*?"

Her breath hitched as he stroked his thumb

across her bottom lip, and she forced her tongue to stay behind her teeth when she desperately wanted to taste him again.

"Why didn't you fight me when I kissed you?" he asked in a quiet seductive voice that sent shivers tingling along her spine and warmth curling in the pit of her stomach.

"I . . ." She swallowed hard, determined to lie so he would never know the intensity with which she desired him, a fervor that frightened with its unfamiliarity, but lured her with a promise of fulfillment. "I was afraid you might take offense and decide not to leave me."

He leaned closer, and his chest pressed against her breast. Her entire body reacted quite differently than it had to the closeness of the man in the clearing. Where before she'd experienced revulsion, now profound desire swamped her.

He brushed his lips across the corner of her mouth. "So . . . if I were to kiss you now, you would fight?"

Closing her eyes, she wished she could gaze into his. Were they the brown of pecans or the black of rich soil? "I'd fight you," she whispered with a breathless voice that belied her words, "but my head hurts."

He pressed his mouth to her temple. "It is a shame we are far from home. Juanita could give you a potion for your head, and I would call your bluff."

Her heart very nearly stilled. Like every word he spoke about home, this woman's name had been surrounded by love. "Juanita?"

"My sister. She knows much about herbs."

Unwarranted relief flooded her. So incredibly stupid. This man was a notorious outlaw. Kit Montgomery had spent his life searching for men such as this, to bring them to justice, to ensure that the people of Texas were safe. Even her father and Grayson Rhodes . . . years ago, they had stood beside Kit and survived a gunfight against a band of outlaws that had become legendary.

As for his threat to call her bluff, not even her father had ever been able to read her with the astute accuracy that Raven did. She didn't want to contemplate the intimacy growing between them or the reason she welcomed it even though it terrified her. "Lee, put out the fire," she repeated.

"Not until you have eaten."

He retreated, and she mourned the loss of his touch, even though she knew danger resided within the desires swirling through her. "You're risking capture."

"They will find me anyway, my stomach is growling so loud."

Sitting up, she moaned low as pain ricocheted across the base of her skull.

"Is it bad?" he asked.

She shook her head slightly.

"You never complain," he said with amazement.

"I seem to recall voicing several objections—"

"That I took you in the dead of night, *sí*, but that you are hungry or cold or weary, no. You are a remarkable woman, Angela Bainbridge."

As his footsteps faded in the distance, she

scooted back until she could lean against a tree. A remarkable woman? Hardly. Her head throbbed with an agony that made it difficult to hold the demons of her past failures at bay.

Fifteen years had passed, but she could see the moment as clearly as if it were yesterday. And the child they had entrusted to her keeping, Damon Montgomery. With his mother's blond hair and his father's pale blue eyes, eyes that had sparkled with merriment whenever they had played together.

She had been four years older, old enough to know better than to stray far, but he had been searching for the perfect hiding place. When the renegades had attacked, he'd been at their mercy.

Angela shuddered. No matter how tightly she closed her eyes, she couldn't prevent the image from appearing. Fair-skinned Damon, trapped beneath the bronzed arm of a warrior as his horse galloped away.

Now, men just as treacherous were closing in on Lee, and she felt as helpless. She contemplated putting out the fire, but the stubborn man would probably only rebuild it. Based on the tales she'd heard, she'd expected him to behave as the man in the clearing had . . . ruthlessly, unmercifully. Yet at every turn, he'd failed to meet her expectations.

"I hope rabbit appeals to you," he announced, interrupting her thoughts. His knees popped, and she envisioned him crouched before the fire, preparing the meal.

"I can't believe you're taking time to cook."

"It won't take long, and my horse can use the additional rest. It will be his last for a while."

"You didn't take that man's horse?"

"They hang horse thieves."

Her stomach tightened. "What difference does that make when you'll probably hang anyway?"

"I would not like to see a noose slipped around your pretty neck if someone mistakenly thought you were the one who stole it."

"How can you joke about it?"

"For a long time I have lived with the knowledge that I'll hang. I do not welcome it, but that is the way of it."

She heard the fire crackle, and a tantalizing aroma wafted toward her. Lee sat beside her, and she realized because of her, he had lost valuable time, had shortened the distance between himself and capture. In the beginning, as much as she'd hated being bound, she'd found satisfaction in the fact that he obviously thought she was capable of escaping. She had managed to slow him down, but now guilt pricked her conscience. He had not abandoned her even though she'd wanted to ensure his capture.

"Lee," she said quietly, "I'm sorry that I asked you to leave me behind. I just wanted to go home so badly."

He cradled her face with such tenderness that she almost wept again. "I know, *querida*. I am not angry with you, and I regret that I must return to my home before I take you to Fortune."

Her heart slammed against her ribs. "What are you talking about? You told Alejandro that as soon as you lost sight of these men—"

"I know what I told him, but before the sun set,

long before I made camp, I spotted another group of riders."

With her hope spiraling, she sat up straighter. "They could be men my father hired."

"Possibly. Or if indeed your father contacted Montgomery, they might be Rangers. Either way, now I know that many are in pursuit, and I cannot take the time to return you until I know for certain that my brothers made it home safely."

She sank against the tree, acknowledging his unasked question. "I'll cooperate."

"*Gracias*. Once I know all is well with them, I will return you to Fortune."

He moved away from her and she listened to the sounds of him preparing a meal. Her mind drifted. She knew the first group of riders hadn't been hired by her father; the man never would have attacked her. But the second group . . . if there was any chance at all that they were more interested in her than Lee . . . and yet she understood fully his need to check on his family. Her own family was constantly in her thoughts. Her parents would be frantic with worry. If only she could somehow let them know no harm had come to her . . .

She removed the deck from her pocket and searched for her favorite card, the two of hearts. Her father had won her mother's hand in marriage with that card. Dare she leave it behind as a signal to ease their troubled hearts? Slipping it beneath the previous winter's leaves, she could only hope that it would be found and the message understood.

She nearly leapt out of her skin when Lee set a plate on her lap. "Sometimes you move so quietly."

"I am a man of many talents. Eat."

Gingerly she searched for a strip of meat. She'd always been self-conscious eating in front of people, but from the beginning it hadn't bothered her to eat while Lee watched. She assumed her need to survive was stronger than her aversion to embarrassment. She slipped the succulent meat into her mouth, and almost groaned from the pleasure of eating something besides jerky. "Why did you turn to a life of crime?"

Sensing his stillness, she could well imagine his dark eyes boring into her. "It is not so much a life of crime as it is one of revenge."

"Against Vernon Shelby?"

"*Sí.*"

Slowly she chewed while contemplating what she knew. He had killed Vernon Shelby's son. He signed his name to the bank robberies, always indicating that he was only taking Shelby's money. But when questioned, Shelby had no idea who Lee Raven was or why he'd singled him out. "I overheard Kit and Spence talking once—"

"Who is Spence?" he interrupted.

"Uncle Kit's son."

"I thought his son had died."

She set the plate aside, her appetite suddenly deserting her with the reminder of her failure to protect Kit's firstborn, the initial heir to his family's English estate. "Spence is his younger son."

"You speak of him as though you care for him."

Was Lee jealous? No man had ever expressed the slightest bit of envy where she'd been concerned. She suddenly understood why her sisters found it thrilling to have an abundance of gentlemen vying for their attention. "Spence is simply a good friend."

"Has he ever kissed you?"

She laughed self-consciously. He *was* jealous. "No. He's considerably younger than I am."

"What has age got to do with anything?"

She could not believe she was in the middle of nowhere with an aching head and a curious outlaw. "Do you prefer older women?"

"I enjoy women of all ages. Do you prefer older men?"

She sighed. "I was the one asking questions."

"Now *I* am the one asking. How old is this Spence?"

The man was infuriating beyond measure. "Eighteen."

"How old are you?"

"Twenty-four. How old are you?" she fired back.

"As old as my tongue, and a little bit older than my teeth."

Stunned, she sat in silence. Did the man have to be so damned mysterious? "You can't trust me enough to tell me your age?"

"The less you know, the better."

She folded her arms and tucked them beneath

her breasts. "Oh, that's right. The bad men will do anything to find out what you look like." Based on the nearness of his voice, she leaned toward him. "Don't you understand that *you're* the bad man?"

"Have you forgotten the man who attacked you?"

"Maybe you didn't notice, but he wasn't exactly asking me to describe you!"

She jerked at the sound of a plate crashing against a tree. Lee's thundering footsteps vibrated against the ground. Against her better judgment she decided to press her advantage. She rose and fisted her hands against her sides. "You abducted me. You killed a man. You steal another man's money—"

His pacing came to an abrupt halt. "He stole from us!"

His harsh breathing surrounded her, and she could envision his chest heaving, his eyes filled with anger. "Are you saying that you're stealing your own money?"

"No." She heard him swallow. Tension strained the air between them. "He stole our land. He took our cattle . . . he shattered our innocence."

The anguish in his voice weakened her knees and she sank against the tree. "If what you say is true—"

"Do you think I would lie?"

Of all the things she didn't know about this man, the one thing she did know was that he'd always been truthful. "No, I don't think you're lying. But why not go to the authorities?"

"It's his word against ours. He said *we* stole the cattle, *we* stole the land. Then they lynched our father and oldest brother while the sheriff stood there and announced that justice had been served. When our mother tried to stop them, they killed her."

Her stomach roiled. "But Shelby claims he never *heard* of Lee Raven before you committed crimes against him."

"A man cannot give a description of someone if he does not recognize the name."

The more she learned about him, the less she seemed to know. She should have realized that an outlaw wouldn't use his true name. "What is your name?"

"I've told you too much already. Finish eating so we can leave."

She heard him covering the fire with dirt and felt its radiating warmth retreat. She was a fool to care for this man, to desire any knowledge of him; all she would ever receive from him was heartache.

Would she—could she—betray him if she acquired the knowledge he so jealously guarded? Or as she feared, was she developing a fondness for him that might threaten her dedication to justice?

Lee despised the thick silence stretching between them and the stiffness in Angela's body. Revealing his name would give away not only his identity, but his past—a past he could barely remember, but wanted desperately to forget.

He and Angela had ridden for hours, taking only a few short breaks. He could not afford to rest for long or to sleep. He had lost precious distance between himself and the men who followed him. For an inexplicable reason, he was more concerned about the second group. If there were Rangers searching for Angela, they would be relentless in their pursuit, driven by loyalty, not money.

He withdrew his poncho from his saddlebag. Angela stirred as he slipped it over her head to offer her some protection against the cool night air. He worried about the blow she'd taken to the head. He should never have left her unprotected and alone.

"Settle against me so you are more comfortable," he said, pressing on her shoulder until her back eased against his chest and her head nestled within the crook of his shoulder. As dangerous as it was, he enjoyed the way she fit against him. "How is your head?" he asked.

"It just aches a little." She released a small laugh, a delightful sound that gave him hope she might have forgiven him. "I saw stars when my head hit the ground. I haven't seen stars since I was twelve."

"It is a clear night. A thousand stars twinkle in the heavens." A perfect night to kiss a woman, and he was incredibly tempted to kiss Angela again, to feel her pliant, warm lips moving against his.

When he was younger and his days were marked by hard toil and the loving embrace of a complete family, he'd dared to sneak a kiss or two when a pretty girl was willing. But as a man, he'd never known the full flavor of a woman's mouth . . . until Angela. Her sweet, tempting taste haunted him still. He could easily become obsessed with her, and that obsession would endanger them both.

"Why did you stay?" she asked softly.

"I told you. I realized I couldn't go. Since I did not know the man, I could not trust him not to harm you."

"And if he hadn't knocked me to the ground?"

"I would have slipped farther into the shadows." And have never seen her again, but he would have thought of her constantly. Whenever he heard a mockingbird or watched a sunrise or wrapped his poncho around his body. Whenever the wind wailed, the leaves in the trees rustled, or he sat alone in his saddle. She would be there, taunting him with dreams that lay beyond his grasp.

"I don't understand why you risked capture when I've been nothing but trouble."

"I have a bad habit of always wanting to protect women," he murmured. "Even when they are aggravating." Especially when they intrigued him, challenged him, made him wish he was a rancher, a teacher, a merchant . . . a simple man with a simple life that allowed him to sleep at night with a woman in his arms.

"So I assume you've had a lot of women in your life."

He couldn't determine if she'd issued a statement or asked a question, but he was fairly certain she didn't welcome the thought that he might have had a life filled with women. The realization made him smile. "Not too many."

"How many?"

He shrugged. "A hundred. Maybe two."

A startling realization hit her. It was the first time he hadn't been honest with her. "Did you know that your accent thickens when you lie?"

"Then my accent must forever be thick."

"Not really. Sometimes it's as though it's not there at all. That's part of the reason that I thought it was fake that first morning."

"And the rest of the reason?"

She shook her head. "I can't quite put my finger on it."

And he hoped she never would because that one bit of information had the power to unleash all that he wanted to forget.

"I could have gotten you killed today," she said quietly, leaning back and tilting her face slightly.

"But you did not. I am an extremely cautious man."

"You saved me, and I don't even know what you look like."

She lifted her hand and he quickly wrapped his fingers around her wrist.

"Let me touch your face," she pleaded gently.

"No."

"Are you hideously ugly?"

Her tart voice made him smile. He much preferred her anger to her sadness.

"If you know what I look like, *querida*, I cannot return you to your father."

"I would never tell anyone."

"I never thought that I would murder a man. You cannot know what you would do, *querida*, until you are in the situation."

"Why *did* you kill Floyd Shelby?"

Not even for her would he break the vow he'd taken that long ago night. "He aggravated me."

"*He* aggravated you? It sounds as though you weren't trying to get even with Vernon Shelby. What did his son do?"

The woman's mind was like a steel trap, latching onto the most insignificant of things and twisting them around until she discovered their significance. "It is best to forget that night."

"But you're not forgetting it. You're on a quest for revenge—"

"Some things are to be remembered, some forgotten, and that is all I will say on the matter. Now, go to sleep."

Miraculously, she did as he ordered. He could only assume that her head still ached, and she welcomed the opportunity to escape the pain. Her head dropped forward and he positioned it at a more comfortable angle.

For one insane moment, he considered pressing her palm against his cheek, even though she'd fallen asleep and would never know. But if she ever touched his face, he feared her caress would reach into his heart.

Chapter 8

With Grayson Rhodes standing beside him, Christian Montgomery watched helplessly beneath the boughs of an ancient oak tree. There, Jessye Bainbridge clung to the scrap of green material that had once been part of her daughter's dress. A woman's tears had the ability to bring him to his knees, but this woman's tears were especially painful to witness.

Other than his wife, Jessye was the most courageous woman he knew. He had not been surprised when he'd met up with Harry and Gray to find Jessye was with them. It was fortunate that he'd been at the Rangers' Austin headquarters when the telegram had arrived alerting him to Angela's abduction. Since he'd had less distance to travel, he'd been able to begin the search sooner.

Harry had his arms wrapped around his wife, and Kit could see that he was fighting back despair. The evidence—disturbed ground, a bloody rock, the scrap of cloth—suggested that a struggle had taken place in the clearing.

"I want this man found, Kit, I want him found, and by God, I want to be the one to kill him," Harry said.

Kit cast a quick glance at his son, crouched in the center of the clearing, a pensive expression causing deep furrows to crease his brow. A thinker. Spence would make an excellent earl to Ravenleigh, the family estate in England. Four of his men were fanning out on foot, rummaging for evidence. He'd sent two other Rangers, Sean Cartwright and Adam Smith, on horse to search the surrounding area.

"I brought my best men, Harry."

Jessye met his gaze, her eyes limpid pools of green. "What do you think happened here?"

God help him, he should have known she wouldn't be content until she knew all. Kit combed his fingers through his hair. He was in dire need of a haircut, but ever since he'd received word of Angela's abduction, he'd thought of nothing except finding her. "In all honesty, I don't know what to make of this situation, but I don't think Raven has hurt Angela."

"Why?" Jessye asked, the relief in her voice like a sharp knife to Kit's heart as her fingers tightened around the scrap of cloth. He hated dealing out false optimism, yet he wanted to lessen their worry. He could only pray that it wasn't for naught.

"If his intent was to attack Angela, why wait almost a week? It makes no sense."

"Does taking our daughter make sense?" Harry asked.

Kit shook his head. "No, no, it doesn't. Especially since he hasn't asked for a ransom."

"Perhaps because he hasn't had time," Gray suggested. "After all, we've determined there's a group of bounty hunters between him and us."

"Which makes it even less likely he attacked her, not when the men following were at their closest."

Jessye tightened her fingers around the green cloth until her knuckles turned white. "Why did he rip off a portion of her bodice?"

"I don't think he did," Spence said.

Jessye looked at him as she did her own children, with affection. "Two buttonholes, Spence, tell me that this piece came from the bodice of her favorite dress. She'd never tear it off."

"I'm not suggesting that she did. I'm only saying that Raven didn't." He shifted his body and pointed to the ground. "I believe these grooves were made by spurs when someone rolled a few times."

Kit, Harry, and Gray exchanged furtive glances.

"Spence, I don't think we want to travel this line of analysis," Kit said quietly. He had no desire for Jessye to hear any speculative details regarding her daughter's attack.

Spence met his gaze with eyes the same shade of light blue as his own. "I know where you think I'm headed with this, but when a man leaves a woman he's bedded, he doesn't usually roll several times. I think she and Raven stopped here. Perhaps he went in search of food; I'm not sure. But I think she was alone. Another man attacked her. Raven then attacked him, shoved him off her, and the man rolled, repeatedly, his rowels scoring the earth."

"Possibly," Kit acknowledged. "We'll ask him when we find them. And we will find them."

A movement caught his attention, and he watched Cartwright and Adams ride into the clearing and dismount. "What did you discover?"

Cartwright approached him. "We located the fire that we spotted two nights ago. Our guess is that it was Raven. We found this."

Kit took the dirt-covered card he extended.

"Good Lord," Harry said, as he limped across the clearing, leaning heavily on his cane. He snatched the card from Kit's fingers and skimmed his thumb across it. "It's Angela's." He looked at Cartwright. "Did you find the others?"

"No, sir. We almost missed this one. Dried leaves were covering most of it," Cartwright said.

A contemplative expression on her face, Jessye took the card from Harry. "The two of hearts," she murmured.

"Does that mean something?" Kit asked.

"I won Jessye's love with that card."

"You already had my love, Harry, you just earned the right to make me your wife." She met

Harry's gaze with her troubled one. "You don't reckon she was trying to tell us that she loves this man."

"Good God, no! He's an outlaw, Jessye—"

"You were a scoundrel. That didn't stop me from loving you."

"A scoundrel and an outlaw are worlds apart. It must have accidentally fallen out of her pocket," Harry said.

"Harry, from the moment you gave her that deck of marked cards, she insisted on wearing a dress with a pocket so she could carry it with her. If I bought her a dress without a pocket, she'd sewn one in it. Angela deliberately left this card, hoping someone would find it and know what it meant. I'd bet my life on it."

"All right, let's assume for a moment that Angela didn't lose it, but left it on purpose," Kit said. "I think we can safely assume she doesn't love the desperado. So what message was she attempting to convey?"

"It obviously has sentimental meaning to your family. Perhaps she just wanted to reassure you that she was unharmed," Grayson offered.

" 'Not to worry, I'm simply traipsing across the countryside with a murderer'?" Harry asked sharply.

Kit held up his hands. "All right, we don't need to be snapping at each other." He glanced at his son, who was good at deducing. "What do you make of all this?"

"I agree with Gray."

If Spence had been ten years younger, Kit

would have ruffled his burnished hair for that "ask me why I think as I do" look in his eyes. "Because?"

"Why didn't he make camp here?" Spence tossed out, before turning to Jessye. "All we've discovered falls in line with my theory. They stopped here. Perhaps he intended to camp here, but then someone attacked Angela. So they moved on and made camp elsewhere. She left the card to let you know that she's okay."

"Now what do we do?" Jessye asked.

"I propose that we continue on. Raven will be avoiding any populated areas, but that doesn't mean we have to. One of my men can go to the nearest town and send one telegram to your daughters and one to Ashton to allay their worries a little." He knew his wife would be anxious to receive news regarding their search.

Jessye wound her arms around him and released a tiny sob. "Oh, Kit, all those years ago, I thought I knew what you and Ashton were going through. I didn't have a clue."

He hugged her tightly. "We'll find her, Jessye. I won't fail this time."

She lifted her gaze to him. "You didn't fail last time."

He stepped out of her embrace, understanding that an argument was not what she needed at this moment, but reassurances. "Let's prepare to ride."

He walked to Harry's horse and waited for his friend to join him. He knew it grated on his pride that he needed help mounting his horse. He heard Harry's halting footsteps, the cane he used beating out an unsteady tattoo. Then silence.

"At least we have hope that Angela is alive, and perhaps he isn't treating her too shabbily. There's some comfort in not knowing everything, I suppose."

Kit turned and faced his friend of many years. "No, Harry. There's no comfort at all in not knowing. It's been fifteen years since my firstborn son disappeared, and there isn't a damn day when I don't wake up and wonder if what I found was evidence he'd been killed. As painful as the absolute certainty will be, it's better to know."

Chapter 9

Angela ran her swollen tongue over her cracked lips. The unmerciful sun beat down with a vengeance. She was grateful for the shade Lee's hat provided. They seldom galloped now, but simply plodded along over unforgiving terrain. She had lost count of the number of days and nights they'd been together. She had to focus all her effort on remaining in the saddle when she desperately wanted to lie down on the ground and sleep until she was an old woman.

He shoved the canteen into her hands.

"Drink. Once. Hold the water in your mouth for a while before swallowing," he ordered in a voice that sounded like sand brushed over rocks.

She welcomed the drops of moisture coating her tongue, knowing she didn't have the luxury of coating her lips. She handed the canteen back

to him and heard him put it away. She swallowed. "I didn't hear you drink."

"I'm not thirsty," he rasped.

"Lee, you have to drink some water."

"It is not a hard thing to do without when you
have grown accustomed to it," he said.

"I'm very sorry."

With his palm, he tenderly cupped her cheek.
"I have told you before, you have nothing to apologize for. You are courageous, *querida*. You make
me wish . . ."

"What do you wish?"

"For things that can never be. If I do not see the
riders today, tomorrow we'll head home and toward fresh water."

Home. His home, not hers, although now she
had absolutely no fear. She knew as surely as she
knew the moment twilight arrived that he would
return her to her family.

He was not a soft man, yet he gave her moments of softness. She sensed he'd been shaped
more by the one night he'd watched the murder
of his family than all the years that had come before. What would his life be like now if no one
had killed those he loved? She had a thousand
questions to ask him, and a throat that hurt with
each word spoken. The time would come, soon,
when she would gain the answers she sought.

A lightning bolt quickly zigzagged across the
midnight sky. A slow smile eased over Lee's face
as some of the tension that had been mounting
for days left him. Thunder resounded.

"We're in luck, *querida*. A storm."

"I can smell the rain."

"It will be here soon."

He urged his horse into a gallop. With any luck, he could cover some distance before the first raindrop fell, and the drops that followed would wash away his passing.

Because he had grown accustomed to being with Angela he had a difficult time imagining riding alone. He knew a time would come when again he would, but he did not welcome it. He wondered about the men who had passed through her life. Although she claimed to have no one waiting for her, surely many men had courted her.

A raindrop splattered on his thigh. Another hit his hand. Lightning burst through the blackened clouds, thunder boomed, and a torrential rain deluged them. Lee slowed the horse to a walk, swept his hat from his head, and removed hers. "Enjoy the rain, *querida*."

She tilted her face up, her head nestled within the crook of his shoulder as though it had been specifically created with her in mind. It amazed him whenever he studied her, which he did with increasing frequency, to realize that every aspect of her complemented him. Where she was soft, he was hard. Where she was curved, he was flat.

For no more than a heartbeat, a sheet of lightning illuminated her features and he committed each one to memory. The rain hitting her face, her lips spread slightly apart, her tongue darting out to capture the water, the droplets clinging to her eyelashes like tiny pearls.

The freckles over her nose tugged at his heart, made her seem younger, innocent. But she was no child. She was a woman who had fought, beguiled, and shot him. She had slept in his arms, touched the loneliness in his heart with soft words, and impressed him with her courage.

All his life, he'd thought he was incredibly strong, and now he was learning that he was humbly weak. Where she was concerned, he seemed to have no willpower, no strength to resist the enticing temptation she offered.

Skimming his thumb along her cheek, cooled by the rain, he gathered the fine dew of moisture that remained. The heat of her breath warmed his hand. Like a desperate man he slowly lowered his mouth to hers, not with the heated passion that had burned through him before—that had done nothing to sate his desires—but with a patience born of needing one moment in his life where time stood still.

The rain eased up just enough that the gentle patter mingling with the humming of the slight wind became a melody. Her lips yielded to his. With one arm, he drew her more closely into the curve of his body, while his other palm rested against her cheek, his thumb continuing to stroke the velvety softness. Where before he had thrust his tongue into her mouth, now he entered slowly, relishing each passage of the journey, the various textures, the burning recesses that were in direct contrast to her cool cheek. He didn't know if the sigh he heard had come from her or the wind, but he deepened the kiss, and her responding moan shimmered through him clear down to his boots.

What had been merely a spark suddenly ignited into an inferno. He pressed her more firmly against his chest, their drenched clothes absorbing the heat from their bodies until he felt as though they wore nothing at all. He could feel her nipple hardening and straining against the fabric of her dress flattened against his chest.

Lowering his hand, he cupped the firm mound of her breast, his fingers kneading, reshaping, but none of his actions altered her perfection. A guttural growl reverberated through his throat, his breathing grew harsh and rapid. He tore his mouth from hers, bent her slightly, closed his lips around the sweetest bud, and suckled gently through the cloth. She almost came off his lap, whimpering, digging her fingers into his shoulder. He lifted his gaze as lightning revealed a woman entranced, and need shot through him with heart-pounding force.

God help him, he wanted her, wanted her as he'd never wanted anything in his life.

A crack of thunder that resounded around him like the retort of a rifle brought his senses reeling back. As much as he wanted her, he couldn't have her. Not tonight, not ever. For what woman would desire a man who had dug his own grave and knew that he must soon lie in it?

Taking a deep, shuddering breath, he eased her back into the safety of his shoulder.

"Lee?" Her voice quivered, her body trembled.

"Shh," he whispered, pressing his cheek against the top of her head. "I should not have done that."

Her agreement was only silence and a clutching of his shirt as she bowed her head.

He kicked his horse into a lope, toward Mexico and home, fearing he had waited too late to return her to her family, not certain where he would find the strength or the willingness to remove her from his life.

Angela felt as though tender bruises covered every inch of her weary body. Heat had blasted her for more days than she cared to count. Sweat had dried on sweat. She had never in her entire life been so incredibly miserable, physically or mentally.

The kiss Lee had bestowed on her in the rain haunted her, the sensations he had stirred to life continued to brew. She had wanted his mouth on her then, she wanted it now. Yet she knew desires were a danger to them and had to be banked, abandoned, forgotten.

She heard horses trotting in the distance. She smelled a pleasant aroma that made her mouth water and her stomach tighten.

The tension in Lee's body seemed to drain away. "We're nearly home, *querida*," he said quietly. "It is late, almost everyone will be in bed, and I don't want to disturb them, so we must be very quiet."

The thought of sleeping in a bed almost made her weep. "I can be as quiet as a mouse."

He brought his horse to a halt. She heard footsteps on planked flooring. A porch.

"Keeping watch, Alejandro?" he asked.

"I thought you planned to take the woman home first," Alejandro said, displeasure evident in his voice.

"We ran into some trouble and I wanted to make sure you were all right." Lee dismounted, then helped her climb off the horse.

"What sort of trouble?" Alejandro asked.

Lee placed his hand on the small of her back and guided her forward. "There was more than one group . . . step up, *querida* . . . of riders . . . step up. I was afraid you might have run into an ambush."

"We saw no one."

"Good. Then they must have all been following us. See to the comfort of my horse while I show Angela where she can sleep." With his hand still on her back, he prodded her gently. "Come, *querida*, welcome to our humble abode."

The hinges moaned as he opened the door. Angela ran her hand quickly across wood. She had expected adobe. Inside the doorway, a rug muffled her passing.

She heard Lee pick up a lamp as he led her across a large room. Her feet hit wood and then another rug. Wood again. The echo of her footsteps changed, indicating the walls were closer together. A hallway. Snoring.

"Eduardo snores," Lee whispered.

"Eduardo?" He had yet another brother.

"*Sí.* You will meet him tomorrow."

He led her into a room. "You can sleep in here."

Her fingers skimmed the carved post of a bed. She sank onto the mattress. Heaven. She ran her hand over the quilt, noting the stitching, the design, varying scraps of cloth joined together to create a whole. She gave into temptation and curled onto her side. Lee's scent rose up from the pillow and wafted around her. Her eyelids immediately grew heavy, her mind dull. As sleep overcame her, she had a vague notion that Lee had slept here before.

Lee sauntered to the last stall in the barn, where he found Alejandro brushing Lee's horse like a man possessed. He leaned against the beam and crossed his arms over his chest. "You are scraping off his hide."

Alejandro took only a second to glare at him before returning his attention to the animal. "I cannot believe you brought the woman here."

"Her name is Angela."

"And because of her, you will hang. How long do you think it will take her to figure out who you are?"

"She is blind."

"Then that makes two of you."

Alejandro's retort stung Lee's pride. He'd always put his family first. Perhaps, Alejandro was right and this time he hadn't. "I know I cannot have her."

"But that does not stop you from wanting her."

Lee clenched his teeth, refusing to acknowledge his brother's comment, wondering if his desire for Angela was apparent or if Alejandro was
only guessing.

Alejandro stopped brushing and met his gaze.
"Ramon knew he could not have Christine
Shelby, but he did not have the strength to deny
her and look what his love cost us."

"No!" Lee stepped into the stall. He refused to
accept that his oldest brother and the woman he
had loved were responsible for the tragedy that
had befallen the family. Shelby's hatred and
greed had guided his actions. "You cannot blame
Ramon—"

"All I know is that Shelby made idle threats
until he discovered Ramon and Christine by the
river. Why do you think he hanged Ramon instead of you or me?"

With a weary sigh, Lee plowed his fingers
through his hair. Sometimes, it was impossible to
carry on a conversation with Alejandro.

"When was the last time you slept?" Alejandro
asked quietly.

Lee forced a corner of his mouth to curl into a
mock smile. "I slept here and there."

Alejandro shook his head. "You would not let
yourself sleep because you would not want her to
hear your screams."

Lee never knew if they were the cries of a
frightened child or a terrified man. "A man attacked her."

Just as Lee knew it would, all the anger
drained from Alejandro. "What?"

"A man broke away from the pack of wolves following us. Since Angela thought her father had sent him, I let her wait for his arrival, but he was one of Shelby's men. I knocked him out before he did much harm."

"You should have killed him."

"One man's death on my conscience is enough, Alejandro."

"You had no choice where his death was concerned."

Lee nodded, not wanting to remember the horror of that night, but it was always there, skulking in the shadows of his memory, waiting for someone to cast the light upon it. Alejandro was skilled at doing just that, determined to remind him that he had been given no choice . . . but a part of him wondered, always wondered.

"Try to get some sleep," Alejandro ordered before turning back to the horse, stroking the brush over the animal's flank with a bit more gentleness.

"Once I have rested, I will take her home."

"See that you do, brother. Her presence here threatens all of us."

When he was a boy, Lee had learned the value of quietly creeping toward his prey. He could never remember who had taught him or why he'd determined that his very existence depended on silence, but it was a skill that he put into practice when the mood suited him . . . as it did now. Like smoke on a gentle soughing wind, he crept across his sister's room and eased onto the mattress.

With a touch as light as a butterfly landing on a petal, he brushed Juanita's dark strands away from her lovely face. Slowly, she opened her eyes.

"It's Lee," he whispered softly, not wanting to alarm her. She frightened so easily.

She bolted upright and wrapped her arms tightly around his neck. "You're home."

He wanted desperately to hug her in return, as he had when they were children, but he understood too well her aversion to being held, so he kept his arms at his sides, unthreatening. He would give his life to return to her the innocence she'd lost that fateful night.

She leaned back slightly. "Do you want me to cook you something to eat?"

"No. I'm tired, but I wanted to see you before I went to bed."

"I was very worried when Alejandro returned without you. He said you had to take a woman home . . . he made no sense."

He could well imagine that Alejandro had been vague, trying not to worry her. They all sought to protect her, and now he wondered if their solicitude was causing more harm than good. "Her name is Angela. She is here."

"You brought her here?"

"*Sí*. Soon, I will take her home, but first I wanted to make certain everyone made it home safely. You will like her. She is very strong."

"She is a big woman?"

Lee smiled warmly and touched his chest. "In here, she is very strong."

"I will make her most welcome."

"I know you will." And perhaps Angela could teach Juanita not to be afraid. He glanced toward the narrow bed nestled against the wall beneath the window where a small boy slept. "How is Miguel?"

"He missed you. He asked about you every day."

"I will visit with him tomorrow. Now, go back to sleep."

She settled down onto the mattress. "Will you watch over me for a while?"

"Always." A promise that he knew was a lie, because a time would come when he would answer for his crimes, and the revelation would require a sacrifice. Although he often felt that he'd made one five years ago. He continued to breathe, to exist, but he did not live . . . did not dream . . . did not dare hope that he would ever have all he had once longed for.

He watched as her eyes drifted closed and waited until her breathing grew faint. Then he leaned over and kissed her brow before quietly quitting the room.

In the hallway, he contemplated using Alejandro's bed. The worrier would probably keep watch outside the house for the remainder of the night, but Lee had no desire to be alone, and he doubted he would sleep anyway. On the few occasions when sleep came, it was too troubled to be restful, and Alejandro was right. With Angela near, he would not succumb to the deep well of slumber where his nightmares held vigil.

Silently he made his way down the corridor. He and his brothers had built this house. It was not fancy, but it was comfortable. It could not replace the *hacienda* they had shared with their parents in southern Texas, but one day he would give them a home as grand as they'd once had. Reaching his bedroom, he stood in the doorway, mesmerized by a sight he'd never thought to see.

The lamp he'd left on the table beside his bed earlier burned low. Beyond the window beckoned the darkness of night, and in his bed, a woman unknowingly lured him. Her hair fanned out across his pillow. With one hand tucked beneath her cheek, she was curled on her side. His chest tightened. How quickly she had stolen into his life, how difficult it would be to send her home. But he knew he must. He'd managed to elude this group of henchmen . . . but what about the next?

He'd left his boots at the front door. He walked in bare feet across a familiar floor and sat on the mattress where an incredibly courageous woman slept. He imagined the kind of man who would marry her, a man who had not shed blood, who had not violated the laws of God and man.

He knew he should make himself a pallet on the floor or retire to Alejandro's bed. Listening to her soft, even breathing, he stretched out beside her. When she didn't stir, he circled his arm around her waist and pressed his cheek against the top of her head. Since when—where she was concerned—had he done what he should do?

*   *   *

Angela awoke, her eyes gritty, her neck stiff, her body weighted down with the pressure of Lee's arm draped over her side, his leg slung over hers. The times they had slept on the ground, she'd nestled her body against his to ward off the chill of the night, but this position seemed much more scandalous, especially since they were in what she was certain was his bed, the sheets creating a cocoon of intimacy. His warm breath skimmed along the nape of her neck, producing delicious hot shivers along her spine.

She became aware of someone else's breath, quick, shallow, and near. Incredibly near.

"Lee, are you awake?" a child whispered loudly.

Beside her, Lee stirred. "Do I look awake, Miguel?" he mumbled.

"No, but you sound awake. *La señorita es muy bonita.*"

"*Sí,*" Lee replied. "But you must be very quiet so you do not wake her."

"She's already awake," Angela informed him.

Lee groaned. "Sorry, *querida*, I wanted you to be able to sleep late, but I do not think the sun has been up for long." He yawned. "Meet my brother Miguel."

She would have scrambled to a sitting position, but Lee still had her pinned in place. Even though Miguel was only a child, she felt the heat burn her cheeks with the thought of his seeing her in this compromising position. She swallowed and spoke calmly as though being caught in bed with a man to whom she was not married wasn't disgraceful. "Hello."

"*Buenos días, señorita.*"

"You must speak English, Miguel," Lee chided gently.

"Why?"

"Because she does not know as much Spanish as you do."

"Why?"

"Her mother and father are not Mexican."

"Oh."

She heard Lee breathe a sigh of relief and decided to ask her own question. "How old are you?"

Silence. She wondered if perhaps he had a limited knowledge of English.

"Miguel, she cannot see your fingers," Lee said quietly. "You must always speak to her."

"Why can't she see my fingers?" Miguel asked.

"She is blind."

"And she is present," Angela reminded him, "so you don't have to talk about her as though she can't speak for herself."

Lee chuckled. "She gets mad easily." She felt Lee shift as though he was reaching across her and ruffling someone's hair. "But not at you, only at me. Tell her how old you are."

"Soon I will be four." He made it sound as though the age was so much more important than three years, as though three were not even worth acknowledging.

"Now, go tell Juanita that I am hungry," Lee said.

The child padded out of the room with bare feet.

"He seems incredibly sweet," Angela mused.

"He is a good boy."

"And you've raised him," she said.

"We've all helped to raise him."

She knew women who had children late in life, but it was obvious that many years separated this little one from his siblings.

Lee rolled off the mattress. "I will bring you some breakfast and then you can have the bath I promised you."

She listened as he left the room. Then she threw back the covers and scrambled out of bed. She could feel the heat of the sun on her face. Carefully, she began crossing the room to the window. Her fingers touched the smooth surface of the glass just as her toes made contact with a wooden box.

She knelt and ran her hand over the ragged edges of the contents. Books. Small books. She lifted one and riffled the frayed pages. Based on their diminutive size, she guessed that she'd discovered his cache of dime novels. She felt along the edge of the box and found another box beside it. The books here were larger, with leather covers. Beside it she located another box of books. Why didn't he place them on shelves?

Cautiously she circled the room. A bureau with four drawers. She was curious enough to open them and discovered only two had clothes in them; the others were empty. Nothing sat on top of the dresser. The walls were bare. She found a table beside the bed, its only adornment a solitary lamp.

Remembering the rug that had muffled her passing the night before, and the aromas that had greeted her when she'd first walked through the door, she sank onto the bed. The house possessed a definite feeling of being lived in, but not this room. It was as lonely as the man who slept here, a temporary haven that showed no signs of permanence because Lee Raven knew his days were numbered.

She listened for the whirl of wheels as wagons or carriages traveled by, the laughter of people, the din of conversation. She heard nothing but the soughing sigh of the wind and the unmistakable quiet of isolation.

Chapter 10

One Sunday afternoon shortly after her nineteenth birthday, Angela had sat in the front parlor awaiting the arrival of her first gentleman caller, an out-of-town friend to one of the men who had been courting her younger sister Heather. Nervous, anxious, fearful that he would find her lacking, she had been more relieved than disappointed when he never arrived.

But all her concerns then paled in comparison to her worries now. She sat on the edge of Lee's bed, the breakfast he'd brought her sitting heavy in her stomach, while she awaited the arrival of his sister. She had faced unknown suitors, even an outlaw, with more confidence. Her favorite dress was torn beyond repair, her hair was a tangled mess, and she carried the fragrance of too many days' travel.

For the life of her, she couldn't determine why she had any desire to impress Lee's sister. For pity's sake, the woman probably possessed no morals at all. She no doubt entertained other outlaws, perhaps warmed their beds. Maybe she drank, cussed, and wore a gun slung low on her hip. She would not be living with her brother now if she did not condone his actions, and that sanction made her as guilty as he was.

Angela's mouth went dry when she heard boots and slippered feet in the hallway. Slowly she rose, wiped her damp palms on her filthy skirt, and pasted on a false smile as the footsteps came to a halt.

"Oh, Lee, you did not tell me she was in pain," a soft voice exclaimed. A rush of movement followed, and then hands, smaller than Lee's, were resting on her shoulders. "Please sit, *señorita*, and tell me where you hurt. I will make you a poultice or a brew—"

"I'm not hurting," Angela assured her.

"Then why do you grimace?" she asked quietly.

"I was smiling."

"Oh, *señorita, lo siento mucho*. I misunderstood. You have a . . . a beautiful smile."

Angela felt her face transform as all her apprehension melted away and she truly smiled. "I doubt that. It was a nervous grin. I wasn't certain what to expect."

"But what I see now *is* a beautiful smile, Angela," Lee said in a seductive voice, as though they were the only two people in the room. "I do not think you have ever shown me this smile."

"I haven't had many reasons to be happy since you abducted me," she pointed out.

"That is my regret and my loss. Juanita will see to your needs. Don't ask my family what I look like."

The order had been gently given, but she knew it allowed no room for compromise. He left the room and she dropped onto the bed. "I find your brother extremely irritating."

"He would die for you, *señorita*."

Although Angela entertained the possibility that the words were true, she did not dare hope that she would ever mean that much to a man. "I hardly think so."

"Then you do not know him."

But what she *did* know was that she had taken an instant liking to Juanita. Smiling, she held out her hand. "I'm very happy to meet you."

Juanita squeezed her hand and said, "*Mi casa es su casa.*"

Angela sank into the wooden tub, allowing the steaming hot water to lap at her throat. Eduardo had hauled in the tub and filled it with buckets of water. He was almost as shy as Juanita was, muttering a greeting to her before hastily leaving the room. Angela supposed the younger siblings had little choice when the older ones appeared to be so forceful.

She rested her head against the back of the tub where Juanita had set a rolled-up blanket to cushion her neck. She thought she might stay here forever.

She felt the tug on her hair as Juanita worked a comb through the tangles. "We should probably just chop it off," Angela murmured lethargically.

"Oh, no, *señorita*. You have beautiful hair, and I have nothing else to do this morning. Besides, I think it would please Lee. He smiles whenever he speaks of you, and it has been a long time since I have seen him smile."

Angela rolled her eyes, not daring to believe that she had the power to make a man smile with little more than the mention of her name. "Are you sure it wasn't a grimace?" she asked teasingly, thinking of her earlier debacle when she had tried to appear calm.

"Oh, very sure, *señorita*. It is a small smile, sort of wistful as though he was afraid that if he smiled too big, fate would take away his reason to smile at all."

Angela hesitated and then decided that the question she wanted to ask wouldn't exactly address what he looked like. "Does he have a nice smile?"

"A very nice smile. It always warms me inside to see it."

"But you said that he doesn't smile often."

"Not for many years now," Juanita said softly, but Angela heard the sadness in her voice.

She was struck again by how much everyone cared for Lee. It was not fear for the outlaw that drove them. No, it was a deep bond.

She knew she should have chastised him this morning when she awoke in his intimate embrace. Instead, she had wished desperately that he'd allow her to roll over and touch him, hold him as he held her. She wanted to know the cut of his jaw, the shape of his nose, the angles that formed his chin. She knew his height, the breadth of his shoulders, the sturdiness of his arms. But she wanted to know all of him.

She considered asking Juanita to describe him, but she would not allow Lee's sister to unknowingly betray him. Although she despised his need to keep his appearance hidden from her, she also respected his right to want it.

"Lee is the oldest," she speculated.

"Oh, no," Juanita said. "Alejandro is older, although not by much."

Angela sat up slightly. "But Lee seems to be in charge."

"*Sí*. He is good at giving orders."

"So it's Alejandro, then Lee . . ." She trailed off, not certain where to go from there.

"Roberto. Jorge. Me, then Eduardo," Juanita finished.

"And Miguel," Angela added.

"Oh, *sí*. Miguel is the youngest."

"He must have been a baby when your mother died." She cringed when Juanita pulled the comb through her hair, making her scalp sting.

"He was just a baby," she acknowledged.

"When were your parents killed?" Angela asked, unable to remember when she'd first heard of the outlaw.

"I said no questions, *querida*," Lee said sternly.

Angela squeaked and dipped lower into the water. "I didn't hear you come in."

"Because you were too busy interrogating my sister."

"I wasn't interrogating her. Besides, you didn't say I couldn't ask questions. You only said that I couldn't ask what you looked like."

She heard his footsteps echoing loudly now as he came farther into the room. She could clearly imagine him bearing down on her.

"You can go, Juanita."

"What are you going to do to her?" Juanita asked. The tremble in her voice surprised Angela.

"I am going to get the tangles out of her hair."

Juanita quickly attacked her hair with the comb. "I can get the tangles out."

"Juanita," Lee chided gently. "It is my fault they are there. I removed the pins."

His knees creaked, and she knew the moment he took the comb and her hair out of Juanita's hands.

"I do not think it is right for a man to be in a room alone with a woman," Juanita said in a small voice.

"She and I were alone for many nights, Juanita," he said quietly.

"You promised me that you would never hurt a woman."

"And I kept that promise. I will keep it until the day I die. But this one here, she is a smart one. She will find answers to questions she is better off not knowing."

She heard Juanita rise to her feet. "I will never forgive you if you hurt her."

"Juanita, you know me. Do you honestly think I would hurt her even if I had not given you that promise?"

"I'm sorry, Lee, I know you would not hurt her."

She heard tears in Juanita's voice, his knees pop as he stood, and she envisioned him taking his sister within his arms.

"It's all right, Juanita," he murmured. "It's all right."

Juanita sniffed. "I need to fix the midday meal. Do not worry, *señorita*, he will not hurt you."

She listened as Juanita walked out of the room, and Lee once again crouched beside the tub. "She was afraid of you," Angela said.

"She is afraid of the memories. You must not ask my family about that night. It is better that they forget."

"How can they forget if you're constantly seeking revenge?" She felt the teeth of the comb dig into her crown just before he yanked it through her hair. "*Ow!*" she cried, and slapped her hand over his.

"I do not know how to do this," he barked.

"Give me the comb." She held out her hand.

"I can do it. Just tell me how."

She sighed. He was the most aggravating man. "Start at the end and ease—gently—the tangles out until you work your way to the top."

"Sounds simple enough."

The back of his hand came to rest on her bare

shoulder, and she felt the movements as he repeatedly jerked the comb through a section of her hair. She wanted to press her chin against his hand, cradle it within the hollow of her neck. She was grateful the water lapped above her chest, wondered where his gaze wandered. Was he smiling now?

During their kisses, she'd ascertained that he had straight teeth and full lips, and she could well imagine that his smile would beguile any woman fortunate enough to have it directed her way. Had he ever grinned at her? Without permission to touch his face, she had no way of knowing. For all she knew, he was scowling, that fine mouth of his turned down in annoyance, not up in appreciation.

His efforts gentled, slowed. She became aware of his forearm touching her arm, heat radiating near her shoulder, warmth that didn't have to pass through cloth. "You're not wearing a shirt?"

He stilled. "No, I came in to get a clean one. I did not expect to find you in the bath already."

She'd been so desperate to wash away the grime that she'd practically ripped off her clothes. "I was eager to be clean."

Skimming his fingers along the shell of her ear, he moved aside her hair. "Is the water too hot?" he asked quietly.

She shook her head slightly. "Why would you think that?"

"Because dew has gathered along your throat, a drop trails down . . . right here . . ." He nuzzled her neck.

She was acutely aware of the wanton desire pooling deep within her, his lower lip capturing the moisture as his heated mouth journeyed higher, his eyelashes fluttering against her ear as though he'd closed his eyes, his teeth nibbling at her lobe, his rapid, harsh breathing. She heard him swallow hard as his fingers fisted around her hair. "Maybe . . . maybe I'd better comb out the tangles," she offered softly, breathlessly.

"*Sí*, I need to take a bath," he rasped.

She halfway expected him to leap into the water with her. Instead, she heard the familiar pop of his knees as he stood and noted that his hand shook when he pressed the comb against her palm. She listened to the heavy tread of his boots as he quit the room and sought what comfort she could in the knowledge that she'd determined he had large feet.

Smiling, she sank further into the water. He also had long eyelashes, long, thick eyelashes that tickled like the fragile petals of a dandelion when her mother would blow them into her face. Her smile of wonder spread throughout her body. Of all the things about an outlaw to discover.

A small sound caught her attention, the brush of a body against a wall. "Miguel?"

She heard him catch his breath. "How did you know, *señorita*?"

She touched a finger to her ear. "I have very good hearing."

He padded across the floor, and the warmth of his body hovered near her shoulder. She thought about telling him that he shouldn't be in here, but a child's innocence was incredibly disarming.

"Lee said I could have a *piñata* for my birthday," he announced, as though it was the most natural thing in the world to talk to a woman who sat in a bathtub. "Will you come to my birthday party?"

She heard the yearning in his young voice, but she didn't know exactly when his birthday was or if she'd still be here.

"Will there be lots of children there?" she asked.

"My brothers and Juanita."

Her stomach tightened with the knowledge that she should have understood. He could have no friends here because his brother was an outlaw. With a sadness for all he could not have, she smiled, knowing no matter how long it took, she wouldn't leave until she'd fulfilled this obligation. "I'll be here for your birthday."

"*Gracias, señorita.* I will let you try to break the *piñata.*" He flung his thin arms around her neck and planted a slobbery kiss on her cheek. He released her abruptly, and she heard his hasty retreat, no doubt eager to share the news that he would have a guest for his birthday celebration, news that would probably not be welcomed by many family members. But she would deal with them when the time came.

Besides, that little boy with his eagerness filled an aching chasm in her heart, a chasm created that awful day she'd lost Damon Montgomery. She couldn't believe she'd told Lee about it. She had been nine, old enough to watch him. He had been a year older than Miguel would soon be. Five. Equally eager, equally enthusiastic, equally giving of his hugs and kisses.

He'd had nothing to fear because his father was one of the most respected Texas Rangers in the state. He'd had nothing to fear except the carelessness of a friend who had ignored the sound of approaching horses until she'd heard his yell, who'd hid out of fear at being captured by the renegades who had caught him and ridden away with him. Her head knew that it had been too late to rescue him, and that her only recourse had been to sneak away and find her family. Her head knew that she'd done all she could.

But her heart had never forgiven her.

Standing by the stone well, Lee dumped another bucket of cool water over his head. He had to get the woman away from here before she made him *loco*. How could he possibly have touched his mouth to her soft neck, to be so close that all he could smell was the delicate scent that belonged to her alone, to nibble on her ear as though he were a starving man sitting down to his first meal? It had taken all the willpower he possessed not to dip his hand beneath the water to take pleasure from the weight of her breast within his palm. Her alabaster flesh demanded a man's mouth pay homage to it. He had never in his life yearned for anything as much as he longed to possess Angela.

But his quest for revenge would ensure that he

never had her. She was not the type of woman to give herself lightly . . . to lift her skirts for him. Only he did not want her to merely lift her skirts. He wanted her to bare her body, every inch of flesh revealed so his gaze could feast on her perfection.

The water had teased her nipples into hardened buds that he had longed to close his mouth around, to run his tongue over, to tempt his lips with. Bared, with no cloth to separate their flesh this time. The water had not been clear enough for him to see anything else, but his imagination had not stopped with only what he could see. He had held her for so many nights that he could envision every curve, every dip, every slope that promised a man heaven . . . especially a man who lived in hell.

He dropped the bucket into the well and began to crank the handle to bring it back up. He doubted that a fourth dousing would cool his heated flesh, but he could always hope.

"What are you doing?" Alejandro asked.

Lee released the handle and glared at his brother. "Taking a bath."

"I thought I saw you bathing earlier."

But then he'd gone to his room to get a clean shirt . . . "So? Now I am taking another one. Is there some law that says a man cannot take two baths in one day?" he demanded.

Alejandro lifted a brow in speculation as he planted his butt on the stone ledge of the well. "I remember Ramon used to spend a lot of time in the river after Christine caught his eye."

Lee plowed his hands through his drenched hair, flinging out droplets. "Will you stop comparing this situation to Ramon's? It is nothing like his. He loved Christine, she loved him. Even if I loved Angela—which I do not—but if I did . . . I know"—with a heavy sigh, he sat beside Alejandro, barely aware of the hard edge biting into his backside—"I know she is a fine lady, and I . . . I am an outlaw. She could never love a man such as me." He looked toward the house and swallowed. "I have to take her home. Tomorrow."

Alejandro slapped his back. "Good. When you return, maybe we will go to Laredo. Visit a cantina, find a lovely *señorita*—"

Lee reached for the shirt he'd snatched off a peg by the door when he'd walked out of his room. "Another woman will not satisfy me." Slipping the shirt over his head, he acknowledged that unfortunately, he couldn't have the one who would.

"So you have fallen in love her." Alejandro's question came out as a statement.

"I don't know. I just know that sometimes it is like there is a hole in me, and when she is near, it is no longer empty."

"You have always been too poetic. You are a man; she is a woman. It is that simple."

"If it were that simple, I would have already bedded her. But nothing about Angela is simple. She is incredibly brave."

"She tried to slow you down, get you captured."

"Would you have not done the same thing in her place?"

"She shot you."

A smile played at the corner of his mouth. "That, I think was a mistake. She would not have sewn me up otherwise. When I told her that I had to delay taking her home, that I had to come here first, she did not protest."

"She is blind."

"She sees more than I do."

Alejandro released a great gust of air. "Then keep her."

"I cannot do that. Do you remember how Christine grieved when Ramon died? I could not ask Angela to endure that suffering. And she would, for a day will come when my luck will run out."

"No one knows what you look like. I could become Lee Raven."

Lee stood, faced his brother, and held his gaze. "No, *hombre*. It is my price to pay. I knew it when I squeezed the trigger."

"Lee!"

Turning, Lee smiled as Miguel's churning legs brought him nearer. Everything in his life was done in such a hurry. As soon as the boy was within range, Lee scooped him up and held him high above his head. The child squealed with delight. "What is it, little Miguel?"

"Juanita says it is time to eat."

Lee swung him around and settled him on his shoulders. "Then we must go eat."

Miguel dug his fingers into Lee's hair. "Your hair is wet."

"I was bathing. Perhaps you need a bath, heh?"

"No!" The child laughed, a delightful sound

that caused Lee's chest to ache. Ah, to possess such innocence again.

"Lee, when will Hector have his babies?" Miguel asked.

When they'd let Miguel name the cat, they hadn't known how to explain about its gender, but apparently that didn't matter to a child. Since Lee had not yet looked in on the critter, he cast a glance at Alejandro, who shrugged and mouthed, "Soon."

"Any time now. We will check on him after our *siesta*," Lee assured him. The boy was almost jumping on his back with anticipation.

They caught up with the others as they neared the front porch. Lee swept Miguel off his shoulders and set him on the porch.

With his brothers in his wake, Lee followed Miguel inside, to a room that housed a large oaken table and several chairs. He stumbled to a stop at the arched doorway, and his brothers rammed into him one by one like a line of dominoes being knocked down.

"*Dios mío*," someone whispered, accurately echoing his thoughts.

Angela gingerly walked around the table, skimming her fingers over a plate, setting a fork and knife on either side, before moving on to the next. She wore one of Juanita's blouses with puffy sleeves and a scooped neck, revealing the barest hint of the swells he'd seen before. One of Juanita's skirts was cinched in tightly at her waist, a bright red sash emphasizing its narrowness. And her hair. Her glorious hair. On either side of her head, one of Juanita's combs kept it from falling into her face, allowing every strand to cascade down her back past her waist.

"You're welcome to sit down," she said, when she had completed her circle of the table.

Miguel scrambled into his chair. "You can sit by me, *señorita*."

She bestowed upon him the most beautiful smile that Lee had ever seen, more lovely than the one she'd given Juanita that morning, so full of happiness and joy that it caused a profound ache in his chest. He had yearned to see such a smile grace her face; now he knew he would have been better off never setting eyes on it.

"All right," she told Miguel. "Keep talking until I find you."

"I am here, I am here . . ." Miguel repeated over and over while her laughter filled the room with the sweetest lyrical music.

As she walked around the table, she moved her hand from chair to chair until it lighted on Miguel's shoulder. Beaming with triumph, she pulled out the chair and sat gracefully. That the one she'd taken happened to be right beside Lee's usual place at the head of the table was unsettling.

Juanita walked in from the kitchen carrying a crock of beans. "What are you waiting for?" she asked. "Sit."

His brothers eased past him, taking chairs, leaving the one beside *her* empty.

"Are you going to join us, Lee?" Angela asked innocently.

He narrowed his eyes. "How do you know I am not already sitting at the table?"

"Because you have big feet, and I know the sound of your footsteps. They always sound angry."

"They do not sound angry." He started toward his chair and stopped. His footsteps did sound angry. Treading more lightly, he reached his chair and sat. "And I do not have big feet."

"Yes, you do, Lee," Jorge said. "You are bigger than all of us. That is why you could never wear anyone's hand-me-downs."

"Jorge! You have said too much."

"You're a little over six feet tall and weigh approximately one hundred and seventy-five pounds," Angela said calmly.

Anger boiled within Lee. "Who told you this?" He glared at each of member of his family. "Who has been telling her these things?"

"You told me," she said with irritating tranquillity.

"I told you nothing."

"When you held me . . . I know where my head comes against my father's chest and how tall he is. I know where the top of my head touches your chest. I merely had to calculate the difference. He's not quite as tall as you are. I'm familiar with the breadth of your chest, the width of your shoulders, the corded muscles in your arms—"

"Enough! You have made your point." He reached for the basket of tortillas and extended it toward her. "Take a tortilla. Tomorrow we leave for Fortune."

She took it, removed a tortilla, set it on her plate, and handed the basket back to him. He reached inside.

"I can't do that," she said softly.

He stilled and glared at her. "What do you mean, you cannot do that?"

She took the bowl Eduardo offered her and began to scoop beans onto her tortilla. "I mean I can't leave. I promised Miguel that I'd be here for his birthday."

"That is not for two more weeks!"

"Then I guess I'll be here for two more weeks." She set down the bowl.

"I thought you wanted to go home."

"I do, but I keep my promises."

"What about your mother and father, who are supposedly worried about you?" he asked sarcastically.

"We'll send them a telegram to let them know that I'm all right."

He slapped his hands on the table. "Why did I not think of this before? We'll send a telegram telling them you are here and then everyone will know. The posse, any men your father hired, the Texas Rangers . . . they will all know right where to come."

She sighed as though she were dealing with a dull child. "The telegram will simply say, 'The two of hearts wins all.' Then no one will know that I'm here."

"What does that mean? 'The two of hearts wins all'?"

She turned her head so that if he didn't know

better, he would have sworn she was looking at him. "My parents know what it means and they'll know that I'm safe."

"But you will not tell me what it means?"

"I was under the impression that our relationship was one of secrets."

"We have no relationship, *querida*."

"Then don't call me '*querida*.' "

"I don't call you—" But he did ... God help him, he did, without thinking, because somewhere along the way she had become a part of his heart.

"Lee, I could send the telegram tomorrow when I go to town for supplies," Roberto said.

"You are not sending the telegram, Roberto. She is not staying."

"But I want her here for my birthday," Miguel said.

Lee shifted his gaze to Miguel. The boy had such large expressive chocolate-colored eyes, just like his mother's. "We cannot always have what we want, Miguel."

"Why?"

"Because there are mean men—"

"But you are not mean."

Miguel looked at him with innocence, trust, and the belief that he was a better man than he was. He didn't know about the wanted poster, the bounty, or the man Lee had killed. The boy would probably hate him when he did learn everything, but right now, he simply wanted to believe that Lee was a good man.

His brothers' and sister's gazes bore into him. No one ate. He wasn't even certain anyone breathed. "I will not risk my family by sending a telegram. For Miguel, though, we will have the birthday celebration early."

"When?" Miguel asked, with the naïveté of a child who could not detect that much more was at stake.

"When I decide." He shifted his gaze to Angela. She wore a satisfied smile as she rolled her tortilla. He wished he did not enjoy her smiles so much. A man could easily be convinced to do anything to have one directed his way.

Chapter 11

Angela lay on the bed with Juanita stretched out beside her. Lee's family apparently had an afternoon ritual of taking a *siesta* after the noonday meal. She knew this room belonged to Juanita because her vanilla fragrance hovered in the air. She supposed that when one could not afford perfumes, one made do with what could be found. With all the money Lee had stolen, he could at least have purchased his sister a bottle of scented water.

Miguel had walked her around the bedroom so she could become familiar with it. Angela hadn't been surprised to discover that Miguel slept in the same room. Juanita was the only woman in his life, a sister who was more of a mother.

As quietly as she could, she eased off the mattress and slipped across the room to the small bed where Miguel slept. She inhaled his child's innocent scent of milk, cat, hay, and earth. It was reckless, agreeing to attend his birthday celebration. She didn't know why she'd been determined to accept his invitation, unless it was because she feared she'd never have children.

Maybe Lee was right and her blindness wasn't a punishment; it had simply been a means to achieve her true penalty: a life without children of her own. For what man would trust her to bear his children and raise them? She'd failed when she had sight; how could she possibly succeed now?

With a feathery touch, she skimmed her fingers over Miguel's hair. She refrained from touching his face, although she dearly wanted to know the contours. Children were such a joy. How would she manage to live without her own to hold close against her bosom?

Slowly, she rose and carefully tiptoed from the room. She felt her way along the hall. She considered going into Lee's room, but for what purpose? She simply had a strong need to be held, and he was so damned skilled at holding. She hated to admit that she would indeed miss him once he returned her to Fortune. Was that the reason that she'd quickly agreed to stay? Because in truth, she didn't want to leave Lee?

Cautiously, she made her way across the front room, searching until she finally found the door. She opened it slowly and slipped onto the porch. She walked to the edge, located the beam, and wrapped her arms around it. Although it was warmed by the afternoon sun, it provided little solace.

"Why are you sad?" A deep voice reverberated behind her.

With a tiny squeal, she swung around. "Why aren't you taking a *siesta*?"

A rocker squeaked. Apparently Lee had stilled when he'd heard her open the door. She listened to his footsteps; he needed only three to cross the porch. Hearing the rasp of cotton against wood, she could envision him leaning against the beam opposite hers, his arms folded across his broad chest.

"I wasn't tired," he said.

"When Miguel voiced that same objection, you said that it didn't matter. It was time for a *siesta*."

"Miguel is a boy. I am a man."

His tangible presence made that fact obvious. Her mouth suddenly went dry. She wound one arm around the beam and skimmed her other hand across the rough wood, anything to distract her thoughts. "Your brothers are sleeping, and they're men as well," she pointed out.

"Sleep brings them peace. They are welcome to it."

She stilled. "It doesn't bring you peace?"

"No."

She swallowed hard and asked hesitantly, "Do you dream about the man you killed?"

"You are searching for a conscience within me when none exists. I would kill him a hundred times if I could."

"It sounds as though he did more than *aggravate* you."

"He is not worth the breath it takes to discuss him. Why are you intent on staying?" he asked quietly.

"I don't know. Tired of traveling I guess." A lie. When he returned her home, she would never again hear his deep intriguing voice. She wished she could identify what it was about his accent that fascinated her. The manner in which he spoke, while carrying a Mexican accent, was still subtly different from his brothers'. She knew dwelling on his past would get her nowhere so she decided to try a different tactic. "I think my father would like you."

"I am just what every father wants for his daughter," he said, self-derision in his voice.

"More, I think you'd like him."

"A gambler who lets his daughter walk the streets at midnight, use profanity, play with marked cards—"

"They're only marked because I can't see them." She smiled with the fond memory. "Although before my blindness, he'd promised me that I could be a dealer at the Texas Lady."

"The Texas Lady . . ." His voice trailed off.

"My father's saloon."

He took a step closer as though suddenly intrigued. "I read a story once about a cattle drive and the venture was called Texas Lady."

"That was my father and mother . . . and Kit Montgomery. They were part of a handful of drives that successfully got cattle north in 1866. They wrote a dime novel about their adventure."

"Bainbridge."

She could almost hear the wheels clicking in his mind.

"Bainbridge." He snapped his fingers. "I knew the name was familiar the first time you told me. I read a story about a gunfight—"

"*Duel Under the Sun.*"

"*Sí!* It was Bainbridge and Montgomery and another man—"

"Rhodes."

"Do you know him as well?"

"Of course, Grayson Rhodes is a very good friend of the family's. He, Kit, and my father came here together from England."

Lee chuckled low. "You should have told me that you know such legendary men. I would have thought twice before hauling you away."

"How was I to know you'd even heard of them? I certainly never would have considered that you were well read."

"I love to read. Anything I can get my hands on. *Mi madre* would tease me and say that I was like the ground in the desert when the rain comes, absorbing every drop of knowledge that came my way."

A description that suited her as well, because she was desperate to gain any scrap of knowledge about him. "Were you a good student in school?"

"The best. Alejandro and I had plans to attend the University of Texas together."

"What would you have studied?" she asked quietly.

"I don't know. Everything."

She suddenly realized with startling clarity that the night when his family was attacked, the men not only had killed his brother, father, and mother, but they had murdered his dreams. She ached for the young man who had wanted to learn, had desired a higher education. Now, he knew how to sneak into banks, steal money, and kidnap women.

"Since no one knows what you look like, you could still go."

"I am living on borrowed time, *querida*. Now that you cannot be a dealer, what are *your* dreams?"

She scowled in frustration. "You're very skilled at turning the subject off yourself."

"I am a man of many talents. Share your dreams with me."

She shrugged. "Now, I have no dreams."

"You must long for something."

She couldn't bare her heart to a man who was little more than a shadow in her mind. Shaking her head, she skimmed her hand along the pillar and felt the bite of a splinter. "Oh!"

The porch reverberated as he stepped nearer. "What is it?"

She moved her finger over her palm. "I caught a little sliver—"

"Here, let me see." He took her hand.

"Really, it's all right. It's just so small that I can't find it."

He pressed his fingers against hers, opening her hand fully. "Did you know that the tongue is more sensitive than the fingers?"

She felt the tip of his tongue trail over her palm like damp velvet. His hot breath created a silken mist over her flesh. If his hold hadn't been so firm, she would have curled her fingers against his mouth. His tongue roamed slowly, resolutely, sensually. She leaned back against the beam, seeking support as her knees weakened. Each stroke of his tongue sent desire cascading through her. She considered pulling her hand loose of his hold. Instead, she lifted her other hand.

He grabbed her wrist, and the sensual haze lifted like fog touched by the sun.

"Please?" she rasped. "Let me touch you."

"I'll take you inside."

She jerked her hands free. "Don't you realize that you've already given me enough information to betray you?"

"Enough perhaps, but I haven't given you everything."

"No," she croaked past her tightening throat. "You didn't give me everything." She moved away from him, her chest aching because for the smallest of moments, while he'd trusted her with his dreams, she'd forgotten that he didn't trust her with his face. "I can find my way back inside. But you, Lee Raven, you're more lost in the darkness than I am, and when they slip that noose around your neck, I hope you won't regret all that you sacrificed for revenge."

She turned on her heel, strode forward,

bumped her shoulder against the doorway, but kept marching on. She wouldn't let him see how much he had hurt her, how she longed for what he wouldn't give her.

Kneeling in the dirt, Angela skimmed her fingers over the vine until she located the tomato. She cradled it between her hands, gently feeling for its ripeness. She'd offered to help Juanita in the garden because she'd desperately needed something to do. Like her mother, she'd never been one for standing still. When her finger touched a squashy portion, she grimaced with revulsion. There was something about the slimy feel of rotten vegetables that curdled her stomach. She plucked it loose and gauged its weight. It might work.

"That one is rotten, *señorita*," Juanita said.

"I know. I'm trying to decide if I want to throw it in your brother's face."

"Lee has made you angry."

Angela tossed the vegetable aside before beginning another search for a ripe tomato. "He has a habit of doing that," she mumbled.

"During the midday meal, he was upset that you did not want to leave."

Upset? Not angry? Angela was curious to know the reason Juanita thought he was merely upset that she wanted to stay. His voice had conveyed irritation, but she'd also noted something she couldn't quite identify. Angela rocked back on her heels. "Upset in what way?"

"I'm not sure. He almost looked as though he

was . . . afraid, and I have never seen him look like that. He is the bravest of men."

He was also an outlaw, but his family seemed unable to acknowledge that. "He's worried that I'll discover what he looks like."

"*Sí*, he has told me many times not to tell you. But then, his appearance has always bothered him."

Her attention sharpened. "Why?"

She heard Juanita plowing her trowel into the ground.

"I have said too much already, *señorita*."

Reaching out, she stopped Juanita's frantic efforts to dig herself a hole in which to hide. "I wish you'd call me Angela."

Juanita stilled. "It would not be right."

"But I'd like for us to be friends." She could sense Juanita's hesitation. "I promise not to ask you anything else about Lee."

Juanita released what sounded like a self-conscious chuckle. "I have almost forgotten how to be a friend."

"So no one visits you here?"

"You are the first. Alejandro is not happy that you are here."

"I don't think anyone is glad except maybe Miguel." She turned back to the plant, searching for another tomato. "I take it then that you don't have a beau."

"Oh, no. I would not want a beau."

Astonished by the determination reflected in Juanita's voice, Angela asked, "Ever?"

"I never want a man to call on me."

"What about getting married and having children?"

"I have Miguel."

Furrowing her brow, Angela turned her attention completely on Juanita. "But he's your brother."

"But I am able to love him and care for him as though he were my son. He is all I need. What about you, *señorita* . . . Angela? Do you want children?"

A soft smile played across Angela's mouth. "Very much, but first I have to find a man with the compassion to look beyond my blindness."

"I do not understand. If I did not know you were blind, to watch you pick tomatoes, I would not know you were blind."

"In Fortune, everyone knows, and my blindness tends to make men apprehensive. One man—his name was Marcus—took me for a stroll through town, but he was so nervous that I'd bump into something and embarrass him that he was the one who ended up bumping into something." Her smile broadened at the memory. "I guess he was watching me instead of where he was going, and he bumped into the wooden Indian statue that's outside the general store. It toppled over onto the bench that sits in front of the store. Mr. Farrington was sitting on the bench, and apparently he leapt up and backward to avoid being crushed by the statue . . . and he went through the window of the store."

"Was he badly hurt?"

The compassion Juanita exhibited touched Angela deeply. "No, miraculously, he came away with only a couple of scratches, but there was a stack of canned goods in front of the window. Every can crashed to the floor and rolled through the building. People were scrambling to get out of the way . . . thuds, bangs, and curses echoed into the street . . . I'd never heard so much commotion in my entire life."

"How awful! You must have been embarrassed."

Angela shook her head. She imagined that most women would appreciate how incredibly solicitous men were around her, but she was more often insulted by their constant hovering and quickly lost interest in them. They spoke to her as though she were a child. Lee had certainly never done that. "I wasn't embarrassed. It wasn't my doing. I knew the statue was there. I would have avoided it. But poor Marcus. He had to pay for all the damage."

"Did you see him again? I mean, did you—"

"It's all right, Juanita. I know what you meant. And no, he never called on me again. He said I was an expense he couldn't afford."

"I think he was just a clumsy oaf."

"My sisters thought the same thing. He asked permission to call on my youngest sister, Crystal, but she refused his suit."

"So you have sisters?" she asked eagerly.

"Two. Heather and Crystal, both younger." She angled her head thoughtfully. "Actually, I have a third sister who is older. Mary Ellen. My mother gave birth to her out of wedlock, and a very nice couple adopted her."

"Your mother told you of this shameful thing she did?" Juanita asked, clearly in shock.

"She never considered it shameful. She was seventeen, and loved the man, but he went off to war. When her daughter was born, she did what she thought was best. But I grew up always knowing that Mary Ellen was my sister. As a matter of fact, she married a duke."

"A duke?"

Angela shook her head. She was jumping from topic to topic, trying to establish a friendship in such a short time. "In England, men of rank carry titles—"

"I know about the peerage."

Now it was Angela's turn to be stunned. "You do?"

"*Sí.* Lee explained it to us. He is fascinated with England and its history."

"Really? I would have thought he'd be fascinated with Spain or Mexico."

"Oh, he is. He knows everything."

Except how to escape the memories that haunted him. She rolled her palm over one of the smooth-skinned tomatoes in her lap. Her curiosity about Lee seemed to know no bounds. She'd promised not to ask anything about him, and here she was prodding for tidbits of information. "He doesn't seem to sleep much."

"He has bad dreams. They are much worse since we moved here. They shame him."

"He's ashamed of his dreams, but proud that he murdered a man?"

Juanita put her hand over Angela's. It was such a small, delicate hand. "Oh, no, *señorita*, he is not proud that he killed a man."

"That's not the impression I got. He was practically bragging about his actions."

"He only pretends because he thinks it makes him . . . I cannot think of the word to explain . . . tough."

She was having a difficult time reconciling what she knew of the legend with what she was learning of the man.

"Where is he now?"

"He took Miguel to the barn to look at his cat."

"I'd like to talk to him. Can you take me?"

"You will not tell him what I told you, will you?"

She squeezed Juanita's hand in reassurance. "Of course not. I just want to assure him that I will leave after the party. I don't want Miguel's birthday tainted with Lee's bad mood."

Juanita removed the tomatoes from Angela's lap. "I need to finish gathering the vegetables for supper, but Alejandro can take you. Alejandro!"

She heard his footsteps growing nearer. "How long has he been watching us?"

"A while. He is very protective."

"And he doesn't like me."

"But he will not hurt you."

She hadn't thought he would. She couldn't deny that she'd been terrified when Lee had first grabbed her outside the bank, but after they'd made their initial stop to rest the horses, her fears had ebbed. She'd never stopped wanting to be free of them, but she'd no longer been afraid. Even now, she felt remarkably safe.

"Alejandro, will you take Angela to the barn?"

"Why?" he asked curtly.

"I want to speak to Lee," Angela answered, rising to her feet.

"Perhaps he does not want to speak to you."

"Are you going to escort me or not?"

"If he wanted you in the barn, he would have invited you to join him."

"Fine." She dusted off her hands. "I'll just take myself."

She allowed the furrows between the rows to guide her out of the garden.

"Alejandro! Take her," Juanita ordered.

With a low growl, he grabbed her arm and propelled her forward. Short tempers obviously ran in this family.

"I'm not a dog to be led around," she informed him.

"You are much worse," he assured her, his grip tightening. "He should never have brought you here."

"You're bruising me."

His hold loosened and his steps slowed. "My apologies, *señorita*."

"I'm not a danger to you or your family," she told him.

"You will get him killed."

Nearby, someone chopped wood with a steady rhythm. Someone turned the creaking handle of a bucket at a well. She understood now why Lee had referred to this place as home. With the exception of the isolation, life here was no different than anywhere else.

Alejandro came to an abrupt halt and released her. "We are at the barn. I leave it to you to find him."

She heard his retreat. "Alejandro?" He stopped. "I won't do anything to endanger him."

"I fear your promises come too late, *señorita*."

His footsteps faded, leaving Angela forlorn. She didn't want to feel that whatever destiny befell Lee was her doing. He'd chosen a life of crime long before he knew her; she hadn't directed his journey.

Cautiously testing each step with the pointed toe of her shoe before moving forward, she inched her way into the barn. Juanita's clothing was not nearly as confining as Angela's had been, and she thought if she were able to glimpse her reflection in the mirror, she'd decide the shoes looked out of place, but she'd never been one to go barefoot.

The sun had warmed her face, but now cooler air welcomed her along with the odor of straw and animals. She envisioned the barn, large and cavernous. Dust motes tickled her nose. When her sight had died, it seemed as though every other sense had burst to life. Nearby, a horse sounded as though it was blowing air past its quivering lips. In the distance, she heard the muted voices of Lee and Miguel.

The last thing she had ever expected of an outlaw was to discover that he possessed a profound loyalty to family. What had happened that caused him to take a life? He couldn't claim self-defense. He'd shot the man in the back. A cowardly action. Yet Lee Raven seemed anything but a coward.

She allowed their voices to guide her. She detected the throaty mewling of a cat warning away intruders.

"Can you count the kittens, Miguel?" Lee asked.

"One, two, three, four."

"Good."

"When can I hold them?"

"Not until I say."

"When will you say?"

"When the mama cat tells me."

Their voices traveled upward to reach her ears, and she imagined Lee hunkered inside the stall, Miguel squatting beside him, mirroring his actions. The boy's voice held so much admiration for his older brother that it was obvious he would never consider disobeying any command Lee gave. But then, that was true for all his brothers. He commanded them as though he'd been born to lead. A shame he'd decided to lead a band of outlaws instead of a community.

"Did it hurt Hector to have babies?" Miguel asked.

Hector? Angela wondered why he would think the male cat would be in pain when it was the female who suffered?

"*Sí*, that is the way of birthing," Lee said quietly.

Lee's answer completely baffled her. Trust a man to make it sound as though he did all the work.

"Did it hurt my mama when I was born?"

Angela held her breath. How could a man ever explain—?

"*Sí*. As I said, it is the way of things, but, oh, Miguel . . . when I put you in her arms for the first time . . . her smile . . . it was beautiful, the most beautiful smile that I have ever seen."

Angela stepped closer, drawn by the love re-sounding not only in Lee's words, but in his voice . . . and something that went beyond love.

"*Señorita*! You are here! We have babies!" Miguel exclaimed before taking her hand. "Come see!"

She heard Lee's knees pop and knew she'd guessed correctly. He'd been crouching.

"She will have to wait to see, Miguel, until she can touch them."

"Can I tell Juanita?" the child asked.

"*Sí*."

His rapidly retreating footsteps alerted her that all was forgotten except the news he had to impart.

"You were there when he was born?" she asked softly.

"Is that strange?"

"Most parents don't want their children around."

"I was not a child when he was born."

She nodded thoughtfully. "I guess you weren't. Was your father there as well?"

"No."

"Where was he?"

"He was not available." He took her arm. "Come. I'm certain Hector is tired of having an audience."

"Hector is the female cat?"

"*Sí*. Some things are difficult to explain to a child."

Humor laced his voice, and she imaged him smiling wryly. How she wished that in her mind she could create a true vision of him, but just as she could not "see" the kittens until the cat allowed her to touch them, so she could not "see" Lee until he trusted her.

Chapter 12

"I don't believe it!" Jorge roared, before tossing his cards onto the center of the table.

With Miguel curled up in his lap asleep, Lee watched the exchange from the sofa, Juanita beside him. With a fierce scowl marring what otherwise was a darkly handsome face, Alejandro sat in a nearby chair. Jorge, Eduardo, and Roberto had been trying to beat Angela at poker for more than two hours. Although she insisted the brothers utter the name of each card shown, since she was not dealing the cards, Lee couldn't determine how she could be cheating.

"She seems to have a knack for remembering what has been played," Lee mused.

"What else has she memorized?" Alejandro asked in a low voice. "The layout of the house?

The land? She could describe too many things that would give away our location."

"You worry too much." Besides, they did not own the land. They could easily leave, would have to leave if the Mexican government discovered them here.

"What have you told her?" Alejandro asked.

"Very little."

"For her that is probably enough."

"Do you remember what it was like to trust someone outside the family?" Lee asked.

"*Sí*." Alejandro stood. "And I remember what it was like to watch the soil soak up our blood."

Lee sighed as Alejandro stormed out the front door.

"What troubles Alejandro?" Roberto asked, looking up.

Lee shrugged. "Who knows with Alejandro?"

His brothers cast furtive glances at each other before turning their attention back to the cards they held. How could Angela not know what they looked like? They were Mexican through and through, their heritage reflected in their chiseled features. What did she want to do? Touch her fingers to their faces? His gut clenched at the thought of them experiencing what he so desperately wanted: her caresses, and more, her love.

But love was lost to him. All that remained was retribution and it was slow in coming. Whenever Shelby placed money in a bank, Lee removed it. His plan had been to exact his revenge by crippling Shelby financially. He had heard that Shelby was hurting, but not to the extent Lee wanted, the degree to which he deserved to suffer.

"You should play with them," Juanita said softly. "You could beat her."

"When she gets cocky, maybe then I will join them."

"I do not think she will get cocky," Juanita told him. "She is very nice, Lee. I am glad she will stay a few more days."

Because like Miguel, Juanita had no friends. She had been but twelve the night that their parents died. She contented herself with keeping house and caring for her brothers, but surely a day would come when she would crave a family of her own, a husband. She would require a very special man. Unfortunately, Lee doubted that a man with enough patience and understanding existed. "You should go to town with Roberto tomorrow."

She shook her head and stared at her hands folded on her lap. "I like it here."

"You can come back, Juanita. It would just be for the day."

"I need to watch Miguel."

"I would watch him."

"I do not want to go. Please do not make me go," she whispered.

Slipping his arm around her shoulders, he hated the way she stiffened, but still he drew her near and pressed a kiss to her temple. "I will not force you to go. I just want you to be happy."

"I am happy. I like it here. We are safe."

But for how long? What would happen if he

could not shake the next set of hunters? He would never lead them here intentionally . . .

"That's it! I am through," Jorge exclaimed. "I don't know how you do it, *señorita*, but you do cheat."

Smiling and sweeping her hand around the table, she gathered the cards. When she had them all together, she shuffled with one hand, palmed the deck, cut it, and stacked it—while her other hand remained in her lap. "Now, why would you think that?" she asked, cockily. "Another round?"

Lee eased Miguel onto Juanita's lap. "She is going to put us in the poorhouse." He stood and sauntered across the room. "*Querida*, go for a walk with me before you take all my brothers' hard-earned money."

She lifted her face, her attention honing in on him. It was remarkable the way it seemed that she was looking at him. She scoffed. "Hard-earned? I know exactly how hard-earned it is."

His brothers gave him knowing smiles and smirks. He wrapped his hand around her arm and drew her to her feet. "There is a lot you do not know, *querida*. Perhaps I am the man to teach you."

Angela couldn't recall ever walking with a man's rough palm pressed against hers, his fingers threaded through hers. She had followed Lee through the house and into the yard, trying to concentrate on the number of steps, the twists, the turns, but his scent of horses and leather had distracted her as much as the roughness of his palm against hers. She imagined him as a rancher instead of a man with a bounty on his head. She couldn't envision him being anything but successful.

More than was wise, she enjoyed the sensation of belonging—or at least the sensation of belonging with this man at this moment in time. He could never be a permanent part of her life nor she a part of his. They were worlds apart. She respected the law, and he seemed to believe it was meant to be broken.

Yet his brothers hadn't cheated when they'd played cards with her. Otherwise they wouldn't have lost every hand. Initially, she'd worried that they'd realize a card was missing from the deck, but she'd quickly determined that they didn't have a knack for remembering the cards that had been played.

In silence, with nothing but the creatures of the night to serenade them, she and Lee continued their trek, distancing themselves from the house, the barn, and the corral.

"What were you doing walking through town the night we robbed the bank?" he asked.

She tightened her hold on his hand. "I like to stroll at night. The air is different, calmer, quieter. And I don't—" She released a soft chuckle.

"You don't what?"

She smiled and turned her head toward him. "I don't usually bump into people at night."

"I haven't noticed you bumping into things."

She shrugged. "I haven't had much chance to explore. Usually when I'm in a new place, I end up with a lot of bruises. But in Fortune, I know every street, every building, the exact number of steps that will take me to the general store, or the boardinghouse, or my father's saloon. I like to slip into the shadows and listen to the noises inside. I can see everything clearly. The bar that my grandfather used to polish until it shined. The crystal chandelier that my father moved from my mother's bedroom to the front of the saloon the day after he won the building from my grandfather. He'd promised to order a new one so my mother could have it back . . . but he never did. I think because it reminds him of the time when they lived in the saloon. Now every room in their house has a chandelier."

"Your house sounds like a fancy place," he said.

She gnawed on her lip. How to explain? "It's a beautiful house. It rings of laughter and tears. Smiles keep it warm more than the fires within the hearths. It's filled with so much love." She hesitated before reaching out to rub his arm. "Your house is like that. I hadn't expected it to be."

"It is not as it once was."

The tall grass caught on her skirt as she inhaled the lingering scent of flowers in bloom.

"So you go out at night to listen to the sounds in a saloon?" he prodded.

"It's more than that. When I press my ear to the window, I can see everyone. The cowboys, the farmers, the merchants, the gamblers . . . but they're always the same people. People who visited the saloon when I was twelve, but they haven't aged in all these years. Sometimes, I want to walk through the saloon and touch their faces, discover new ones, recognize old ones, ask them what color their hair is now. The things I don't touch again never change . . . and the things I've never touched . . . I don't know what they look like."

"It bothers you not knowing what everyone looks like."

"It's like living in a cave, isolated. I live in the darkness, but my life can be more than shadows."

"I cannot see you living in shadows. You have fought me, insulted me, stood up to me . . . slept in my arms."

The last was said in a low, sensual voice that sent desire curling throughout her. He stopped walking. Her heart pounded with her acute awareness of him.

"If my brothers will allow it, you may touch their faces. Juanita's, too."

"But not yours."

"No, not mine."

Disappointment reeled through her. He released her hand, and she heard his knees pop. She knelt beside him, taking a deep breath to stay the tears. She couldn't recall ever wanting anything as desperately as she wanted his trust, unless it was his love, but she knew that she couldn't possess true love without trust. If he wouldn't entrust her with his appearance, how could he possibly trust her with his heart? An odor assailed her, not unpleasant, but unexpected. Lowing of cattle echoed around her.

"There are cattle out there," she said, unable to keep the surprise out of her voice.

"*Sí.*"

Now that she'd turned her attention away from him, she could detect the clack of horns hitting, hooves stomping the ground. "A lot of cattle."

"Two thousand head."

She was taken aback by the pride reflected in his voice, the pride she'd often heard in cowboys' voices when they sauntered into the saloon to take a breather before herding the cattle farther north. "Your cattle?"

"My brothers'."

"They're ranchers?"

"You sound surprised. This family has always been ranchers. Our father. His father before him. Shelby destroyed our home, but he could not rob us of our past. We saved what cattle we could from our father's range—those that were not slaughtered. The rest we gathered where we could, if they belonged to no one. We have bred some. Building the herd. Next spring, they will drive the cattle up to the rail yards in Fort Worth."

She heard the longing in his voice. They would take the cattle while he was relegated to stay behind because he couldn't risk being captured or endangering them.

He hadn't mentioned that they used the stolen money to purchase livestock. "If you don't buy cattle, what do you do with the money you steal?"

She could sense his hesitation, his unwilling-ness to tell her. She wanted something from him, a corner of trust. "You spend it on women?"

"No."

She didn't know why there was a touch of hu-mor in his voice. "Liquor? Gambling?"

"I do not spend it."

"You're just hoarding it away, then—"

"No."

She released a sigh of frustration. "Why can't you ever give me a straightforward answer? Why do you have to be secretive with every aspect of your life?"

He wrapped his hand around hers, lifted it slightly, and placed the most tender of kisses on the tips of her fingers. His soft lips formed the perfect frame for the heat of his mouth. His warm breath skimmed over her knuckles, sending shiv-ers of pleasure rippling through her.

"I will tell you a secret, but you must swear that you will never tell a soul," he demanded.

Joy spiraled through her with the thought of one secret revealed. In time, perhaps he would share others, including the mystery of his appear-ance. "I promise."

"I have never told anyone this."

Holding her breath, she tightened her fingers around his. "You can trust me."

He kissed her fingers again. "When I was a boy . . . a very, very young boy, like Miguel . . . I imagined that an angel visited me."

"An angel?" she whispered.

"*Sí*. The sun would shine in her hair, and she

would smile at me. I loved this angel, but then one day, she stopped coming. For a long time, I thought I had done something wrong, something to make her angry—or worse, sad. Then one day, I realized that I had simply grown too old, and the angel had always been only in my imagination. But she had seemed so real."

"Imaginary friends are like that." She experienced an incredible sense of kinship, could understand completely how a child might confuse reality with make-believe. She'd done it enough times herself. "When I was a child, I had a friend called Dastardly Pete. Whenever my mother caught me doing something that I shouldn't do, I'd tell her that Dastardly Pete had made me do it." Her heart tightened with a memory. "When I awoke from being sick for so long, and the world was still dark, and my father explained that it would remain dark, Dastardly Pete was the only friend who treated me like I hadn't changed. To everyone else, I was suddenly fragile."

He kissed her hand again, and she sensed that he was desperately fighting to hold himself in check, to keep the kiss warm when he wanted it to be scorching. "You are not fragile, but delicate in the ways of a woman. You have such strength, such courage. You would not break easily. Juanita . . . Juanita is fragile. If a man treated her as I treated you that first night, she would have curled into a ball and died." His voice carried a ragged edge, a vulnerability she never would have suspected he possessed. "I do not know what to do for her."

She wanted to comfort him beyond reason, this man she knew she should loathe, this man who caressed her hand as though it were an object of marvel. "You love her. That's obvious. Sometimes that's enough."

"In this case it's *not* enough. That night haunts her, more than any of us. She was so young. Only twelve. She cannot forget it."

She desperately wanted to reach out and touch him, offer him the compassion of her caress. "It haunts you too."

"I choose not to forget. That is the difference."

With his fingers still threaded through hers, she brought his hand to her mouth and kissed the back of his hand. She would have sworn she felt a tremor ripple through him. "Tell me what happened that night," she urged softly, wanting, needing to know his past so she could understand him.

"It is not a pretty story, *querida*."

She craved a glimpse into his soul, but knew he would tell her nothing if she confessed that. "All I'm asking for, Lee, is a glimmer of light in my darkness."

He swore harshly beneath his breath before the silence blanketed them. She wouldn't press him. His inner turmoil was almost palpable, shimmering between them. Finally, he released a long, deep sigh.

"They rode in from the north, in the dead of night. *Gringos* with more land than they knew what to do with. Our ranch bordered theirs. They were not fond of having Mexicans for neighbors, but they tolerated us. It did not matter that the family had lived there for two generations, with the third already putting down roots. They saw us as outsiders. Then my older brother Ramon committed a grave sin."

She didn't prod, but simply knelt beside him, rubbing her hand up and down his tense forearm, the corded muscles firm beneath her palm. She heard him swallow hard.

"He fell in love with Shelby's daughter, Christine. They tried to keep what was happening between them a secret. But someone saw them. They accused my family of stealing cattle. We had no need to steal cattle; we had double what they had. Our grandfather had been there when Texas had fought for its independence."

"He fought with the Mexican army under Santa Anna?" she asked.

"No, he fought with Sam Houston to defeat the Mexican army and gain independence for Texas. He purchased that land with his blood, and Shelby stole it away with the blood of our grandfather's son."

His voice had grown gritty. She wanted desperately to cradle his cheek, smooth away the lines that she was certain marred his brow, but she could not betray his desire for her not to know what he looked like. So she contented herself with fighting back her tears at his painful memories and inadequately offering comfort by stroking his arm.

"They hanged Ramon first." He moved his hand to his thigh. She placed hers over his and felt his hand ball into a fist within hers. "Can you imagine the anguish that would tear through your chest as you watched your son hang?" A drop of moisture hit her wrist. She squeezed her eyes shut, wishing she could wipe away his tears.

"My mother was screaming . . . my father shouting. They put the noose around his neck next. While he struggled against death, he had to watch them shoot each of his remaining sons and then the woman of his heart."

Her breath caught. "They shot you?"

"*Sí*." His voice had grown hoarse as though he had to push each word through a throat knotted with emotion. "Like our mother, we tried to stop them, but they were too many. We lay on the ground, our blood flowing into the dirt while our mother's cries for mercy echoed around us."

Another tear landed onto her hand. She tightened her hold on his arm. "Was Floyd Shelby there that night?"

She heard him breathe in deeply before clearing his throat.

"At first, but he did not stay long. He had other things he wished to accomplish. I found him later that night and killed him."

Confusion swamped her. "But you were hurt."

"*Sí*. They set fire to our house before they rode off into the night, leaving us with our blood seeping into the earth. Our parents were dead. My brothers . . . except for Ramon . . . were holding on."

"Did you tell the authorities what happened?"

"The authorities? Shelby had men willing to

swear with their hands on the Bible that we were thieves."

She was shivering, but the tremors had nothing to do with the cool night air, and everything to do with the horror of his tale. "I'm not saying you should have killed Shelby's son, but under the circumstances, your need for revenge could be understood—"

"I did not kill him for revenge. I killed him because he was a rabid animal."

Abruptly he stood and she grieved the loss of contact.

"I have told you enough," he barked. She heard his harsh breathing, the steady pounding of his boot heels over the ground as he paced. "I told you more than I should have."

She slowly rose to her feet, desperately wanting to take away his pain and if she couldn't accomplish that, at least to share it. "Lee—"

"Do not say my name like that," he ordered.

"Like what?"

"Like you care for me."

The tears burst free of her dam of control. "God help me, but I *do* care for you."

He grabbed her arm and jerked her close. She felt the wall of his chest pressing against her breasts. "Don't, *querida*. Don't weep for me, and don't care for me."

Then as though to mock his order, his mouth swooped down to cover hers, hard, demanding. She wrapped her arms around his waist, spreading her fingers over his broad back, relishing the manner in which his muscles bunched with his movements. With one hand, he cradled her face, his thumb stroking the corner of her mouth as though it wasn't enough to have his tongue slowly exploring every nook and cranny. She dug her fingers into his back, fearful that her legs might buckle as desire consumed her.

"I want you, *querida*," he whispered, his voice raw. "I want you beneath me ... but I cannot have you."

Profound regret laced his words. A man of honor he'd called himself and she'd scoffed.

"I have nothing to offer you," he said quietly just before he took her hand and led her back into the night.

And like ashes held within her palm and with a breath of kindness blown gently onto the wind, she discarded all she knew of the legend and accepted into her heart all she understood of the man.

Chapter 13

Lee lay in the bed, staring at the pale moon-light spilling through the window. Angela was nestled within the circle of his arms, her back pressed flat against his chest. She wore one of Juanita's nightgowns, the cloth soft against his bare chest. She had braided her hair into a thick rope that left the enticing nape of her neck visible. She had suggested that she sleep with Juanita, but he had forbidden it. She had recommended he sleep with his brothers. He had promised to keep his britches on.

He was tempted to roll her over and blanket her body with his own, bury himself so deeply within her that he might actually find the man he should have become.

"I don't know why I couldn't sleep with Juanita," she said.

"Because I did not wish it."

"And everything has to be your way."

"If everything were my way, I would not now be wearing my britches."

"I think it's a good thing that you are," she said softly.

Clothing could not hide his desire for her. He lifted his head and gazed at her profile limned by the moonlight. "I am a weak man. You should let me take you back tomorrow, *querida*."

A corner of her mouth curled up, and he could have sworn she was blushing. "But I promised Miguel I would be here for his birthday."

He settled back on the pillow and tucked her head beneath his chin. "Do not grow fond of him."

"Too late."

He feared it was too late for a great many things. Love. Contentment. A normal life.

"The moon pours in through the window. Even though it is after midnight, I can see your face," he murmured, skimming his knuckles along her chin, her throat.

"You can outline my face, but I can't outline yours."

Sighing heavily, he curled his arm over her side and spread his fingers over her belly. "Must you always bring that up?"

"My father says I'm stubborn. My mother says I'm determined."

"I think you just like to have your way."

"If I had my way, I wouldn't be here now, would I? You would have returned me to Fortune when I demanded it."

"But now that I want to take you, you do not want to go."

She chuckled softly. "It seems like sometimes you have your way and sometimes I have my way. It's like that with my parents."

"It was that way with mine as well. They were good people. They did not deserve all that happened that night."

She shifted slightly. "Still, that doesn't justify you robbing banks."

"I do not rob banks. I only take the money that Vernon Shelby deposited."

She rolled onto her back. He longed to loosen the buttons on the nightgown, slip his hand beneath the fabric—

"How do you know how much money he's deposited?" she asked.

He groaned. The next thing he knew, he'd confess everything to this woman. "Someone tells me."

"He doesn't know what you look like?"

"Perhaps."

She sat up. "What kind of answer is that? I'm not stupid. He has to know, which means you have an accomplice."

"No," he stated flatly.

"What do you think your brothers are? Don't you realize that you are risking their being sent to prison?"

He sighed in aggravation. "I leave a note so they know I only took Shelby's money, and I sign my name so no one else is accused of taking the money."

"But your brothers—"

"Are not responsible for my actions. I am the one who takes the money. I am the thief."

She flopped back on the bed. Her face was easy to read. Right now she was furious. He imagined most men liked their women smiling, but he enjoyed all of Angela's moods.

"You shouldn't take them with you," she said curtly.

"I know. This time, they felt a need to do something, so they came."

"Except Eduardo. He is apparently the only one with any smarts."

"We would not leave Juanita all alone. They know that would make me angrier than them following me," he said.

She turned onto her side, presenting him with her back. He slipped his arm around her and drew her against his chest.

"Since no one knows what you look like, if you stopped stealing money and changed your name—"

"I have unfinished business, *querida*."

She growled. "You are so stubborn!"

"Determined." He pressed a kiss to the nape of her neck. She went absolutely still. "Why do you seek to save me?"

"I don't know."

Confusion laced her voice. Did she really not know or did she just not wish to reveal the truth? He trailed his fingers along the curve of her neck. She shivered, and he felt tiny ridges rise just beneath the surface of her skin. Her reaction pleased him. "I cannot be saved, *querida*." He skimmed his breath across the sensitive spot below her ear. "Now, go to sleep before we both discover that you are beyond saving as well."

Angela felt a trifle wicked, a bit deceptive, and incredibly excited as she lightly touched her fingers to Miguel's face. He was the last to sit before her. Juanita had already taken a turn. As had Eduardo, Roberto, and Jorge. She wasn't surprised that Alejandro had refused. Other than Lee, Miguel was the only one who had a face she wanted to memorize. The others . . . she hated to admit it, even to herself, but she had used them. It was as simple and as deceitful as that. Memorizing each feature instead of the face as a whole, she'd taken the common characteristics and applied them in a mosaic portrait to create an image of Lee. Thick, straight hair. Broad nose. Rounded cheeks. Square jaw. Features chiseled over the centuries, since the first conquistador had set foot on Texas soil.

They had each confirmed what she'd already surmised: black hair and dark eyes. She didn't ask about their olive complexion. She could envision it perfectly. So unlike her paleness and that of her family and most of their friends. Her father and his friends had arrived from England unaccustomed to the relentless heat of the Texas sun, her father the darkest but even he burned on occasion.

With Miguel, she saw Lee as he might have

been as a child. Too thin, with sharp corners and eyes much too large for his narrow face. A mouth that he fought to keep serious, its quivering betraying his struggle.

"You can smile, Miguel," she said kindly and smoothed her fingertips over the crescent moon shape of his lips. "You have a pretty smile."

"Pretty?" he snapped, indignation evident in his tiny child's voice.

How could she forget how masculine even the youngest male wanted to be?

"Handsome," she corrected herself, tiptoeing her fingers lightly over his lips, her own smile bright with gladness because he filled a spot within her heart that had been empty for far too long. She imagined Lee at this age and wished she had known him then, before the night that he'd turned to a life of committing crimes and hiding from the world. For all the wrong things he'd done, she sensed he contained an inherent goodness that life had reshaped but could not destroy.

At the echo of approaching footsteps, beneath her fingertips Miguel's smile broadened, and she knew who had entered Lee's bedroom before the child spoke.

"Lee, Angela says I am handsome."

"You must call her *Miss* Angela, Miguel."

The boy's smile withered. "Why?"

"Because that is the polite thing to do."

Knees popped and she felt the warmth of Lee's body as he crouched beside her. "Do you intend to spend all morning doing this?" he asked brusquely.

She folded her hands into her lap. "Thank you, Miguel."

"You're welcome, *señorita*."

A rush of air brushed over her and tiny feet pounded the floor in retreat.

"He's such a sweet child," she said softly. "You're doing an excellent job raising him."

"Mostly it is Juanita's doing."

She nibbled on her lip. "But you're the one instructing him on manners. Who would have thought an outlaw would care about being polite?"

"I am not your ordinary outlaw," he stated confidently.

"No, you're not." Neither did she think he was an ordinary man. Why couldn't he have put his talents toward achieving greatness instead of notoriety? Why was he so protective of his identity? "I don't understand how it is that no one knew what you looked like. Weren't you at your trial?"

"No."

"How could you not attend your own trial?"

"Shortly after I murdered Floyd Shelby, I sent Vernon Shelby a letter. I signed my name. I wanted him to know Lee Raven knew what he had done and would make him pay. I also thought it would ensure that they never went after my brothers. I heard that Shelby took the letter to a judge. He was able to get a conviction and a sentence."

It wasn't unheard of for judges to pass down sentences without actual trials—especially in the less populated areas of Texas.

Her breathing stilled as he took her hand, turned it slightly, and trailed his fingers across her fingertips. "No calluses." Creating tiny figure eights, his callused fingers journeyed slowly over her palm, eliciting delicious responses throughout her body. "Incredibly soft, white. Hands that have not had to toil in the sun."

"I worked in the garden with Juanita yesterday." She felt the heat rise in her face with her breathless response. Why did she forget to breathe whenever he touched her?

"I was not insulting you, *querida*. I was simply pointing out that yours are the hands of a lady." And his were the hands of an outlaw. A fact she found easy to overlook because they were much more. They were the hands of an older brother who had taken on the role of father, those of a son striving to find justice, those of a man who had risked his own capture to protect her.

He continued to caress her as though he wanted to memorize every line that cut across her palm, every groove in her fingertip. "What did your fingers see when they looked at my brothers?"

Unmistakable longing echoed in his voice, and her heart constricted with the knowledge that he'd allowed his brothers to experience what he desired. He wanted her to touch him, but his inability to trust her forced him to hold his desires at bay; and in so doing, he tethered hers as well.

She lifted her free hand. "Lee, I could show you—"

"No."

He took her hand. Now, holding both, he circled his thumb within the center of her palm. "Tell me what you saw," he implored quietly.

Her throat tightened and she fought back the tears for what they could both never have: the other.

"Roberto is a worrier."

"How do you know?"

"The furrows in his brow are deep."

"And Jorge?"

"He was the only one besides Miguel who smiled. The lines in his face seemed fainter, as though he were more carefree—"

"Reckless. He is reckless."

"Eduardo is shy. I think he must have been blushing because I could feel his face growing warm."

"Can you not tell that my flesh heats up whenever you are near?"

She shook her head slightly. "I . . . I"—she had noticed how hot his body was, but she'd never dared hope she was responsible—"I just thought you were naturally hot."

"Touching you, even in a way as innocent as this"—he trailed his finger along her collarbone—"is enough to make my blood boil. My skin grows fevered, as though I were sick . . . *dios mío*, you are making me *loco*."

Abruptly he stood, and she heard him retreat in the direction of the window. She pressed her palms against her own warm cheeks. She repeated her silent litany—he was an outlaw—but her heart no longer cared. Slowly she rose to her feet and cautiously worked her way to his side. "Lee—"·

"We are having Miguel's party tonight. Tomorrow I'm taking you home."

"It's not right, Lee," she said quietly.

"You wanted to go home—"

"I'm talking about Miguel."

"What is wrong with him?"

"Nothing is wrong with *him*, but everything is wrong with his *life*."

"What do you mean?"

She thought she detected a measure of fear in his voice. Reaching out, she touched his arm, surprised to find him so tense. She wanted to reassure him, but at the same time she felt a responsibility to make him aware of the harm he was causing. "Who does he play with?" she asked gently.

"He has us," he replied, clearly baffled. "We play with him."

"But he needs to play with other children."

"Jorge is like a child. Always getting into trouble—"

"Jorge is reckless, not a child. Miguel needs someone near his age."

"You said yourself that we were doing a good job raising him."

"And you are," she rushed to assure him. "But he acts more like a little adult than a small boy.

What happens when it's time for him to start school?"

"I will teach him. I can read and cipher. I'll teach him what he needs to know."

"I understand that you're wanted for murder, but you can't punish your whole family—"

"I am not punishing them! I am trying to protect them."

"By giving them a life that allows no one else in? How will Miguel learn about the world?"

"I will tell him."

"Just like you've told me what you want me to know?"

"I've told you many things."

"But not everything. If you trusted me—"

"It's not a matter of trust; it's a matter of protection."

"How are you protecting those you love? By hiding them away? What kind of life is this?"

"It's the best I can give them."

"But it's not enough, Lee. Their world is as empty as mine."

"Better it be empty than not exist at all."

He brushed past her, and she listened to the heavy tread of his boots as he stormed away. She pressed her palm against the window, desperate to touch the impossible dream: of capturing Lee Raven, not with shackles, but with her heart.

Chapter 14

Angela grew dizzy as Miguel, with his small hands pressed against her knees, encouraged her to go round and round. She wore a bandanna over her eyes because no one trusted her blindness completely. She couldn't explain why that fact made her happy, perhaps because the action made her seem like everyone else.

Although Lee had not spoken to her for the remainder of the day except to bark out that it was time to celebrate Miguel's birthday, she knew he stood nearby, could feel the heat of his gaze on her.

She stumbled and laughed. "I think that's enough, Miguel. I'll never find the *piñata* now."

Miguel giggled. Someone thrust a pole into her hand. Before the person could retreat, she bopped him on the head. Miguel guffawed. She so loved his trills of delight. She would miss him when she left, and she knew that moment was coming sooner than she wanted, probably tomorrow.

She listened intently for the wind whispering across what Juanita had described as brightly colored streamers dangling from a clay pot. Angela had no plans to hit the *piñata* hard. She would leave the thrill of actually cracking it open to Miguel, but she did want to tap it just to prove that she was an equal at this child's game. She swung out and sliced the pole through the air . . . at nothing. She regained her balance and dignity.

"You moved it up!" she yelled. She'd heard hemp scraping across bark.

"Of course, *señorita*," Jorge said. "That is the way the game is played."

She straightened her shoulders and took a deep breath, determined to move more quickly. A few swipes and stumbles later, she was breathing heavily and losing whatever semblance of patience she might have had. She clenched her teeth and swung the stick as quickly as she could with all her might—and it came to a dead halt as she hit an immovable object.

"Your turn is over, Angela," Lee said in a low voice just before he snatched the pole from her. "Miguel, it is time for you." Lee unwound the bandanna from her head.

"She was funny to watch," Miguel said.

Lee took her arm and led her aside. "Stand out of harm's way," he ordered.

As soon as she supposed she was in a safe

place, he released her. "Tomorrow, we leave for Fortune. Tonight you will sleep with Juanita."

His plans should have had her jumping with joy instead of feeling a keen sense of loss. "How long do you intend to remain angry with me?" she demanded.

"How can you accuse me of being angry when I am granting your wishes?"

"I know you, Lee."

"You know nothing."

"You've avoided me for most of the day," she pointed out quietly.

"I had chores to do."

"Liar."

"Don't aggravate me, Angela," he said in a tightly controlled voice.

Angela, not *querida*. He was definitely upset with her.

"Where is it? Where is it?" Miguel cried out.

"Lee, I'm not going to tell anyone what I've learned about you or your family."

"I know that."

"Then why remain upset with me?"

He sighed deeply. "Because you made me realize that I have put my family in danger with my selfishness and my quest for revenge. I must find a way to change that."

"Are you going to give Shelby back his money?"

"Never." She heard his scorn explode in the single word. "I must simply remove myself from them and continue my quest alone."

Thwack!

"I hit it!" Miguel cried.

"Hit it again, Miguel," Alejandro yelled.

Thwack! Thwack!

"Good job!" Alejandro said.

And she wondered if before her arrival, Lee would have been the one shouting encouragement, and she suddenly realized that he wasn't only withdrawing himself from her, but from his family.

For as long as he could remember, Lee had loved these people who sat beneath the stars with him. He had always foolishly thought that when he was captured, he alone would pay and that they would be left in peace.

Youth, fury, and pain had blinded him to the truth. Angela saw more clearly than he did. He had thought to keep his family with him for as long as he could. Now, he realized that he needed to separate himself from them and ensure that no one suspected them—ever. Otherwise, he risked betraying the generous hearts of his parents.

"Lee, play us a song," Juanita said softly, breaking into his thoughts.

He smiled warmly at her. She so seldom asked for anything that he could deny her nothing. He would have tonight with his family, surround himself with their love, share his own . . . a night to remember that he would carry with him always.

He took the guitar that she offered him. Their mother had taught them all to play, but there was little doubt that Lee's voice was the most melodi-

ous. He strummed his fingers over the strings before singing Juanita's favorite song.

Angela wasn't surprised that Lee sang beauti-
fully. She was surprised that he'd chosen such a
sad song: "Red River Valley." Yet, she could almost hear him saying farewell himself as his
voice carried the words into the night.

She sensed an underlying current among the
older brothers, as though they all recognized that
a change was hovering just beyond the horizon.
She was certain Juanita was unaware of it. Juanita
seemed in a way separate from them. As far as
Angela could tell, Juanita never ventured far
from the house. And of course, Miguel was still
wrapped in the innocence of a child.

If only she could convince Lee to seek out Kit
Montgomery. She was certain Kit would listen to
his tale. She didn't think Lee could get away
without any punishment at all, but a few years in
prison would be better than a noose around his
neck. She shuddered with the thought and
shoved it out of her mind.

She wanted to enjoy what she was certain was
going to be her last night here. They had celebrated Miguel's birthday. He'd broken his *piñata*.
Her time with the notorious outlaw was coming
to a close.

Swaying gently, she became immersed in Lee's
rich voice. She heard no trace of his accent as he
sang and wondered again if maybe his accent
was fake, designed to throw her off. But this was
his family . . . or was it? Perhaps they'd hired
someone . . . the thoughts began swirling so fast

that she became as dizzy as she had earlier when Miguel had spun her around. Something was off, but what?

Lee's voice drifted into silence, the final chords hummed on the breeze, and her suspicions faded.

"Dance with me, *querida*," Lee ordered, taking her hand and pulling her to her feet.

Her heart leapt into her throat. "What? I can't dance."

"Play something fast, Alejandro," Lee said as he drew her body flush against his.

She shook her head vigorously. "I can't dance."

"If there is one truth I know, it is that you can do anything."

Alejandro strummed the guitar, the chords rippled through the air, and Angela tightened her hold on Lee, her left hand digging into his shoulder while the fingers on her right hand clutched his, his thighs brushing against hers as he guided her through the rapid steps of the dance.

If she could see, Lee thought, their gazes would be locked. Her face was angled back slightly so it appeared she was looking at him while he was unable to stop watching her. Her body moved in rhythm to his, as though they were one—exactly as he'd envisioned it. With each beat of the music, the warmth from her body seeped more deeply into his.

With grace, she glided through the movements as though she knew how he would turn, how he would twist, before he did. Only once did he push her away from him and spin her under his arm before bringing her back to the place where he had the irrational thought that she truly belonged—with him.

He slowed his steps, no longer following the rhythm of the music, but listening instead to the insistent murmuring of his heart. He tightened his hold on her while his gaze slowly moved over her face, noting her slightly open mouth, her wondrous eyes, the delicate features that masked a determination he admired.

The music stopped and only then did he realize that he had stopped dancing long before. He watched her chest heaving with her rapid breaths, breaths not created by movement, but by anticipation. Her tongue darted out and touched her upper lip. God help him, he wanted to lift her into his arms, carry her to his bed, and make her his, completely and absolutely.

Instead, he released her. She staggered back. Within the torches' glow, he saw the confusion and disappointment fill her eyes.

"The party is over," he snapped. Then he strode away from the house, away from his family, away from the only woman who possessed the power to destroy him.

Sitting on the bed, braiding her hair, Angela listened as Juanita helped Miguel recite his prayers. Calming him after his successful busting of the *piñata* had been a challenge, one Juanita had handled with incredible patience.

Angela would miss them, would long for the moments when she was wrapped in the arms of a man who never seemed to view her blindness as a shortcoming.

They had danced. Never in her life had any man, not even her father, swept her onto a dance floor and guided her movements with his body's subtle directions: the nudge of a knee, the closing of his fingers around hers, his chest brushing against her breasts. Her nipples had tightened with the first stroke and sent desire coiling deep within her. She grew warm just remembering his breath quickening, not from the speed of their actions, but from the intimacy of their contact. For a time, it had seemed as though they were one, inseparable. His heat had become hers. His motions had carried her toward ecstasy. Had her eyes reflected her wanton craving for his touch?

They must have, for surely that was the reason he'd left abruptly. He'd been wise to banish her to Juanita's bed for the night because she'd been acutely aware of the passion shimmering between them, like the desert sun creating walls of heat, and just like that sun, destroying all that it touched.

Did he fear his destruction as much as she did? Did he desire her with the intensity that she did him?

"Goodnight, Miz Angela."

Angela snapped to the present. She crossed the short expanse to Miguel's bed. Zoning in on where his voice had traveled from, she knelt, touched the pillow, and detected his nearby warmth. He was already lying down. She combed her fingers through his hair. "Did you have a good birthday?"

"*Sí*. I will break the *piñata* at *your* birthday," he said with such eagerness that she loathed disappointing him.

"My birthday isn't for a while yet."

"How old are you?" he asked.

"Twenty-four."

"Juanita, how old are you?" he asked.

"Seventeen."

Startled, Angela stopped brushing her fingers through Miguel's hair. She'd touched Juanita's face, knew she was young. But to be seventeen and so isolated. This life seemed almost cruel.

"When is your birthday? I will break your *piñata*," Miguel assured Juanita.

"My birthday is not for many, many months. Now, go to sleep and break *piñatas* in your dreams," Juanita ordered him gently.

Angela bent down and kissed his forehead. "Have pleasant dreams, little one."

He rolled over, and she waited, listening for shallow, even breathing that meant he'd drifted off to sleep. The mattress moaned slightly as Juanita climbed into bed. Slowly, Angela rose to her feet and returned to the bed. She slipped beneath the covers.

"It is good that you are sleeping here tonight," Juanita whispered. "It is not right for a man to have a woman in his bed if he is not married to her."

"We only slept," she said quietly, surprised by

the stab of disappointment that the truth caused. If he had welcomed her into his bed tonight, she couldn't be certain that all she would have done was sleep. He stirred something deep within her, something more compelling than desire. "Juanita, when Lee and I danced, was he smiling?"

"No. I have never seen him look as he did tonight," Juanita said, her voice low, as though she feared she was imparting a secret.

"Angry?"

"Oh, no. I have seen Lee angry. Tonight it was like he was under a spell."

Angela shifted on the mattress. "What do you mean?"

"While you danced, he never took his eyes off you. He watched you as though you were the light in his darkness."

She was just beginning to understand how bleak that blackness might be. He had told her that Juanita had been twelve the night Shelby attacked. Now she was seventeen. Five years had passed, yet Miguel was only now turning four.

Turning onto her side, she squeezed her eyes shut and pressed her fist to her mouth to stop herself from asking Juanita how it was possible that her mother had given birth to Miguel after she died.

He was lost, so lost, stumbling in the darkness, searching for home . . . warmth, security, love . . . but they remained beyond reach. Perhaps he didn't deserve them.

Shaking, cold . . . blood, too damned much blood.
Screams, cries . . . tears. An explosion. The loss of all
his dreams.

Angela jerked awake, the heartrending wail
that had ripped into her dreams still shimmering
expectantly in the air like lightning streaking
across the sky to forewarn the clap of thunder.

"What in God's name was that?" she whispered, not daring to breathe.

"Lee . . . dreaming," Juanita mumbled.

Dreaming? That terrified howl had come from
someone trapped in the throes of a nightmare, a
cry she'd made often enough after Damon had
been taken. Years had passed before the nightmares had lessened and eventually succumbed to
oblivion.

Angela scrambled out of bed and crossed over
to Miguel's bed. The child still slept peacefully.
Were Lee's cries in the night so common that
everyone was accustomed to them and simply
slept on?

Quietly she crept into the hallway. Somewhere
a bed moaned. Someone stirred. Then silence,
thick, heavy, unnatural . . . as though at any moment it would give way to something terrifying.

Her mouth grew dryer with each tentative step
she took to Lee's room. She wrapped her hand
around the doorknob, turned it, and slowly
pushed open the door. Harsh breathing echoed in
the room like the constant pumping sound of bel-
lows in a forge feeding the flames. "Lee?"

"Get out!"

The savageness of his order couldn't hide the fear. Stepping farther into the room, she closed the door.

"Damn it, Angela, get the hell out!"

But in his trembling voice, she heard a strong man fighting to remain valiant. A man who might not understand that strength sometimes came from challenging his weaknesses, and that this time, at least, he didn't have to confront them alone.

Concentrating on the location of his voice near the window, she glided toward him until she felt the heat of his body so close to her own, too much heat. He wasn't wearing a shirt, and only Juanita's thin nightgown served as a barrier between her flesh and his.

"Does it not bother you to have a man standing before you who wears not a stitch of clothing?" he asked severely.

Her suspicions confirmed, she shook her head. Did he now fear something more than his nightmare? "No. You don't frighten me, Lee. You haven't for a long time."

In that moment, she would have sold her soul to be able to see him, standing in the shadows, silhouetted against the night. Yet in a way, he was only a shadow himself; she knew his shape but not the details. "Let me help you."

"You can't help me."

"I'm willing to try."

"Don't you understand? No one can help me."

"Then at least let me comfort you." Touching his arm, she became aware of the tiny tremors rip-

pling through him, the clammy dampness of his
skin. "I know the reason that you killed Floyd
Shelby," she said softly.

His corded muscles tensed into hard knots.
"You can't know," he insisted.

But she did. All the facts had tumbled through
her mind late into the night, long after Juanita
drifted off to sleep. In her mind, she clearly saw a
young girl forced into womanhood, and a brother
who had sacrificed his own dreams to save her.
"Miguel isn't your brother as you claim. He's
your nephew. You killed that man because of
what he did to Juanita."

A shudder coursed through him, his breathing
grew more labored as though with each breath he
fought the memories. "She was a child when he
took her into the night. I could not stop him."

Her heart constricted painfully with his ravaged agony. It shouldn't have been his place to
have to stop anyone. Where had the law been?
Sanctioning the murder of a father and son, allowing the violation of a young girl. Lee had
tried to stop the murders and been shot. He'd
been unable to protect Juanita. She understood
how failings fueled the flames of guilt, how they
could eat at you, distort your memory until you
knew what you should have done and forgot
that you'd taken the only choice open to you. In
retrospect, choices increased. In reality, only one
ever existed, the one chosen. Until now, standing
here with this man, she hadn't realized it as
clearly.

"Hush now," she cooed, much as he had when she'd been attacked. Little wonder he'd refused to leave her to the mercies of the men who'd followed them. He'd learned long ago of the ugliness that some men carried within them. She rubbed his arm, desperately wanting to comfort him in any way she could. "Shh, you did the only thing you could do."

"I failed her."

"No, Lee, the law failed her—not you." He had rescued her, and then he had brought her son into the world. For five years, he had carried the torment of a perceived failure with him. She had called him a vicious murderer when in truth he'd been Juanita's salvation. She placed her hand on his chest, over his pounding heart. "It's over now."

"It'll never be over." Growling, he drew her close with one arm while his free hand cradled her face. "Make me forget," he croaked hoarsely. "For God's sake, make me forget."

He blanketed her mouth with his own, his lips desperate, his tongue demanding. She opened herself up to the kiss, but more she completely welcomed the man. Even as she sank against him, willing to comfort him in any way necessary, wanting to offer solace, she understood the undeniable message she conveyed: absolute surrender. She would give him all she could, do what she could to help him forget, and in the process, create memories of this one night that she would hold close to her heart through the years.

Gasping, he broke away. "You have to go."

But some decisions were hers and hers alone. The most important of all: who she would love.

"No, Lee, I have to stay." Slowly, with fingers that were deft at turning a card, she began loosening the buttons on her nightgown. She heard his sharp intake of breath and was acutely aware of his gaze, intense and smoldering to such a degree that it almost felt as though he was touching her. She stilled her fingers when she'd given freedom to the last button, and knew that with her next action there would be no turning back.

With his shoulder denting the wall, his hands clenched into tightened fists at his side, Lee had watched each slow, torturous movement of her fingers, had felt his body grow more taut with each button she slipped through its mooring. The pale moonlight spilling in through the window waltzed softly over the inner swells of her breasts, just the barest glimpse of creamy skin that hinted at what remained hidden. He knew that if she wasn't willing to leave, then he should. But he couldn't. He didn't have the strength to refuse what she was offering, what he so desperately wanted, to journey with her to a place where his nightmares had never been.

"Be sure, Angela," he rasped, his blood humming so loudly that he couldn't be certain he'd spoken loudly enough for her to hear him.

She angled her head slightly as though she was amused that he would even question her intent. As her stilled fingers began to move once more, he sucked in his breath. Her hands didn't shake, no doubts creased her brow. Her face was serene, expectant, and he hoped he wouldn't disappoint her.

She parted the material further until the gown glided slowly, sensually off the delicate slope of her shoulders, over the tempting mounds of her breasts, along her tiny waist, across her flattened belly. Past her narrow, rounded hips, slender thighs, enticing calves, dainty ankles, stopping only when it pooled at her tiny feet.

The midnight breeze blew through the window and traveled lightly over her exposed skin. Little bumps erupted over her flesh; her nipples puckered. His mouth went dry. "*Dios mío*," he said hoarsely. "You probably have no idea how beautiful you are."

Tears stung Angela's eyes at the reverence in Lee's voice. No man, other than her father, had ever hinted that she was beautiful. She took a step toward him, more sure of her course than she'd ever been. Of all the actions she'd expected of him at this moment, reaching behind her to take her braid was the last. He unwound her hair until it cascaded around her.

"I like the way the moonlight glistens on your hair."

He drew her close, his strong arms like bands around her as his mouth possessed hers. Just as they had danced earlier, he now guided her. The backs of her knees hit the bed, and she sank onto the mattress, his body covering hers as early morning sunlight touched the earth, awakening all in its path. Her remaining senses seemed to heighten with incredible awareness, her skin prickling. When he cradled her bare breast with his roughened palm, a shaft of pleasure speared her.

She reached for him, and he captured her wrist. "Let me touch you," she implored.

In gentle rebuke, he took her other wrist, clamped both within his large hand, and raised them over her head, resting them on the pillow. "Let me touch you first," he said quietly, his hand skimming a virgin trail from her throat to her knee.

Simply touching her bared skin brought Lee close to losing control. He wanted to savor the moment, to relish every line, every curve, every dip. A woman's body was a marvel of velvety hills and secretive valleys, each to be treasured for the incredible pleasure that gazing upon them brought to a man. He grazed his fingers up her thigh. Like satin, but warm, almost hot, as though she too burned with his needs. She whimpered softly and he felt a shiver pass beneath his callused fingers. Did he excite her as she excited him?

Moving up, he plowed his hand through her hair, angled his mouth over hers, and kissed her deeply. The succulent recesses of her mouth inflamed him, sent desire hot and blinding rushing through him. His restraint was close to snapping. Her hands strained against his hold as though hers was as well. He tore his lips from hers, burning a path along the column of her throat.

Angela moaned, her body caught up in the maelstrom he created as his fiery mouth paid homage to her, trailing hot, moist kisses over her flesh, his tongue darting, swirling, taunting, teasing until she was squirming and arching toward him. He splayed the fingers of his free hand over her stomach and slowly moved them lower, lower until he cupped her intimately.

With heat surging through every nerve, she strained harder against the vice-like grip that still held her hands over her head. "Lee—"

"Shh, *querida*, enjoy what I have to offer."

What he had to offer were sensations she'd never imagined, tendrils of pleasure weaving their way through her as his fingers stroked and teased her amorously. She gasped. "Lee—"

"Shh." With his knee, he nudged her thighs apart, and then he was nestled between her legs, his chest rubbing her breasts as he returned his mouth to hers, kissing her voraciously, his tongue mimicking the slow actions of his body as he cautiously tested her body's defenses.

She had none. Where he was concerned, emotionally and physically, she had lowered the barriers to her heart. Squeezing her legs against his hips, she urged him on.

As he slid into her body, she felt the slightest bit of discomfort. Then nothing existed beyond the fullness of him. He stilled and she was aware of his labored breathing and his tenseness, the light sprinkling of hair on his chest. "Dear Lord, but you feel good," he rasped.

Releasing her wrists, he intertwined his fingers through hers, the backs of her hands cradled within his palms just as he was now cradled tightly between her thighs.

Slowly, ever so slowly, he rocked against her, his chest brushing over hers with each thrust, his tongue delving into her mouth, his fingers tightening around hers. It was like a pebble thrown into a pond, with sensations rippling through her, growing, widening until they encompassed all of her. He had taken her on a journey through Texas, but the road they now traveled was unlike anything she'd ever experienced; the joy of it, the rightness of it, as though her body had been created to house his. Her passionate responses mounted, growing stronger and increasingly intense, until they exploded like the Fourth of July fireworks she'd seen the year before she'd lost her sight. Arching beneath him, she cried out, but his mouth, still hovering over hers, captured her declaration of exultation. He released a guttural groan with his final thrust, his body shuddering almost violently. Beside her ear, he breathed heavily, and she felt the fine sheen of sweat beading his flesh.

He placed a kiss beneath her jaw before easing off her. He released her hands, turned her onto her side, and pressed his chest against her back, her backside nestled within his lap while his palm cradled her breast.

She could hear his breathing growing slower, fainter, until it became the steady, soft rhythm of a sound sleep. A solitary tear rolled from the corner of her eye. For all they had just shared, he'd never let her touch his face.

Chapter 15

Lee couldn't remember the last time that he'd slept soundly. Indeed, he had no memory of a sleep that carried him under as deeply as this one had.

As a child, he'd always been prone to unexplained nightmares. He had learned to awaken himself at the first hint that the demons causing them were going to play havoc with his mind. Even now, as a man, he constantly warded them off.

Except for last night. He'd gone too long without giving in to his usual restless sleep. He'd been too exhausted to keep his guard up, and the nightmares had arrived with a vengeance. Only this time when he'd awakened trembling and ashamed, still caught in the web of their horror, his angel had returned as well.

Angela. Incredibly giving and loving, she had gifted him with herself . . . a gift he treasured beyond measure, but in the harsh reality of day, knew he did not rightfully deserve.

Languidly, he stretched, relishing the slaked sensation of a sated body that had loved long and hard. Intending to draw Angela back into the circle of his embrace, he turned onto his side, only to discover he was alone. His heart thundering, he bolted upright. The early morning sunlight streamed in through the window while the slight breeze toyed with the curtains.

What spell had she cast over him to make him oblivious to her leaving?

He scrambled out of bed, snatched his britches off the floor, and worked his way into them. Buttoning them as he went, he strode from the room. The aroma of hot sweetbread teased his nostrils. He peered into the kitchen.

Juanita turned from the oven. *"Buenos días."*

"Have you seen Angela?" he asked.

"She went outside."

"By herself?"

Juanita nodded.

"You let her go by herself?"

"She didn't ask me for help. She just walked out."

Lee stormed out of the house, past the corral and the barn, frantically searching for the woman who had somehow managed to snare him from the moment he'd stumbled into her. In the field beyond, he spotted the red hue of her hair and hoped the morning sun would not burn her fair skin. Heat saturated his body as he remembered how smooth that flesh had felt beneath his hands, against his mouth. Already he wanted her again, in his bed, beneath his body, writhing, gasping. He'd never meant to possess her, but still struggling against his nightmare, he'd been a man drowning, and she'd offered a tether toward a dream that he should have ignored.

He knew that undeniable truth in his head, but his heart . . . his heart preached otherwise.

Kneeling before her, he was caught off-guard by the sadness reflected in her eyes. He couldn't blame her for regretting what had passed between them last night. He had been her first, an honor that should have gone to a man far better than he was, a man who could give her his name and offer her a world deserving of her.

He took her hand, the ache in his chest growing as it remained limp in his. "Angela?"

She didn't tilt her face toward him as she usually did so that it appeared she was looking at him. He pressed a kiss to her fingers, and she snatched her hand away.

"Regrets, *querida*?" he asked gently.

She shook her head slowly. "I hurt."

Guilt stabbed him with the evidence of his failure. "I tried to be gentle."

Shaking her head, she pressed a clenched fist to her breast. "Here. I hurt so badly here. Last night, I was willing to give you everything, and you manipulated my body in ways that ensured I never touched your face."

He squeezed his eyes shut. He'd held her

hands and when she'd asked for freedom, he'd distracted her—easily, if her moans and cries had been any indication. He opened his eyes. "It's for the best, Angela."

"The hell it is. You keep a false wall between us, Lee. I don't know why. I don't know what you're hiding, but it's a lot more than your identity."

"You don't know what you're talking about," he snapped, the anger rising because she'd hit the mark.

"Then let me touch your face."

"I can't."

"You can't? Or you won't?"

He had hidden his identity for so long that it was now his nature to do so. He would not change for her, risk himself, risk his family. He surged to his feet. "Tomorrow I'm taking you home."

"Rot in hell."

He strode away from her, his feet pounding the ground unmercifully. If he let her touch his face, let her into his heart completely, how would he ever bear to face the hangman's noose? If he removed the last barrier between them, where would he find the strength to give her up?

The air shimmered differently when night began to fall. The heat lingered as long as it could, but eventually it was forced into retreat. Angela had long ago learned to measure the night by the absence of heat.

She had remained in her self-imposed exile all day. Shortly after the sun moved from being directly over her head, Miguel had brought her a tortilla wrapped around beans, rice, and meat. Awkwardly, he'd placed Lee's hat on her head. The tears she'd been holding at bay had surfaced then. A man had made love to her, and she had little knowledge regarding his appearance. She wasn't concerned with his actual features, she only cared what her ignorance divulged: that he was keeping a portion of himself secret, that he wasn't willing to reveal every flaw, every perfection. That he didn't trust her, and without that, he could never truly love her.

Yet he had managed to lure her into loving him with a voice that reminded her of whiskey going down, tales of loss that had touched her heart, and a respect toward her that no other man had ever shown.

She heard rocks and pebbles sliding away beneath the tread of heavy boots. The familiar pop of knees bending. The warmth from a body scant inches away seeping into hers.

"So even eyes that cannot see can weep," Lee said quietly.

"Have you any idea how much trust it takes for a woman to open herself up to a man as I did for you last night?" she asked, her voice catching, betraying the agonizing ache in her chest that threatened to suffocate her. She wanted to be angry—furious, in fact—but she only felt the deep pain and wondered how long it would last. No doubt for the remainder of her life.

He slid his hands beneath hers and stroked his

thumbs across her knuckles. "Angela, come into the house."

She didn't want to remember how those glorious hands had elicited pleasure in her last night, and yet she couldn't deny that she treasured the memory. She shook her head slightly. "I want to go home."

Slowly, very slowly, he lifted her hands and pressed her fingers against his mouth. His warm, moist breath skimmed over the back of her hands, and she heated with the memory of his lips gliding tantalizingly over her flesh the night before. Then even more slowly, he turned her hand and kissed the heart of her palm before he flattened her hands against the base of his throat. She felt his Adam's apple bob as he swallowed hard just before his hands drifted away, leaving hers, granting her permission to obtain what she most desired.

Her breath caught, and fresh tears stung her eyes. She scrambled up to her knees and folded her trembling hands around his neck. Beneath his chin, the stubble of his beard barely pricked her. A day's growth, she was certain, although it wasn't nearly as rough as her father's. It was soft, reminiscent of dandelion petals before they were scattered on the wind. Not at all what she'd expected.

She knew she should go slowly, memorize the curves, the lines, each indentation, but she was far too excited, filled with too much happiness. She ran her fingers over his chin, along his tense jaw, stopping briefly at his lips. Those she thought she'd known, but his kisses had distorted the shape. Full on the bottom, thin on top, unsmiling. No upward curve; simply straight as though revealing himself to her brought him absolutely no joy. Tiny grooves along the corners dipped down. Lines etched by sadness. Her heart constricted and she wished she possessed the power to make him smile, to erase the rivulets of a life that she knew he hadn't deserved.

She was momentarily tempted to stop. To give him what he wanted: an identity unknown to her, but she was greedy, greedy to know everything about him. She slid her hands up. His cheekbones were high, much higher than his brothers' . . . And his nose. Chiseled, narrow, aristocratic popped into her mind. She furrowed her brow. "You don't look like your brothers."

"Don't I?" he asked quietly.

Shaking her head, she trailed her fingers over his eyes, over brows not nearly as thick as Jorge's or Roberto's or Eduardo's. Why? Why did he look so different . . . and yet familiar?

Had Alejandro refused to grant her permission to touch his face because he was the brother who most resembled Lee?

Scooting closer, she combed her fingers into his hair, thick like his brothers', but still so unlike theirs. She released a giddy laugh. "Your hair is curly. I thought it would be straight, like Jorge's."

"Did you? Then I must be a disappointment."

His emotionless tone matched his expressionless face. He reminded her of a child stoically accepting his punishment for snitching a cookie before dinner. She desperately wanted him to relish her fingers touching his face, raking through his hair. She cradled his cheek with one hand while the other rested along his crown, where the curling strands had woven around her fingers. "Last night wasn't just about trust. God help me, Lee, I've fallen in love with you."

Groaning, he drew her into his arms, threaded his fingers through her hair, and slashed his mouth across hers, a kiss filled with fervor and desire, wanting, and the knowledge that whatever they built between them would not last, could not last. Wanted posters across the state of Texas demanded his capture, promised his death.

Losing him would be worse than losing her sight. With her eyes, she'd hoarded twelve years of memories crammed with images to sustain her. With Lee, she had only days. How could she fall so fast, so hard, so deeply in love?

He rained kisses over her face, his bearded stubble abrading her skin, but she didn't care. She welcomed the softness and the rough, so much like the man.

"Angel," he whispered, just before he latched his mouth back onto hers, his tongue delving deeply, claiming all she was willing to give.

And she did want to give, everything she owned, all she possessed, for whatever time they had, she would be his totally and completely, knowing it would never be enough, understanding it was all she would ever have.

Suddenly his mouth left hers and he stood, drawing her to her feet. He lifted her into his arms. She wound one arm around his neck and touched his face with her other hand. She found his mouth with ease, kissing him with urgency as he strode over the uneven ground. He broke away and quickened his stride.

"I don't want to break our necks," he murmured.

She traced her fingers over his cheek, his chin, his mouth. His mouth that still didn't smile, but it wasn't as straight as it had been the first time she'd touched it. She wanted to constantly keep her hands pressed to his face, to be aware of the muscles shifting with each expression, to know with a touch if he was happy or sad or angry.

The door creaked on its hinges as he opened it, slammed as he closed it. The aromas of supper teased her nostrils.

"Aren't you going to eat, Lee?" Juanita asked.

"Not yet," he replied, and Angela buried her face in the hollow of his shoulder.

They would know, his entire family would know what was passing between them in his bedroom, in his bed. And she didn't care. God help her she didn't care if her reputation was ruined, if no other man would ever want her, if she was destined to spend the remainder of her life alone. For now she only wanted Lee and whatever time they had, every moment spent within his arms.

Another door slammed shut, and then he laid her down gently on the mattress, his body blanketing hers as his mouth captured hers. She sensed in him an equal desperation, the knowledge she held reflected in the rapacious hunger with which his kiss devoured her. Their love was but a fleeting illusion that could not exist beyond the boundaries of this house. And yet she didn't care, or perhaps it made her care more, made her want him desperately. Since she could not have forever, she would make the most of now.

With her fingers, she etched the lines of his face into her memory as he worked to remove her clothes. She imagined the passion burning in his dark eyes, the appreciation.

"You are so beautiful, *querida*," he whispered hoarsely, before his mouth began its heated sojourn over her bare breasts.

Molten fire flowed through her, and she quivered with desire and burned with hunger. He left her for the briefest of moments, and when he returned, they became flesh against flesh, and she'd never expected anything to feel this perfect. She placed her hands on either side of his beloved face. "I love you, Lee."

His chest rumbled with the force of his moan as he buried his face between her breasts. She threaded her fingers through his hair. "It's all right if you don't love me."

He kissed the inside swell of her breast before levering himself above her. She brushed her fingers over his face, trying to read his thoughts. Regret?

"This is wrong, Angela," he murmured quietly before lowering his mouth to hers. A desolate kiss. "I have nothing to offer you but sorrow."

"I don't care." Her voice cracked and tears filled her eyes. Her fingers felt the corners of his mouth lift slightly.

"I love you, *querida*," he rasped. Her heart leapt with such joy that it was almost painful.

"God help me," he whispered, "God help us both because I do not have the strength to walk out of this room."

"I wouldn't let you leave," she promised, and he laughed, a low, sad laugh. "Love me, Lee, for as long as you can."

His hands, his mouth, worked their magic, touching, teasing, taunting while she basked in the luxury of touching him as well, learning the shape of every corded muscle, tasting the salt of his sweat as his flesh grew slick, marveling at the tenseness that gave way to such tender caresses.

When he rose above her, she was ready, and when he joined his body to hers, she lifted her hips to welcome him. His guttural groan sounded of possession and his arms tightened around her. She skimmed her hands across his shoulders, over his neck, along his face, resting them there lightly, reveling in the passion he had unleashed.

He rocked against her, his body growing more tense as hers heightened with pleasure. She wanted to dig her fingers into his shoulders in order to stay tethered, but she wanted more to know the many facets of passion that played over his features.

Sensations rippled out from her core, and she splayed her fingers over his face as the darkness of her world shattered into a million stars of incredible beauty. She cried out, arching beneath him as he shuddered above her. He lowered himself and buried his face in the crook of her shoulder, his breathing harsh, his breath skimming along her collarbone. With one hand, she stroked his broad back, while with the other she touched his face, creating in her mind the image of contentment.

He groaned, and carefully, with their bodies still joined, he rolled them onto their sides. Never in her life had she resented her blindness more, that at this moment she could not see love reflected in his eyes.

He skimmed his fingers along her side, across her bare hip, down her thigh. "I warned you that I was a weak man."

She smiled softly. "You're anything but weak."

He chuckled low. "Not where you're concerned. I should have returned you to your father the moment I realized you were blind."

"But the posse—"

"I should have risked it."

But she was incredibly glad that he hadn't. To have gone through her life not knowing passion or a love this binding . . . she could not imagine the emptiness. She didn't even have the heart to ask him to stop calling her "Angel." He'd done it twice this evening, and she was surprised that the pain did not come with the reminder of the little boy who had been such a joy. Unexpected sadness rippled through her. She had been Damon's angel and he'd died. Now she was Lee's . . . and death waited slightly beyond reach for him as well.

Raised up on one elbow, lying on the bed, Lee placed a sliver of watermelon into Angela's waiting mouth. Under Alejandro's knowing glare, he'd gone to the kitchen and heaped food onto a plate. His brother wanted to talk; Lee didn't.

He didn't need to hear his misgivings voiced or be told that he trod on dangerous ground. Angela was his tonight, tomorrow, for as long as she wanted to stay. When he had to give her up, he would somehow find the strength to do so.

Her fingers journeyed over his chest, halted, journeyed again, halted. "How did you get all these tiny scars?" she asked.

The small indentations had always dotted his flesh. He shrugged, momentarily forgetting that she couldn't see his movement. "I don't remember. They've always been there."

"There's so many. Whatever happened must have been painful."

"Not so painful if I don't remember it," he reassured her. He saw no point in dwelling on what might be unpleasant, especially when the simple act of gazing upon her brought such intense pleasure.

He slipped a grape between her lips, leaned forward, kissed her, and took it into his mouth. God, he wanted to make love to her again. "Still hungry?" he asked.

Shaking her head, she nestled into the pillow. "No."

Grateful, he set the plate aside before easing his body over hers. If the heavens smiled on him and let him live to be a hundred, he would never have enough of her. She skimmed her fingers along his cheek, a different touch, not searching, but caressing. Last night how could he have even considered making love to her without giving her the freedom to touch him? Without realizing it, he had deprived them both of so much because of his fears of capture. He lowered his mouth to her breast and circled his tongue around the sensitive bud. She combed her fingers through his hair.

"Lee?"

"Mmm?" He suckled gently, relishing the quick intake of her breath.

"Lee, I want to talk."

"So talk. I am a man of many talents. I can kiss you and listen at the same time." He trailed his mouth to the valley between her breasts. The way his hand molded around the soft orb was perfection.

"I don't know . . . I don't know if I can talk while you're doing that."

Chuckling with satisfaction at her admission, he lavished kisses on her other breast. "Then don't talk."

She yanked his hair.

"Ow!" He jerked his head up. "Why did you do that?"

"I want to talk."

He scowled, a wasted action. He flopped onto his back, then rolled to his side, turned her so her breasts could flatten against his chest, and skimmed his fingers up and down her spine. "All right, *talk*."

She ran her tongue over her lips. He leaned forward and planted a hard kiss against them.

"Lee!" she scolded.

"Do not draw my attention to your mouth if you do not want me to kiss it."

Shaking her head slightly, she smiled softly and unerringly laid her palm against his cheek. "Sometimes you remind me of a child."

"Then let's play."

He tucked her beneath him, bracketed his hands on either side of her face, and kissed her soundly, deeply, passionately. Never before in his life had he had time for a woman. He took pride in the fact that he had not fumbled too noticeably, that she had not guessed he was as untutored as she was.

He kissed her cheek, her closed eyes, her brow. He would never grow tired of kissing her.

"My father is an influential man," she muttered as though from far away, as though she'd force the words past the realm of pleasure.

He nibbled on her earlobe. "So you have said."

"Christian Montgomery is even more so."

He stilled, his heart thundering within his chest, a steady staccato beat that seemed to echo within the room. Kit Montgomery's relentless pursuit of justice was legendary. The man had fascinated Lee simply because he was the exact opposite of all that Lee had come to stand for.

"Lee, Kit could help you."

"To the hangman's noose, *querida*," he said, pleased that his voice didn't tremble with the thought of all he would lose if he fell into the legendary Ranger's hands. With the tip of his tongue, he circled the delicate shell of her ear. He wanted to bury himself deep within her, not face the demons that haunted him.

She dug her fingers into his scalp and lifted his head as though she needed to look him straight in the eye; perhaps she only needed him to see her, worried, fearful, holding the knowledge that he was only passing through her life, not staying for any length of time. It hit him hard that as deeply as he cared for her, he should have spared her this torment.

"If you turned yourself over to Kit, willingly gave yourself up, explained that night, exactly why you killed—"

"No!" He rolled out of bed and began to pace, his bare feet pounding against the planked flooring. "I promised Juanita that I would never tell a soul; I would take what happened that night to the grave with me."

"Your brothers—"

"Made the same vow once we discovered she was with child."

She sat up, her hair cascading around her in magnificent glory while tears glimmered within her eyes. "Do you honestly think Juanita wants you to hang?"

"She is not strong like you, Angela." His chest ached with his failure. "I could never learn how to make her strong."

"By making her face facts. My God, Lee, don't you think I was terrified when I discovered that I was blind? I never wanted to leave my bed. I just wanted to lie there and stare at the darkness that my world had become. If the truth would prevent you from hanging—"

"It wouldn't. I did not kill him in self-defense. That is the way of it." She jerked back as though he'd slapped her. The tears rolled onto her cheeks, branding his heart with unbridled pain. He sat on the bed, cupped her cheek, and captured a tear with his thumb. "Oh, my angel, I should have never touched you."

More tears surfaced, dampening her lovely face, pooling at the corners of her mouth. She shook her head. "No, don't say that. I don't regret what's happening between us. I'm just greedy and want more time. The rest of my life. If you'd be willing to meet with my father and Kit, I'm certain that they could prevent your hanging. You might have to go to prison for a while . . ."

The bed dipped as he shifted his weight, and she eased forward until she could press her face to his back and wrap her arms around his waist. "Maybe it would be enough to just tell them what Shelby did to your family without mentioning Juanita," she whispered. "It's a chance for us, Lee."

He closed his hands over her clasped hands

resting against his stomach. "I don't know if it's a chance worth taking. To be with you, *sí*, that would be worth it, but to find myself at the end of a rope if the truth made no difference . . . I would rather die in a blaze of gunfire." He lifted her hands, curled his back, and kissed her fingertips. "I'm going to return you to Fortune tomorrow."

"I no longer want to go back to Fortune. I want to stay here."

He held his breath, not daring to believe that he'd heard correctly. "You would stay here with me?"

"*Sí*. I'll even learn Spanish."

Turning, he combed his fingers through her hair. "What of your parents? Do you not care that they might be worried?"

"I'll write them a letter, explain that I love you, and that I'll be happy—"

"*Would* you be happy, Angela?"

"I'll be happy as long as you're with me."

"Even if I never took another cent of Shelby's money, I am still wanted for murder."

"I know, but if we were to stay here—"

"You said yourself that this is no life."

"And you said it was better than nothing at all. It's where I want to be."

He shot off the bed with such force that it rocked. He had not expected this. Had not expected her to want to stay. His inadequacies suddenly surfaced. He wanted more for her, so much more than what he had to offer. Did she fully understand what she was sacrificing for him?

"Where you want to be? This land is not ours! We are . . . like squatters. When the Mexican government discovers us here, we will have to leave."

She shrugged. "Then we'll leave."

"Where will we go?"

"If you refuse to try to get back the land that is rightfully yours, then we'll go somewhere else. The New Mexico Territory, California, Canada. I don't care. Just so we're together."

His knees hit the floor with a resounding thud and he took her hands. "Angela, I can't give you fancy dresses."

"I don't want fancy dresses. I want you, Lee. I love you."

He groaned low in his throat as he pressed her fingertips to his lips. "I have to think on this."

"Think on it all you want; I'm not leaving."

He chuckled. "You are a stubborn woman, Angela Bainbridge."

"Determined." She bracketed her hands on either side of his face. "Don't take me back to Fortune, Lee. Please."

"You must promise me that if I am ever captured, you will forget me."

He did not pressure her for the promise that she was unwilling to give. Instead, he feathered kisses over her face, tasting her tears, tears wept for him. For once, he wished she could see, could look into his eyes and know the depth of the love he held for her. Because she could not, he would have to show her.

Tenderly, he eased her down to the bed . . .

Chapter 16

"It sounds as though you're packing," Angela said, as she brought the sheet up to her throat. Outside, a rooster crowed.

Lee stilled and she wondered how long he'd been moving about the room before his actions disturbed her, how long he might have gazed at her exposed breasts. The heat suffused her body with the thought of all they'd shared last night.

She'd looked forward to waking in his arms this morning, and somehow she'd managed to lose her opportunity.

"I have to leave for a few days."

She shoved herself into a sitting position. "Where are you going?"

He sighed before dropping onto the edge of the bed. He softly touched his lips to hers. Circling her arm around his neck, she deepened the kiss.

He groaned low in his throat, nudged the sheet aside, and cradled her breast.

She had become a wanton woman, willing to do anything to keep her man beside her. And he had become her man. If she couldn't convince him to save himself, she would find a way to rescue him from the hangman's noose.

He broke off the kiss. "I have to see someone." He stroked his thumb over her lips. "I'll miss you, *querida*."

Fear etched itself into her heart as she grabbed his arm, digging her fingers into his muscles, fearful for what he was about to do and what it might cost them. "Lee, please don't take any more of Shelby's money."

"I won't—not today, at least—but I must dispose of the money I have."

"What are you going to do with it?"

He bussed a quick kiss over her lips. "Don't ask so many questions."

"Damn it, Lee, trust me. You can't truly love me if you don't trust me."

He touched his forehead to hers. She heard him swallow, felt the tension radiating from his body. Why did he find it so difficult to trust?

"I won't betray you," she whispered.

"I know that, it is just that some things are not mine alone to tell. But this I will tell you. In memory of Ramon, we give the money where it is most needed. Shelby hates Mexicans. So his money is used to better their lives, to build a school, a church, a home."

"Why aren't you using the money to bring Shelby to justice?"

"I have told you that it was his word against ours. We did not think anyone would listen to us. So we decided to take his money. He cannot build his empire; slowly it crumbles. Sometimes, I think too slowly, but a day will come when he will leave and we will return."

"There has to be a better way to bring him to justice."

He stood. She heard him pick up his saddlebags. "I'll think on it."

She whispered hoarsely, "*Vaya con dios.*"

"Always."

Lee strode into the barn, where Alejandro had his horse waiting. "*Gracias.*"

"Which one should I saddle for the woman?" Alejandro asked.

Lee slung his saddlebags into place. "I'm not taking Angela."

Alejandro narrowed his eyes. "Why not? It is the perfect opportunity. You deliver the money to Christine on the other side of the border, and then you simply go on to Fortune."

Bending his head and shaking it, Lee scrutinized the scuff marks on his boots, the well-worn heels. He remembered the fancy dress Angela had been wearing the night he had bumped into her outside the bank. What had he been thinking that night? And what had he been thinking when he'd first laid his body over hers? Even if he weren't an outlaw, he had nothing of himself worthy enough for her. "There is nothing simple about this situation."

"Only because you insist on making it difficult. The woman is going to get you hanged."

"The *woman* has a name." He lifted his head and held his brother's gaze. "I love her, Alejandro."

Alejandro looked as though he wanted to smash his fist into something hard. "Just like Ramon."

"Nothing like Ramon, and you know it."

Alejandro seemed to sag. "What are you going to do?"

"That I have not decided. She thinks Kit Montgomery and her father could help us find justice."

"What they will do is get you hanged."

Lee slapped his saddlebag and the horse sidestepped. "What is *this* accomplishing? When we were young, scared, and lost, our plan for revenge seemed very grand. But now we are older, not easily frightened. For the first time in my life, with Angela, I do not feel lost. I see things now that I did not before. What kind of a life is this for Miguel? He has no friends. He knows no children. And Juanita? She is afraid of her shadow. Seeking revenge has only managed to take away our freedom. Even this land we live on is not ours! If the Mexican government discovers us, they will shoo us away like pesky horseflies. They will probably take your cattle. We need to put our efforts toward getting your land back."

"It is your land as well."

"No, it's not." Lee watched the dust motes waltzing through the sunlight filtering into the barn. Running his hand over his shirt, he felt the tiny scars that had been with him for so long that he no longer noticed them, no longer questioned their origin. But Angela had him wondering about a great many things lately. "Do you remember anything about the night your father found me?"

Alejandro shook his head. "Very little. I remember the blood. I had never seen so much. They did not expect you to live, but you have always been stubborn."

"From the beginning, they treated me as though I had been born to them. I often forget that I wasn't."

"They loved you. You were a good son," Alejandro said.

"Not so good when I have brought their children to this." He mounted. "If I do not return, give me your word that you'll protect Angela and take her to her father."

"Why would you not return?"

"The road I travel has many forks in it, Alejandro. Give me your word."

"I will return her to her father. *Vaya con dios.*"

The bells tolled midnight as Lee quietly entered the sanctuary through the front door. He was always amazed at the peace that descended over him as he stood at the back. The simple church had a way of easing a troubled soul. It was a fine testament to the memory of his brother, a gentle man who had never raised his voice in anger or lifted his hand to harm another.

Out of respect for his mother's teachings, Lee crossed himself quickly before walking toward the altar where candles flickered. He knelt before the railing and bowed his head, but he no longer prayed. His soul was beyond redemption, and he wouldn't insult God by asking for His help in seeking vengeance.

"I was afraid you wouldn't come," the woman kneeling beside him whispered.

He had always thought Christine was the most beautiful woman he'd ever seen—until Angela had stumbled into his life.

"I learned too late that the bank in Fortune was a trap," she added, contempt for her father evident in every word.

"I assumed it would be—so far from home. So I was very cautious." He'd anticipated everything except a lady walking at midnight. "Do you know who the men were that your father hired?"

She sighed wearily. "No, I only know that they lost your trail after some storm. Thank goodness."

Lee breathed a sigh relief. The rain had served him well.

"Father was furious. He's planning to increase the bounty he's personally contributing for your capture. With that and the five hundred the state offers, it's getting terribly dangerous." Tears welled in her eyes. "No matter what we do, it doesn't stop the pain, and it doesn't ease the guilt."

"You are not to blame for what happened that night."

"I'll stop blaming myself when you stop blaming yourself."

A corner of his mouth quirked up. "Fair enough."

Concern filled her blue eyes. "I heard that you abducted a lady."

He nodded slowly, his eyes never leaving hers.

"I know you well enough to know you haven't hurt her, but I can't speak out in your defense without giving myself away."

He could argue that he had hurt Angela, feared that he'd caused harm that could never be undone. "I do not need you to speak for me. She is well."

She placed her hand gently over his where he gripped the railing. "I'm sure you have plans to return her, but let someone else do it."

"I do not let others stand in my stead." He relaxed his hand. He knew well how one night could forever alter a life. But every night with Angela seemed to change him. He grinned slightly. "How is your son?"

Her face blossomed into a smile, the warmth and love reflected in her eyes. "As handsome and kind as his father."

He thought of Juanita, how frightened she'd been the first time that she'd felt the ripple of movement that was her child. It had scared the hell out of him, too, until he realized what was happening. They were young, struggling to understand what no one had ever explained. He'd been frantic to comfort her, to uncover the answers.

In desperation, he'd turned to the one person who had nursed their wounds, suggested they leave. Like a thief, he'd sneaked into Christine's room to steal knowledge, only to discover that she, too, was with child. She carried Ramon's child.

She had been equally as frightened as Juanita but for different reasons. She was older—twenty-one— and not afraid of giving birth, but terrified that her father would take the child from her.

So she'd told her father that she was going to tend her ailing aunt who lived near Laredo. Then she'd come to stay with them. In the months that followed, while he'd dealt with two weeping, anxious women, they'd begun planning how she would raise this child without her family knowing and how she would honor the man she still loved.

He had brought his brother's son and Christine's brother's son into the world. He had a responsibility for their future, and thus far, he had to admit he had handled it poorly. If it hadn't been for Angela, he might never have never noticed.

"I've been thinking," he began.

"A dangerous occupation for a man."

His grin broadened. Five years ago, they had all been frightened and weak. Now they were stronger. "It is time we turned our energies elsewhere. You have a son who needs you. I must work to see that the Rodriguez land is reclaimed."

"How are you going to do that?"

"I don't know exactly, but Angela will help."

She arched a brow. "You say her name softly. Don't tell me that the notorious Lee Raven has had his heart stolen."

"Captured," he told her. "She captivated me from the moment I took her in my arms." He passed the saddlebags over to her. "The money from the last robbery is yours alone. We have done enough good deeds. Take your son someplace where you can be with him always and build a life for him that will honor his father."

"I wish you'd come see him."

With regret, Lee shook his head. The child did not need to know his uncle, the outlaw. "It is best if I don't, but I'll send my love." He leaned over and pressed a kiss to her cheek. She hugged him closely as though she feared this meeting would be their last. "*Vaya con dios*," he rasped, hoping that it wasn't.

"Does it hurt Hector when the babies bite him like that?" Miguel asked.

Kneeling in the last stall with Miguel and Juanita, Angela waited for Juanita to answer the question.

"No, little one," Juanita said softly. "It does not hurt Hector. They are not biting. They are suckling."

"When will Hector leave his babies?"

"Hector will not leave her babies," Juanita assured him.

"Why?"

"Because Hector is their mama."

"But my mama left me."

Angela's chest ached with his conclusion. He was fascinated with the cat and she couldn't help but feel that he was more interested in what it must be like to have a mother than in what it was to be a cat. They all assumed he would blithely accept that he had no mother, yet all around him on the ranch he would see female animals with their offspring, watch them caring for their newborns. How could he not help but wonder why his mother had not stayed?

"Miguel, your mama loved you," Juanita stammered. "Very much."

"Why did she leave?"

"It is as we told you. She had to go be an angel."

"Oh." He paused a heartbeat before asking, "*Señorita*, is it time for your birthday yet?" as though he'd completely forgotten the previous conversation.

Smiling warmly, Angela reached out and ruffled his hair. "Not yet."

He released a big gust of air. "That is the way of it."

Her heart turned over in her chest at Lee's oft-repeated phrase. She pulled Miguel close and hugged him tightly. "I love you, Miguel."

"Miguel!" Alejandro called from the entrance to the barn, his voice echoing within the cavernous structure. "It is time for chores."

He squirmed out of her embrace and ran out of the barn.

"I have chores as well," Juanita said.

Angela rested her hand on Juanita's arm, stopping her from rising. "Juanita, I know that I'm new to this family and there is a lot that I don't know, but I do know that you love Miguel."

"He is the light of my life."

She swallowed, not certain how to accomplish what she needed. She smiled softly. "Do you remember your mother?"

"*Sí*. She was kind. She always hugged us and made us laugh and wiped away our tears."

"Can you imagine how hard it would be not to have a mother?"

"That would be a terrible thing."

"Miguel doesn't have a mother."

"He has me."

"But you're his sister."

"Oh," she said in a tiny voice that reminded Angela very much of Miguel when an answer disappointed him. "It is not the same thing, is it?"

Tears burned Angela's eyes as she slowly shook her head. "No." She squeezed Juanita's hand. "All little boys need a mother. I know how difficult it is when our world suddenly changes. Until I was twelve, I could see, and then I got very, very sick. When the sickness left, it took my sight with it. I was scared when I couldn't see, but I was also ashamed."

"You should not have been ashamed, Angela. It was not your fault."

"No, it wasn't my fault, but I was still embarrassed because I was different, I had changed. I wasn't ready for that change. I didn't want to be different. But I got tired of lying in bed, so one day

I climbed out and stubbed my toe on the leg of a chair. And it hurt. But the next day when I climbed out of bed, I remembered where the chair was."

"This time you did not stub your toe," Juanita said.

"That's right. I didn't. I bumped my shin on a little table."

"Oh, Angela, it must have hurt."

"It did. But the next day, I didn't stub my toe and I didn't bump my shin."

Juanita squeezed her hand as though to congratulate her. "That is good."

"I bruised my knee."

Juanita gasped. "No."

"Yes. Every day I was afraid of what I might hurt when I got out of bed. But I still got out of bed because no matter how scary things got, they were never as scary as I thought they *would* be."

"You are very brave."

"I'm not brave. I just got tired of being afraid of the dark." She brushed her fingers across Juanita's brow, combing her hair back from her face. She didn't want to push her too far. Like Lee, she didn't know how to help her without hurting her. "I hope someday you can meet my mother."

"I do not think she would like me."

"She would love you just like I do."

"I do not like to leave this place."

"A slow journey, a cautious journey, is better than no journey at all."

Sitting on the floor in Lee's room, Angela removed Lee's books from their boxes one by one, lining them up along the wall beneath the window. She wanted to build him a shelf, a permanent place to keep his books, where he could still find them when he was an old man.

She was beginning to understand why Lee would not break his vow to Juanita. She had wanted to beg Juanita to tell the authorities what had happened, wanted her to tell Miguel that she was his mother. But in many ways, Juanita was a child herself. Afraid of the world. Angela wanted to help her but she didn't know how.

She closed her eyes. It was an old habit from her days of sight when she'd wished to block out the world to spin her romantic dreams. After so many years of not seeing the world, she still found comfort in the simple gesture.

She touched her fingers to her chin, trying in her mind to re-create the feel of Lee's chin. His features were so unlike his brothers'. Sharper, more defined. Or perhaps they'd only appeared that way because she'd wanted to know them with an urgency that was almost frightening. Yet sitting here, she realized she'd been distracted by his kisses, enamored of his touch, and she'd failed to gather the details that she required to envision him fully. Was his hair black or brown? And the shade of his eyes . . . how deeply did the brown run?

She began making a mental note of brown objects gathered from her memory, concentrating on their hue, hoping he could accurately identify the one that most closely resembled his eyes. She wasn't that concerned with his hair, but his eyes.

Windows to the soul, corridors to the heart. She regretted that she could not hold his gaze and look deeply into his eyes as she'd so often seen her mother do with her father—before she'd lost her sight.

She remembered the many times that they had seemed to become lost in each other, just looking at each other, faraway smiles softening their features as though they shared a magical place of memories that they could travel to at any time regardless of their surroundings.

Did Lee look at her like that? As though she made him complete, as though she were the sum of his existence, the center of his world? Or had she simply fallen under his spell because he was her captor?

She didn't think she was that naïve or that easily fooled.

Familiar footsteps echoed down the hallway and her heart picked up its tempo. The hurried, resounding tread of large feet. Joy burst through her. He was home.

She knew the moment he entered the room. The door banged closed in his wake, providing immediate privacy, promising intimacy. She rose and found herself gathered in his strong arms, his rapacious mouth moving over hers with an intensity that she welcomed. The heat from his body melted into hers as she wound her arms firmly around his neck, running her fingers into his curls. He needed a haircut. She inhaled his familiar musky male scent—and something else. The withering scent of roses.

Pain knifed through her heart as she tore her mouth from his, shoved him back, and scrambled away until her knees hit the bed. She pressed a trembling hand to her mouth. "You were with a woman."

"What?" Bafflement laced his voice.

"You went away to be with another woman. I can smell her."

"I stopped and bathed in the river. How can you smell her?"

He didn't even bother to deny it. "Your clothes carry her stink." A tear rolled onto her cheek. Furiously she swiped it away. "How could I be such a fool?"

"Angela, it's not what you think," he said huskily, his fingers skimming her cheek.

She slapped at him, her palm making contact with his arm. She wanted to withdraw from him, curl into a tightened ball so he could never touch her again. "Get away from me," she spat.

His arms came around her, holding her close against his solid chest. He grunted when she kicked his shin.

"Listen to me," he said.

"No! You've got nothing to say that I want to hear."

"I love you," he rasped.

Words she had longed to hear tainted by his rendezvous with another woman. She twisted madly. "Let me go!"

"Yes, I was with a woman. A friend. She is just a friend. I did not lie with her."

She stilled, sinking against him, shaking her

head. "Then why do your clothes reek of her?"

He skimmed his lips along her temple. "Because she embraced me when we said good-bye."

She supposed that could be true. He'd never lied to her, and would a man who had recently bedded another be so quick to take her in his arms, his body so responsive? Because even now she could feel the clear evidence of his desire pressed against her belly.

He dipped his head and pressed a kiss to the sensitive spot below her ear. "You're the only one, Angel, the only one I've ever made love to."

Her breath caught. "Ever?"

"Ever," he whispered hoarsely beside her ear. "I thought of you every moment I was away. Did you think of me?"

She tipped her head back, touched her hand to his pliant lips. She gave him a tremulous smile. "I thought of you every moment you were away."

His mouth returned to hers with an urgency greater than it had before. And his hands, his roughened, callused hands worked to make their clothes melt away until they were flesh to flesh, shoulder to hip.

She fell onto the bed and he followed her, until they were a tangle of desperate limbs, touching, searching, wanting, desiring.

When his body entered hers, she cried out from the sheer joy of it. He was hers, and she was his. All doubts faded away as she met his thrusts with abandon, their sweat-sheened bodies slick. She moaned and writhed beneath him, climbing higher and higher, while her hands skimmed over his clenched jaws, his flaring nostrils, his open eyes.

Oh, to see as he saw . . .

As he carried her over the precipice into the realm of pleasure, for a fleeting second, she did see—his love. Pure, deep, hers forever.

Sated, his limbs heavy, his breathing slowly returning to normal, Lee rolled to his side and drew Angela into the curve of his body. He threaded his fingers into the tangle of her hair, rested his palm against the curve of her chin, stroked his thumb over her cheek, and pressed a kiss to her brow. He thought about how close he'd come to never knowing this measure of contentment.

The bounty of her love was something he wasn't certain he deserved, but he was still grateful for it, treasured it, and would carry the memory of it with him always.

Chapter 17

The wind blew softly, gently, whispering its secrets to the leaves in the trees that grew haphazardly along the banks of the river. Sitting on a blanket of bright red, orange, and yellow, colors and designs that Lee had described in vivid detail, Angela had never known such contentment. That it was a false happiness, she refused to acknowledge. That it was fleeting she didn't dare contemplate.

She had this moment, this day, with a man whom she knew she would love forever. He'd awakened her at midnight, and again at dawn, his hands, his lips, his hardened body weaving magical sensations, each touch a gift, each moan a song.

As though they were a normal couple with the luxury of courtship, he'd brought her here to enjoy the cool breeze blowing off the Rio Grande, the shade of the trees, and the joy of his company.

"Arrogant, I know," he'd said, as he'd lifted her onto a horse, "to think you would want to spend time with me alone."

"Arrogant," she'd responded with a smile, "but accurate."

Now he was stretched out on the ground, his head nestled within her lap while she skimmed her fingers over his face, his neck, his shoulders, and through his hair. She thought she would never grow weary of touching him. She must have dreamt a hundred times of going on a picnic just as her sisters often did, with a man who didn't stumble over his feet as he tried to ensure that she didn't trip over hers. With Lee, she felt complete. "Is your hair black or brown?" she asked lazily.

"They are so close in color, what does it matter?"

"I'm trying to create a clearer image of you in my mind."

"I think your heart sees me clearly," he murmured as took her hand and kissed each fingertip.

She returned her hands to his head. "I like colors, so tell me something that's the same shade as your hair."

"I will have to think on it to find the perfect object."

"It doesn't have to be perfect."

"But you will put this thing on top of my head, heh? So I must think on it."

She shook her head. Sometimes he was incredibly frustrating. "Who taught you to play the guitar?"

"*Mi madre*. She had a beautiful voice."

"You are apparently the only one of her sons to inherit it."

Beneath her fingers, he seemed to tense. "No, it is Juanita who has her talent, but she no longer sings, except maybe lullabies to Miguel."

She brushed his errant curls off his brow. "Whose idea was it to tell people that Miguel was your brother?"

"Mine. Juanita was so ashamed that I thought it would be easier for her if she did not have to admit to anyone that she had a son."

"But you're denying Miguel a chance to know her as his mother."

Abruptly, he sat up. "I've considered that, but there is no easy way to handle this situation. How do you think he is going to feel if he discovers I murdered his father?"

She heard the pain reflected in his voice and knew he would be lost without that little boy's love. To comfort him, she flattened her palm against his back, the corded muscles bunching beneath the fabric of his shirt. "Miguel will always love you, no matter what happens."

"I did not bring you here to discuss what cannot be changed." Tenderly he cradled her cheek. "I wanted us to have a day with no memories. Teach me how to court you."

She released a burst of laughter. "It's a little late for that, don't you think?"

"It is never too late to court a woman. *Mi padre*

told me that a man should seek to please the lady of his heart for as long as he lives."

"He sounds like a wise man."

"He was. So how shall I court you, Angela Bainbridge?"

Tears stung her eyes for what he'd indirectly told her. "Am I the lady of your heart, then?"

"*Sí*." Lee lowered his mouth to hers, kissing her tenderly, relishing the feel of her lips molding themselves against his while their tongues waltzed to a rhythm dictated by their hearts. "Do you doubt it?"

"No."

"Good. Now, how have other men sought to win your favor?"

Angela smiled with the memories of bungling suitors. "With no success."

"So what would you have me do?"

She skimmed her fingers over his beloved features. "Live to be an old man."

No smile lines formed in his face, no hint of joy. "What can I give you today?" he asked.

Her chest tightened. "Just hold me."

His arms came around her with a sureness as he eased her down to the blanket. "A woman should be greedy when a man is offering her whatever she desires."

She *was* greedy as his mouth teased hers with light pecks before settling in for a deeper kiss. She was starved for the taste of him, the scent of him, the heat of him. She wanted his body moving over hers in slow, heated ecstasy. If they were paupers, with him beside her, she would know wealth. His tongue waltzed with hers before sweeping through her mouth, outlining every curve, every dip.

He drew back. "If I am not careful, I will make love to you out here while the sun watches."

She felt her cheeks grow hot with the thought. "I'm not that daring."

"But you are brave; from the beginning, I admired your bravery."

"I get that from my mother. If she was ever afraid of anything, I never knew."

"Why were you not afraid of me?"

"I was at first, when you grabbed me outside the bank, but then . . ." She laughed self-consciously. "Your voice never sounded cruel, your touch never felt brutal." She shook her head. "I don't know, Lee. I know I should have been terrified, but I never felt threatened. Then when you scolded me for using profanity, I thought, what kind of outlaw is this man?"

"You have gotten much better at not using profanity."

She bracketed her hands on either side of his face. "My God, but I love you."

"And I love that smile." He traced the edges of her lips, then moved his finger down so it could follow the line of her collarbone, exposed by the low neck of the blouse she wore. "Why did it bother you when I called you 'Angel' that first morning?"

She was surprised that she did not feel the usual stab of pain with the memory. "Because of Damon."

He stilled his light caress. "Damon?"

"Damon Montgomery." When he neither responded nor moved, she added, "The little boy I lost."

"His name was Damon?"

"Yes. He called me 'Angel.' I guess 'Angela' was too hard when he was so young."

"He was very fortunate to have had you for a friend."

Now the pain did roll through her. "Not so fortunate."

He gave her a quick kiss. "We are not supposed to talk about memories today, we are supposed to make them."

He moved away from her, took her hand, and pulled her to her feet. "Come. I have decided what I am going to give you."

"Lee, you don't have to give me anything."

"I'd give you the world if I could."

In a way he did. Holding hands, they walked and talked . . . safe subjects all. Books they'd read, people they'd known. He told her of the *vaqueros* who had come up from Mexico each spring to help his father drive the cattle north. She shared stories about the men who visited her father's saloon. Then he surprised her by taking her on a journey through his memory of all the happy times. She could almost hear his father's laughter, feel the warmth of his mother's embrace, the gentle teasing of an older brother tolerant of the younger ones who tagged after him. Within Lee's voice, she heard the longing for what he had once possessed, surprisingly never taken for granted, and the acceptance that it would never come to pass again.

As twilight shadows began to chase away the heat of day, she stood beside a tree, her hands pressed against the bark, the trunk vibrating as Lee scraped a knife against the wood. "What are you doing?" she asked.

"I'll show you in a minute."

She tapped her foot against an exposed root. "Have I ever mentioned that I'm not patient?"

He chuckled low. "That I figured out on my own."

She gnawed on her bottom lip. "My mother used to tell me that men were like barbed wire."

"Like barbed wire?" he asked, obviously distracted.

"Yes, they have their good points."

He laughed then, a rumble that started deep within his chest and echoed around them.

She shrieked as he lifted her in the air. Smiling brightly, she planted her hands on his shoulders as he spun her around.

"Good points? I will share my good points with you later."

Tears burned her eyes. "I've never heard you laugh, not like that. My God, Lee, you almost sound happy."

He stopped twirling then and slowly lowered her to the ground. "I am happy, *querida*." He skimmed his knuckles across her cheek. "When I am with you, I feel . . ."

"What do you feel?" she asked.

"Like I am the man that perhaps I should have

been." He bussed a quick kiss across her lips. "Like I am a man who would do *loco* things like this."

He flattened her hand against the tree. She detected a groove chiseled into the bark.

"What do you think?" he asked.

"Who's being impatient now?" she chided. "I have to concentrate." She ran her finger along the indentation: a slant that eventually curved into a V that curved into a slant that came to a point. Something jutted out from each side. "It's a heart," she whispered, "a heart with an arrow going through it. That's something young sweethearts would do."

"So today I feel young." He took her hand. "What does the center of the heart tell you?"

With her fingertips, she traced the lines. "AB, and beneath that is LR." Tears of joy welled in her eyes and spilled onto her cheeks. "I always wanted someone to carve my initials on a tree." She pressed her hands flat, trying to create an impression against her palms.

"Then you like it?"

"I love it."

"You are too easy to please, *querida*."

She spun around. "But you have to get rid of it. What if someone sees it?"

"That is the whole point."

"You could lead someone straight to you."

"What are the odds that someone will figure it out . . . if they happen to see it?"

"Whatever they are, I don't like them."

"The branches are low, the foliage dense. I do

not think anyone will see it, but it will be here for a thousand years, and if someone *should* spot it, they will spin tales about the outlaw who fell in love with a lady."

She touched her fingers to his mouth. He was smiling, a full beautiful smile that she couldn't bring herself to dim with her worries. "Tell me the story, Lee, tell me the story that you think they'll weave."

He lifted her into his arms. "I think I'll take you to bed and show it to you instead."

He was lost, so lost, stumbling in the darkness, searching for home . . . warmth, security, love . . . but they remained beyond reach. Perhaps he didn't deserve them.

Shaking, cold . . . blood, too damned much blood. Screams, cries . . . tears. An explosion. The loss of all his dreams.

He swirled through the haze until he saw them, waiting for him, arms outstretched, anxious to welcome him home. But he couldn't go home, not now, not after what he had become.

A voice intruded on his nightmare, lulling him away, calling him back. Lee awoke with a start, his breathing harsh and heavy, his body slick with sweat.

"Lee? Are you all right?"

A small hand rested on his heaving chest, another gently stroked his damp hair.

"Angel?" he rasped.

"It was just a dream," she assured him softly, "just a dream."

"It's always so real. I can smell the fear."

"Were you reliving the night your family was attacked?"

"At first, but then . . . I have a long ago memory."

She moved up and pressed his face against the gentle swells of her bosom. "You're crying."

The shame clenched his gut and twisted it into a hardened knot as he shook his head in denial of the truth.

"It's all right, Lee. It's all right," she cooed. "You don't have to be ashamed."

"But I am."

"Don't be. Not with me."

Not with her, not with this woman who saw him more clearly than anyone ever had. He plowed his fingers into her hair and burrowed his face into her pliant flesh.

"What do you dream?"

"I see a man and woman."

"Your parents?"

"No, I don't know who they are, but it saddens me to see them. I hurt when I see them."

"Then don't dream," she whispered. "Just sleep."

She rubbed his tense shoulders, kneaded his stiff neck. He began to drift off, carrying her into his dreams.

Angela sat beside the window, the gentle night breeze ruffling her hair. Lee had finally succumbed to the lure of sleep, so deeply that he hadn't stirred when she'd clambered out of bed.

But how long would he sleep before he awoke with another anguished cry?

They had returned home, and he had indeed taken her to bed, the story of love he had woven with each caress, each kiss had expanded her love for him. She could only hope that in time, her love would heal the wounds of his past.

She didn't want to sleep in case he needed her again, but she'd never been one for idleness. So she contemplated exactly what she would tell her parents. How to explain what she barely understood.

With a book on her lap serving to support the paper, using her left hand as a guide, she began to write.

My dearest Mother and Father,

I have met the most incredible man. In many ways, he reminds me of you, Father, so protective of his family, of those he loves.

In other ways, he's like no one I've ever met before. He sees me as I've always wanted to be seen: not as a woman without sight, but simply as a woman. He challenges me, pricks my temper, then soothes my anger.

No one has to tell me when he looks at me. I feel the intensity of his gaze warming me. His voice calms me. His nearness reassures me. His laughter and smiles become mine.

His love makes me complete.

I don't expect you to understand why I would choose to live with a man who has such a bleak

future and refuses to promise me anything be-
yond heartache. I do hope that you'll respect my
decision to stay here.

I love Lee as I never dared dream to love any-
one . . . with all my heart.

I hope that someday you'll have the opportu-
nity to meet him. Until then, I remain forever
your daughter.

Angela

Setting the paper aside, she rose from the chair
and leaned over the bed. Lee breathed evenly,
calmly. Quietly, she left the room.

Counting her steps, Angela walked away from
the house.

She missed her midnight strolls, but here she
could find no landmarks to identify. No fence, no
wooden Indian, no boisterous laughter drifting
out from the saloon—nothing to guide her. She
could easily lose her way, and knowing the exact
number of steps between the house and her destination was imperative.

She must ask Lee to build her a path. She
would go crazy without the freedom to wander.
Her blindness would not cage her in as much as
Lee's love would. Was that fair to either of them?
Would she come to resent it?

She knew without a doubt that she wanted to
spend the remainder of her life with him, grow
old with him. Bring his children into the world.
But she would have to raise them in isolation, and

she wasn't certain she could deny them access to a world she could no longer see but still loved. Commotion, wagon wheels spinning, the din of conversation, the rumble of laughter. If only she could convince Lee to talk with her father. Then they might have a chance at a normal life, if they could only clear his name.

His name. She wanted him to clear a name that wasn't truly his. What *was* his real name? Why couldn't he go back to being who he was before the night Shelby attacked his family? Why had he chosen the name Lee Raven?

So many questions. He had trusted her with his heart, given her so much already, but she wanted everything, to understand each nuance behind his actions . . . but more, she wanted to save him from the gallows.

Shooting a man in the back might have been cowardly, but she understood his reasons for killing Floyd Shelby. She was convinced that if he would only explain to a judge all that had happened that night, he would be exonerated. Surely her parents would defend his actions. She thought Kit Montgomery would as well. Perhaps then Lee's nightmares would cease.

"Angela?"

She stilled, fear shoving aside what should have been joy. "Spence?"

"Thank God." He tightly wrapped his arms around her while her mind spun with a thousand questions. He moved back slightly, but anchored her to his side with one arm. "Come on. Let's get you out of here."

Resisting, she broke free. "What are you doing here?"

"What the bloody hell do you think we're doing?" he asked.

"We? Who all is here?"

He took her arm. "I'll explain everything once I've gotten you safely away."

Shaking her head, she jerked loose. "Explain now. Who is here?"

He sighed heavily. "Father, Gray, six Rangers, your parents."

"*My* parents are with *you*?"

"Yes. We're spread out so we have the area covered. I was sneaking up for a closer look to see if I could determine the weaknesses. We planned to take the place at dawn. You can well imagine that it was nearly impossible to convince your parents of the value in waiting, in the advantages of following standard Ranger procedure. But we thought it less likely that Raven would use you as a shield if we caught him unawares."

"He'd never use me as a shield."

"It's a moot issue now. Since we have you, we won't have to be cautious when we go in to get him."

"So you'll go in with guns blazing?" she asked, thinking of Lee's comment that he'd rather die by gun than by rope.

"We won't attack quite that dramatically."

"You're in Mexico. You have no jurisdiction here."

"Precedents have been set for Rangers not strictly adhering to the boundaries formed by the

Texas border." He cupped her face between his hands. "Angela, what in the hell is going on? I'm here to rescue you, for which I would think you'd be immensely grateful. Instead, you're arguing."

"Because it's too dangerous for all of you. He has five brothers in the house. One is a little boy. His sister is there." She could well imagine the terror Juanita would experience to see a hoard of unfamiliar men storming the house. "You were searching for me. Why not leave Raven?"

"We can't now that we've found him. He's a murderer. You know Father's reputation and his quest for justice."

Clutching his arm, she wanted desperately to tell him the whole story, but Lee's gentle rebuke whispered to her heart that some things weren't hers to reveal. Although his family's history might be one of them, it still hurt not to vindicate him with the truth. "Justice won't be served if someone gets hurt."

Her stomach knotted as she thought of any of these people being killed. Lee's family. Hers. Kit. Grayson. Spence. Would Lee surrender to protect his family? Would anyone who participated in the search to find her give him a chance? They didn't know him as she did. And he didn't know them. What would anyone's death accomplish? She swallowed hard. "If I promise you that he'll never again rob another bank, he'll never again cross into Texas, will you please just leave us here and pretend you never found us?"

Tenderly he cradled her cheek. "What happened while you were with him?"

Tears stung her eyes. "I fell in love with him."

He drew her close. "Listen to me. That's not uncommon in abductions. I've read where women who were carried off by Indians fell in love with their captors."

She shook her head. "It's not like that. I've written a letter to Mother and Father explaining that I want to stay with him."

"Trust me, sweetheart. What you're feeling is a result of the circumstances, not the man."

"He's a *good* man."

"He's a coward. He shot a man in the back, for God's sake. To be sure, you are our first consideration, but we're not going to leave without him."

And if they tried to take him, they would end up taking him dead. How could she possibly endure his death? "I can deliver him to you," she rasped, her throat aching as she forced out the words.

"Raven?"

She stepped out of his embrace. "There's a spot by the river. You'll find initials carved in a tree. I'll have him take me there shortly after dawn. If we aren't far from the house, his brothers will try to stop you and someone is bound to get killed"— she thought she might be ill—"and you can arrest him at the river." She dug her fingers into his arm. "Just don't hurt him."

He sighed heavily. "I really need to discuss this idiotic idea of yours with Father."

"We don't have time. If Lee wakes up, and I'm not in bed—" Too late she realized what her words had revealed.

"Christ," Spence muttered. "Tell me you're not in his bed."

"Please, Spence. Just go back to the others and tell them what our plan is."

"*Our* plan? I'm not going to take any credit for it."

"I'll take full credit for it, then, but don't you see that it's the only way we can guarantee that no one gets wounded—or worse, killed?"

"All right, but if you haven't left the house by noon, we'll come in and take him—any way we can."

Rising up on the tips of her toes, she kissed Spence's cheek. "Thank you."

"Don't thank me. Your father is going to bloody well kill Raven when he realizes what the man did."

"You use too much profanity, Spence."

"What?"

She shook her head. "Nothing."

"One other thing—don't try to warn him. We'll leave men behind to watch the house. If he tries to escape, my promise to you is voided. We'll do whatever we have to in order to arrest him."

Putting Lee on alert was possibly the worst plan of action. She knew how stealthy he could be when he set his mind to it. Hadn't he sneaked up on her time and time again? And if he truly was as skilled with weapons as he claimed, she knew he would do whatever it took to protect his family. "I'll keep my end of the bargain. Can you turn me so that I'm in a direct line with the house?"

He placed his hands on her shoulders and guided her around. "Be careful."

"You, too. Please tell my parents not to worry. Raven never hurt me. Never."

As she walked back toward the house, she wondered if he'd ever be able to say the same of her.

"Describe the sunrise to me. I want to see it through your eyes," Angela said quietly, too quietly, as they stood beneath the tree where he'd carved their initials.

He wasn't certain what had possessed him when he'd taken his knife to the bark. He'd almost carved his true initials, had almost convinced himself to reveal everything. She made him believe in possibilities, had forced him to realize that his quest for revenge had somehow gone astray, was hurting the wrong people. Perhaps with her by his side, he could redirect his energies, he could find a more satisfying way to make Shelby accountable for his actions.

She'd been somber ever since he'd awakened her before dawn and made love to her. She'd wept afterward and had told him that she wanted to come here. As willing as she was to stay with him, he had to be as willing to open his heart completely.

He watched as she traced her fingers over the ragged gouges he'd made.

"The sunrise," she whispered.

"I'd rather describe you."

"I know what I look like."

"Do you? Do you know that through my eyes you are the loveliest woman I've ever seen?" Taking her hand, he knelt on one knee. "Will you marry me?"

She gasped, not with the joy he'd expected, but with an expression of horror. Tears filled her eyes and spilled onto her cheeks.

The crunch of a boot heel alerted him that they weren't alone. Every nerve in his body felt as though lightning had streaked through it. He shot to his feet and wrapped his fingers around the butt of his gun at the same moment that Angela wound her hand around his wrist.

"No," she pleaded, her face stricken but showing no evidence of surprise, only quiet acceptance.

"Move your hand away from the gun, Raven," someone ordered. "We have half a dozen rifles trained on you."

"Please," Angela rasped hoarsely, "do as Captain Montgomery says. They won't hurt you."

Montgomery. He should have known. "What about my brothers?"

She shook her head as more tears fell. "They only want you."

She'd known, somehow she'd known they would be here waiting for him, had lured him here. Slowly he unfurled his fingers and raised his hands, grateful his hat shadowed his face and enabled him to hide the agony of her betrayal.

"Angela, move away from him."

Montgomery's voice resonated around Lee,

cultured, authoritative, his British accent apparent.

But Angela didn't move. "Promise me you won't do anything to draw their fire," she begged Lee.

"I'm going to remove my gun belt," he announced before cautiously lowering one hand. While he worked the fastenings, he sliced his gaze to Angela. "A man only fights, *querida*, when he has a reason to live."

"Lee, listen to me—"

"You have nothing to say that I want to hear." He dropped his gun belt to the ground and took a step back. Two men immediately emerged from their hiding places behind the trees, spun him around, and wrenched his arms behind his back. His stomach knotted as he heard the clanking of iron. He was grateful that his family wasn't here to witness his shame and humiliation, to see him stripped of dignity as the cold metal was snapped around his wrists.

"You don't have to chain him," Angela said.

"Angela!" a voice boomed.

Lee listened to the hurried halting footsteps and the sound of a cane tapping the ground. Keeping his head bent, his hat rim hiding his face, out of the corner of his eye, he saw the man come to a staggering stop and draw Angela against him with one arm, the cane not merely a prop. He relied on it . . . heavily if the way his knuckles turned white as he gripped the golden lion's head was any indication.

Lee's breath stilled as memories flitted in and out of his mind. A child, studying the lion, frightened of it. Then the memories faded and he doubted that he'd seen them at all.

"Papa, tell them that they don't have to bind him."

"Angela, Kit knows best," her father said, his accent undeniably British. "Are you hurt? Did he harm you in any way?"

"No, Papa, I'm fine but you have to help him."

"I'll help him all right. Straight to the gallows." Her father moved away from her until he stood directly in front of Lee. "I ought to beat you to a bloody pulp."

Dear God, but he wished he would, would beat him black and blue until he was unrecognizable.

"Look at me, you sorry bastard."

"Harry, I'll handle this," Montgomery said. "You take care of Angela."

His head still lowered, he saw Montgomery's boots first. Scuffed, covered in dust, but obviously finely made.

"I'm Captain Christian Montgomery of the Texas—"

"I know who you are," Lee said solemnly. His heart pounding, dreading what he feared he would discover, he slowly lifted his gaze . . .

And found himself staring into eyes the same light blue as his own.

Chapter 18

Slowly, excruciatingly slowly, Kit Montgomery reached out with a trembling hand and swept the black Stetson from his prisoner's head.

Kit had always envisioned Lee Raven with dark hair. Perhaps because his name conjured up images of black birds. He'd never expected him to have hair that curled as his did when he allowed it to grow too long. Hair the color of wheat . . . like his wife's.

"What do you want us to do, Captain?" Sean Cartwright asked.

Kit did what he'd never expected to do at this moment. "Put him on his horse," he ordered before turning his back on his son.

Angela heard the quiver in Kit's voice, the clanging of the chains, and Lee's retreating footsteps. She couldn't remember when she'd felt this lost, could never remember feeling this abandoned. Frantically reaching out, she clutched her father's arm. "Papa—"

"Come along now," he said briskly.

"Papa, what's wrong?" The silence before the Ranger had spoken had been palpable, almost deafening. "Papa?"

"Angela!"

She turned at her mother's urgent plea. "Mama!"

A scent she knew well—the fragrance of affection and caring that she associated with her mother—greeted her a heartbeat before her mother's arms wound tightly around her and her mother's tears dampened her cheek.

"Oh, sweetie," her mother rasped, rocking her slightly. "Oh, my baby."

"Mama, something's wrong."

"Not anymore. We have you back. Are you hurt?"

"No, but what are they doing with Lee?"

"Lee?" her mother asked.

She nodded, her worries increasing. "Something is terribly wrong. Kit was upset. I heard it in his voice."

"Oh, Angela," her mother began, brushing Angela's hair back from her face, a comforting gesture, but also a telling sign that she didn't know exactly how to explain something. "What do you know about Lee Raven?"

"That he probably hates me right now."

"What else?"

"I don't understand. Why are we playing twenty questions? Why don't you just tell me—"

"He looks remarkably like Kit," her father said quietly.

Her heart lurched, her stomach knotted, and bile rose in her throat. "I don't understand. You mean he's a darkened version of Kit? He's Mexican—"

"No, sweetie, he isn't."

She spun around. "Where is he? I have to talk with him."

"They're escorting him across the river," her father said. "We need to follow."

She sank against him, tears stinging her eyes as she pushed the question past the knot in her throat, "What color is his hair?"

"Blond."

Images bombarded her. Damon Montgomery running into her arms. Damon Montgomery chasing her. Damon Montgomery playing hide and seek with her.

Damon Montgomery making passionate love to her.

Angela sat by the fire, listening to the crackling of the flames. Dear God in heaven, Lee Raven was Damon Montgomery. She felt numb from the top of her head to the tips of her toes, had ever since the truth regarding his identify had burst through her with unrelenting anguish. She had failed him as a child. Had she failed him now that he was a man?

Her mother and father sat on either side of her,

each holding her hand. Spence sat beside her mother. Grayson Rhodes was on the other side of her father. She didn't know where Kit was. Lee was somewhere nearby. She'd heard the rattle of his chains, but they'd fallen into silence before she could identify the location.

No one had spoken as they rode. No one had uttered a word when they made camp. No one had talked while they ate. So much needed to be said, yet everyone seemed wary of communicating their thoughts and concerns aloud. As though everyone was in shock, stunned beyond belief.

What was Lee feeling? Did he know who he was? Had he recognized Kit? Discovering that Damon was alive after all these years should have been a cause for jubilation, not mourning.

"I need to speak with Lee," she said. As hard as she tried, she couldn't envision him as Damon. Why hadn't he told her? Had he not realized who he was?

"I'm not sure that's a wise idea," her mother said.

"Is he glaring at me?"

"No," her mother said.

"Is he looking at me?"

"No."

Her heart sank. Not once throughout the day had she felt his gaze on her, and that knowledge chilled her. To have her mother confirm her suspicions—that he was ignoring her—only increased her concern for his welfare. "Did he eat?"

"No," Spence said.

A man only fights, querida, *when he has a reason to live.* So he assumed he had no reason to live, no reason to eat.

"Spence, will you put some food on a plate? I can get him to eat."

"I'm not letting you approach him alone," her father said.

"Isn't he still chained?"

"Yes, but they have his hands in front of him now instead of behind his back. Seems rather risky to me. Even if he should happen to be . . . well, whoever he is—"

"I'll be fine by myself," she interrupted.

"I've no doubt about that, but still I shall accompany you—"

"Papa!" she snapped. Reaching out, she wrapped her hand around his. "I love you with all my heart, but I'm not a little girl any longer. I stood up to an outlaw, shot him—"

"You shot him?" Gray interrupted. "When he attacked you in the clearing?"

"He never attacked me. That was another man. I shot Lee during my botched escape. Then I tended his wound, fell in love with him, and betrayed him. Believe me, I can handle taking him something to eat by myself." To soften the blow of her words, she brought her father's hand to her lips and pressed his knuckles to her cheek. "Even though you were watching, I grew up."

Reaching into her pocket, she withdrew the letter that she'd written when the future held promise. "I want you both to read this."

"What is it?" her mother asked as she took it.

"A letter I wrote to you when I didn't think I'd return to Fortune." She rose to her feet and extended her hand. "Spence, the plate."

"Yes, ma'am," he answered smartly as he gave it to her.

"Don't get cocky."

"Wouldn't dream of it. I will, however, escort you to the prisoner and then leave you."

He intertwined his arm around hers before he started walking. As soon as she no longer felt the heat from the fire and knew her parents weren't close enough to hear, she asked, "If I knew why he killed Floyd Shelby and told a judge, would it make a difference in his sentence?"

"Probably not. Hearsay, and all that. It would be rather like me telling your parents last night that you'd somehow managed to fall in love with an outlaw. I don't think they truly believed it until *you* told them, just now."

"Did they look shocked?"

"Devastated is a more accurate description. I don't think he's exactly what they had in mind for you."

"Did you talk to him when you took him his food earlier?" she asked softly.

"I tried, but he took an instant dislike to me."

She couldn't stop the small smile from playing at the corner of her mouth. "He probably sensed the lawyer in you."

"I'm not a lawyer yet. You have to be twenty-one to go before the licensing board."

"You always wanted to grow up too fast," she reminded him. "Did you like him?"

"Not particularly. He seemed a bit surly, but then under the circumstances, I suppose I would as well."

"How is your father holding up?"

"Judging by the uncharacteristic manner in which he's been avoiding everyone, I'd say not too well. Just so you'll know, we have men standing at the perimeter, rifles at the ready." He stopped walking. "Five steps and you'll be at the entrance to the lion's den. Good luck."

She listened to his retreating footsteps and the pounding of her own heart. She hadn't been this frightened when Lee had first grabbed her outside the bank. Cautiously she strolled forward and then lowered herself to her knees. "I brought you something to eat."

She heard no clanking of chains and detected no movement of air. She set the plate on her lap. Reaching out with a trembling hand, she searched for his face. As soon as she touched his cheek, he jerked away. Pain ripped through her at his rejection. "Lee—"

"You knew they were waiting at the river. I saw it in your face, Angela, so don't deny it."

"Yes, I knew," she whispered, clutching her hands together to stop herself from reaching for him again. "After you had the nightmare, after you drifted off to sleep, I went for a walk. I ran into Spence not far from the house." She leaned toward him. "Lee, all the men you see here were outside waiting for dawn." Tears stung her eyes. "All I could think was that you might be killed. Or Miguel. Juanita. My father."

"You could have told me."

"So you could have gotten killed trying to escape? Or killed someone to protect your family?"

"At least then I might have stood a chance. Your way guarantees me a trip to the gallows."

She refused to believe he would hang. "When I asked you to leave me to the men who were following you, you wouldn't because you didn't know them. Lee, I *know these* men. I trust them. You can trust them." Silence stretched between them. "You have the right to be angry, but not stupid." She held out the plate. "You need to keep up your strength."

The chains clanged as he pulled the plate from her hands.

"Why did you work diligently to convince me you were Mexican?" she asked.

"Because in my heart, I am."

"That first night, after we . . . made love . . . were you afraid that I'd figure out who you were if I touched your face?"

"I thought you might realize what I was not."

"What was that?"

"I thought I was not wanted. I'd always assumed I had been abandoned. I didn't want you to know of my shame."

Her heart constricted at the ravaged echo in his voice. "Do you understand now that you weren't abandoned? I lost you—"

"No. You must stop blaming yourself for what happened before. For what happened today, you can blame yourself."

His words stung just as she was certain he'd intended for them to. "Do you remember anything about your childhood?" she asked softly.

"I remember that I could always beat Alejandro in a scuffle."

She'd assumed so much about his complexion that she hadn't insisted that he reveal every shade of color, every hue. "What color are your eyes?"

"Blue. Like a sky at noon when the sun has washed away most of the color."

Tears welled in her eyes. "Just like Kit's. Just like Spence's. Just like Damon's. They were always so clear. You're Damon," she rasped.

"No. Damon Rodriguez died the night Shelby attacked his family."

The breath backed up painfully in her lungs. "Damon? Damon Rodriguez? They called you Damon?"

"It was my name, all I remembered."

"When I told you that the child I lost was named 'Damon,' why didn't you tell me who you were then?"

"Because I didn't know for certain. It could have just been coincidence."

"But we could have discussed it and determined the truth."

"What then, Angela? Who I was before does not change the destiny of the man I have become. Instead, people will have to grieve the death of their son all over again. Can you imagine a crueler twist of fate?"

No, she couldn't, but she'd learned long ago that Fate didn't have a penchant for dealing a winning hand. "If you don't tell them why you killed Floyd Shelby, I will. I lost you once, I'm not willing to lose you again."

"I have told you I took a vow to take that night to my grave. Betray me once more, and you'll lose me . . . forever."

Standing within the night shadows at the edge of the camp, Kit watched his prisoner. *His prisoner*. His son.

And Lee must truly be his son. It was like looking at his reflection in a distant, smoky mirror. Dear God, but Kit would have recognized him anywhere. Fifteen years. And not a day had passed when he hadn't thought of the son that had been lost to him. Inexplicably, he'd never thought of the lad as growing any older.

He shifted his gaze slightly as Harry came to stand beside him. His trustworthy friend had apparently determined that Kit had wallowed in his misery alone long enough.

"How will I tell Ashton?" Kit rasped. He squeezed his eyes shut, and a hot tear leaked onto his cheek. "Dear God, Harry, when we found his bloodied clothes, I was certain he was dead. How do I tell her now that I was wrong?"

"His clothes were tattered and bloody. I drew the same conclusion. You had to put an end to your suffering and hers. It was time to put the hope to rest."

Wearily Kit shook his head. "The hope never went away. Still, I can't let her watch him hang. I can't let her know now, without any doubt, that our son is dead." He slumped against the tree and dragged his fingers through his hair. "I have spent twenty years enforcing the laws of this state, and my son grew up to represent everything I loathed."

He pressed his clenched fist against his chest. "It bloody well hurts, Harry. The years with him that were lost to us, the man he is, the man I had dreamed of him becoming the first time I held him within my arms."

Harry released a great gust of air. "God help me as well, my daughter has fallen in love with the rapscallion."

Kit grimaced. "She's always loved Damon—"

"She didn't know he was Damon when she fell in love with him. His accent led her to believe he was Mexican. She had only a vague notion of what he looked like and had no hint whatsoever that he might be Damon."

"Regardless, her feelings don't change what he did."

"You've killed."

Kit's stomach lurched. "Don't travel that path, Harry," he warned.

"I've killed. By God, my wife has killed. Who is to say his actions were not as justified as ours?"

"A judge. He has been tried and convicted."

"I studied him the entire time Angela was with him. I've spent too many years learning to gauge the merits of men, and at the risk of sounding arrogant, I'm damn good at it. Take a closer look at him, Kit. He might be worth saving."

* * *

With tears streaming down her lovely face, Angela had returned to her family. Deep inside, Lee wept as well for what they might have shared. He had trusted her, and she had tricked him into being caught by men with the power to destroy him—had she not destroyed him first.

Angela had spoken time and again of trust. Her treachery hurt all the more because he had confided in her, risked his family, and exposed his heart. He had proposed marriage. The moment should have reflected exultation, not humiliation.

He could not shake off his shame. The Rangers had been watching when he'd dropped to his knees before her. He had revealed his unbridled love, and these strangers had witnessed the full extent of his betrayal.

She might succeed in convincing herself that she had done it out of concern for his family and hers, but he would never forgive her for not trusting him to protect those he loved.

He watched as Angela's mother offered comfort by brushing her daughter's hair. He clenched his hands with the memory of those magnificent strands fanned out over his chest.

He tore his gaze away from the women and studied the stars. He could connect the bits of light to create images, but he could not piece together all the fragments of his life.

He refused to accept Angela's claim that he was Damon Montgomery. Although he'd considered the possibility when she'd first mentioned the child's name, he'd quickly dismissed the coincidence. A man with Montgomery's reputation would have found his son—unless he'd been glad to be rid of him. Lee had found that thought too painful to contemplate.

A movement caught his attention, and he watched Montgomery stride confidently across the camp he commanded with little more than a look or a stance. Lee's heart thundered as the older man neared. Until today, he hadn't realized that in the past few years, he'd seen Montgomery every time he looked into the mirror—only the lines in the Ranger's face ran more deeply.

Montgomery crouched before him, scrutinizing him as though he wanted to pierce his soul. "Let's take a walk," he said quietly.

Reaching out, he inserted a key into the shackles' lock. Lee's mouth went dry as he studied the large hands and long, slender fingers that worked to free him. Had they ever been applied to his backside? Held him? Taken his child's hand while the man they belonged to walked beside him explaining the mysteries of the world? They were the hands that should have guided him through life.

"It's true what they say, you do not wear a gun," Lee said inanely for no other reason than that the silence stretching between them was unnerving.

"I find pistols cumbersome, but I have a nasty fist that I'm not afraid to use."

"So do I."

In the dancing light of the fire, Lee thought he saw pain slash across Montgomery's face. The iron bracelets fell away from his wrists and clanked to the ground. Montgomery stood, and Lee slowly did the same, his muscles stiff from sitting still for so long. One of the men standing nearby with a rifle stepped toward them.

"No need to follow, Sean," Montgomery said. "We'll be quite all right."

The two men walked away from the camp, Lee acutely aware of the unexpected sense of familiarity that now overpowered him. He'd always thought that his body bore the scars of truth: he'd been unwanted, neglected, unloved ... until a Mexican family had taken him in and embraced him as one of their own. Now, he no longer knew what to make of his conclusions.

Montgomery came to an abrupt halt and darted a glance at the stars, the tree, and the ground before settling an unwavering gaze on Lee. "Have you any notion as to the reason that you call yourself Lee Raven?"

Lee thought back to the days after Shelby's attack. He'd dug a shallow grave beside his parents' and put up a marker bearing his real name. As long as Shelby thought he was dead, the man would search for a phantom. Then Lee had combed the recesses of his mind for a name to adopt, a name that would mean nothing to Shelby ... but for reasons he'd never been able to comprehend, it meant something to him. "I wanted an alias that couldn't be connected to my family."

"You failed miserably in that regard, then ... or perhaps not. I never spotted the similarity,"

Montgomery murmured as though lost in thought. He smiled sadly. "Ravenleigh is the name of my family's estate in England. From the moment my first son was born, he was taught that he was the heir presumptive and that someday he would become the Earl of Ravenleigh."

Lee's stomach clenched. He took two faltering steps back until he slammed against a tree and could use it to support his quaking legs. He drew in a deep, shuddering breath. "Raven Lee." *Lee Raven*. The words had become entangled in his memory. The name swirling like a gray mist through his memories suddenly settled into place, and he was a boy listening to his father speak with pride about his family home. Ravenleigh. His heritage. All along, the name he'd chosen had reflected his past more than he'd realized.

"Before you were Lee Raven, did you go by another name?"

Slowly Lee nodded. "Damon Rodriguez."

"Damon," he repeated softly. "Your mother selected the name."

Your mother. They were the first words Montgomery had spoken that confirmed what Lee had been unwilling to accept, had not dared to admit. Although Angela had told him, he'd refused to believe, but now the truth took root. The man standing before him *was* his father. No, no, Juan Rodriguez had been his father. He had taught Lee to tend cattle, to show respect toward women, and to love his Mexican heritage.

"Do you remember her?" Montgomery asked,

and within his voice, Lee heard the deep, abiding love he held for his wife.

"No."

"Her hair is the same shade as yours. Much longer, of course. Although, you could do with a haircut."

"Sí." Combing his fingers through his hair, he stilled. He'd seen Montgomery make the same gesture numerous times as they'd set up camp.

"You speak Spanish."

"Without thinking. It is the way I was raised."

Montgomery flinched. Lee didn't know if he'd ever think of him as his father, but perhaps that was for the best. He didn't want Montgomery to see him as his son. He could not imagine the disappointment the man was experiencing to discover his son was an outlaw. And worse, to have thought he was dead once, and to be forced to endure his death again.

"Do you know how you came to be with the Rodriguez family?"

Lee swallowed hard. He found it more difficult to trust after Angela's recent betrayal, but he saw no harm in revealing this information. "Juan Rodriguez found me. I was hurt, sick, and hungry."

"Do you remember anything before that?"

Like wispy gray smoke, a memory eased past his defenses, but vulnerability, sorrow, and shame traveled with it. He remembered pain, paralyzing fear . . . but before that . . . nothing. "No. I'm sorry."

"No need to apologize. You were very young—"

"How old am I?" Lee blurted. They'd always celebrated his birthday on the day that they'd found him, but they'd never added years. They'd assumed Alejandro was older because he was taller, but with a full belly every night, Lee had quickly outsized him.

"Twenty."

He nodded. He was younger than Alejandro. He should have figured it out. Angela had told him that she was four years older than the boy she'd lost—and he had become exactly what he'd feared he was when she'd told him the boy's name—he was that child. "Angela told me what happened, but I don't remember it."

"That's probably for the best. I want you to know that I never stopped looking," Montgomery said somberly.

Lee's gut tightened and he looked away. He had no desire to see the plea for understanding in the man's eyes, the need for Lee to acknowledge that Montgomery was his father.

"I scoured every Indian village and outlaw hideaway. I gained a reputation for being obsessed with justice when my true goal was to locate my son. Damon—"

Lee snapped his gaze to Montgomery's. "No, I must remain Lee Raven. That is the man who must go to the gallows. I will not bring shame to the family who raised me . . . or any other family."

"Your mother—"

"Should never know. It would be cruel to tell her you found a man who resembled your son—"

"Resembled my son? Is that what you bloody well think?" He took a step closer, and Lee saw the faint moonlight glistening within the tears in his father's eyes. "You are my son, by God. I don't give a bloody damn what you call yourself. You are my son!"

Lee bolted away from the tree and began to pace. "I have read your story. I know the kind of man you are. You are a man of honor." He came to an abrupt halt, faced Montgomery, and hit his own chest. "I have killed."

"You think I haven't?"

"You kill within the confines of the law."

"Sometimes situations cannot be defined by law," Montgomery said quietly. "This morning, you could have shot at us."

"Angela might have gotten hurt."

"You could run now."

"I thought you said you had a mean fist?"

Montgomery smiled, actually smiled. "I do, but I have old legs. You'd outdistance me in no time, assuming you're as quick on your feet as Spence. He's your brother, you know."

"I can see the resemblance between the two of you."

"You also have a sister named Mercy who's fifteen. As serene as her mother."

A sister—a sister it would be best if he never met.

Crossing his arms over his chest, Montgomery

leaned against the tree. "So what am I to do with you?"

"Forget you found me."

"Not bloody likely. Why did you kill Floyd Shelby?"

Lee lowered his head and studied the shadowed ground between his feet. "He did not deserve to breathe the same air as my family." He lifted his gaze.

"Care to be a bit more specific?"

He thought of Juanita's pain, her tears, and the vow he'd given her. She'd suffered too much already, and he knew revealing the truth would do little to vindicate his actions. He wasn't willing to risk hurting her further, and he didn't know if Montgomery would respect his desire to protect Juanita. "No. I cannot explain my reasons for killing him, but other things that happened, what Vernon Shelby did, I can explain. Angela said if I told you that you might help my brothers get their land back."

Montgomery shoved himself away from the tree. "Let's walk a bit more. I can think better when I'm walking."

Once again, Lee fell into step beside him.

"I thought of you every day, but never thought of you growing up," Montgomery said. "I used to have to take smaller steps so you could match my stride."

And for a fleeting instant, Lee captured the memory of walking in the tall shadow of a man . . . and holding his hand.

* * *

Lee sat within the circle of the fire, continually reminding himself that he was a prisoner, even though he was no longer shackled. Sooner or later, the manacles would go back on.

"I heard your family stole cattle," Spence said.

"Lies. They were good people."

"Did vigilantes kill them?" Spence asked.

"Shelby and his men—with the sheriff's blessing. Men who came here after the War Between the States and had no respect for the Mexicans who had worked the land before them. They stole what belonged to us, what had been earned with sweat and blood."

Montgomery raised a brow, but Lee wouldn't take back his words. After so many years, he'd begun to think of himself as more Mexican than white, if he thought of the shade of his skin at all. He couldn't have loved the Rodriguez family more if he had been born to them.

"Vigilantes killing rustlers has long been an accepted practice where cattle empires thrive. Barely two years ago in Wyoming, they hanged Cattle Kate and her lover for stealing cattle," Spence said.

Lee had a strong urge to plow his fist into Spence's face. "Are you saying that Shelby's actions were justified?"

"I am simply insinuating that he did not set a precedent with his actions. Nor is he the last do to do what he did."

"Did the family have a deed to the land?" Montgomery asked.

Lee wasn't certain, but surely they possessed some proof of ownership. "Sam Houston deeded the land to them. I would think there would be a record of that somewhere. You will see that the land is returned to them?"

Montgomery gave a long, slow nod. "If indeed we can prove the land is theirs and was wrongfully taken from them. What is your brothers' involvement in Floyd Shelby's death?"

"None at all."

"The bank robberies?"

"I alone am responsible for my crimes. My brothers are not to be held accountable for what I did."

"You leave a hell of a lot of tracks for a man who rides alone," Montgomery said.

"They may ride with me on occasion, but they had no part in the crimes I committed." A small lie, but under the circumstances, he thought it entirely justified.

"They won't be punished," Montgomery said, and Lee heard the reputation for honesty and integrity his father had acquired reverberating in his voice.

His father. For a brief moment, with the relief that his family would be safe, he almost considered allowing his original family back into his heart. But it would be hard enough to walk to the gallows with what he had to give up. Impossible if he were forced to relinquish more.

He thought it a shame that Fate had chosen not to be kind. He wished Kit Montgomery had never learned the truth about him, had been left to believe that his son died all those years ago.

In truth, now he had died twice. The third time would no doubt be, as they said, a charm.

"It's numbing, isn't it?" Gray asked quietly, "when the dead return to life?"

Kit realized that Gray would be the one to know. After all, his wife's first husband had managed the feat.

He and Gray were the only ones remaining by the fire. Except for the men standing guard, everyone else had retired to their bedrolls. Kit's sons lay on opposite sides of the camp. Neither seemed to be sleeping.

"Numb. An apt description. I'd always expected to feel overjoyed, ecstatic, but all I can think is that I'm going to have to watch him hang."

"I supposed you could allow him to escape."

"I've seriously considered it." He stared at the dancing flames. "But all that would gain me is waiting in dread for news that he truly was dead. He still has a crime to answer for. Bounty hunters who would not be as tolerant as us in their treatment of him would continue to search for him. I need to find a few answers, answers he's not willing to provide."

"Why do you suppose that is?"

Kit shook his head. "I'm not sure. Although I've considered that he might be trying to protect someone. Obviously not himself."

"So what's your plan?"

Kit heaved a sigh. "Take him to Emilia." The

small town in south Texas was nestled just south of the Nueces River. "That's the town nearest Shelby's ranch. I'll make some inquiries. But regardless of his reasons, as justified as they might be for killing the man, I can't overlook that he shot him from behind."

"Are you going to tell Ashton?"

"No. This burden I must carry on my heart alone. She is too frail to survive losing Damon again. I'm going to send Spence home, but he's only to tell her that Angela is safe. As for you, my friend, it's time for you to return to Fortune, let Angela's sisters know she is well, and take care of your own family."

"If there's anything at all that you need—"

"I need another miracle."

Chapter 19

"**I** think I spotted a seamstress shop on the other side of the mercantile when we rode in yesterday evening," Angela's mother said, as they walked along the boardwalk in Emilia, their arms looped together.

Emilia. Angela liked the name of the place, but dreaded what the town represented for Lee. Lee. She still couldn't think of him as Damon. To her he was still the outlaw Lee Raven.

From what she'd been able to learn, Kit had taken him to the jail. At first she'd hoped he'd let Lee escape. Instead, he'd explained that he needed to make inquiries into the events that had happened the night Shelby attacked his family.

But would he find enough information to exonerate Lee? And if he didn't, how long could she wait before she destroyed the fragile bond of

Lee's love for her by telling Kit all that she knew? If she told him, would he still want proof from others? Would Juanita be willing to recount the events of that horrible night in order to save her brother?

There were so many avenues for his salvation, none of which he seemed willing to seriously consider—all because of a vow two children had made.

Angela and her parents had taken two rooms at the small hotel. They'd wanted her to return to Fortune, but she couldn't until she knew Lee's fate. Kit had acquired a room as well. He'd told all but two of his men to return to their normal duties, none of which included staying in Emilia.

She'd tried to talk with Lee a few times as they'd journeyed here, but he'd been reticent, aloof, unwilling to understand her actions, unable to forgive her. He'd repeatedly demanded that she not say anything about Juanita. With him turning from her and her heart breaking, how in the world could she enjoy this outing with her mother?

"Perhaps we'll stop at the millinery and order you a new hat as well. You always enjoyed hats," her mother said.

"Mama, I'm really not interested in shopping."

"Angela, you can't continue to wear that outfit. It's filthy."

"We can wash it."

"I'd prefer to replace it. Besides, now that we're in a town, I can't keep wearing britches."

She welcomed the smile of remembrance. "Why not? You prefer them to a dress."

"Yes, well, there are times when I at least like to pretend I'm a lady."

She squeezed her mother's arm. "You are a lady."

Her mother scoffed, before saying, "Here we are. *The Seamstress*. How original."

Angela heard a tiny bell jingle in welcome as her mother opened the door. Taking a deep breath for fortification, Angela followed her mother inside, hoping they'd have some ready-mades.

"Howdy, howdy," a woman called out. "I'm Bonnie. No offense, but you look like you were rode hard and put away wet."

Her mother laughed lightly. "I hope we're not that bad off, but we do need some new clothes as quickly as we can get them."

"Then I'm the one to help you. I got a few ready-mades that I can add a personal touch to if you like, or we can start from scratch."

Angela ran her hand along the counter. The last thing she wanted was to spend any more time in here than necessary.

"Hopefully, we can find one of something you already have made for each of us, and then we'll start from scratch on the others," her mother said.

Angela suppressed a groan. Her father had told her once that getting her mother to shop for clothes was a chore. Over the years, she'd obviously decided it was a chore she enjoyed.

"The others?" Bonnie repeated.

"We're not sure how long we'll be in town," her mother explained.

"Are you here for the hanging?" Bonnie asked.

Angela gripped the edge of the counter as dizziness assailed her. Were they already anticipating this horrifying event?

Her mother slipped her arm around Angela's waist and drew her close, offering support. "No, we're not here for a hanging."

"But you heard, didn't you? Heard that they brought Lee Raven in last night?"

"Yes, we're aware of that," Angela said sharply. "But we're not here to discuss that fact. We're here to get some clothing."

"Oh, of course. With your coloring and all, I bet you both want something in green."

Angela didn't care. She really didn't. Just throw an outfit at her, and she'd take it.

"Green would be fine," her mother said.

"Well, let me see what I got here." Bonnie's voice floated up as though she'd ducked behind the counter. "Funniest thing about that Lee Raven. Turns out that he's Damon Rodriguez. Can't say as I'm really surprised."

Every nerve in Angela's body snapped to attention. "Why do you say that?"

"Well," Bonnie's voice grew louder as she set something on the counter with a thump. "Vernon killing his family and all. I mean, I was surprised when I heard Damon wasn't dead. We thought he'd died that night, along with the rest of 'em. But once I heard he hadn't, then I wasn't surprised that he'd been taking Vernon's money. Still, it shocked me that he'd killed Floyd . . . not that I don't think he needed killing—"

"Why do you think he needed killing?" Angela asked, acutely aware that she sounded like a bloody echo, and not giving a damn that she did.

She heard a hand running over cloth. "He had a mean streak in him a mile wide. I didn't like the way he looked at women, either, even ones as old as me, like he could see clear down to your drawers."

"Did you know Damon well?" Angela asked, desperate to find answers, to know him as he had been.

"Oh, yeah. Knew the whole Rodriguez family. Mrs. Rodriguez came to me for all her clothing. Nicest woman you'd ever meet. Real genteel, like Spanish nobility, or something. Only they didn't lord it over you. Made you feel good just to be around them."

"What was Damon like?"

"Just like his brothers, 'cept for not lookin' like 'em, of course. Polite as you please. Their mother kept a tight rein on them, but never took a switch to 'em. Didn't have to. Those boys adored her. All she had to do was give 'em a look that said 'You've disappointed me' and they'd straighten right up. Never heard a bad word come out of their mouths. Always tipping their hats to the ladies. They'd come to town on Saturday, dressed in their finery. Short black jackets and britches decorated with silver thread. Their best sombreros. I think that's what got Vernon's goat."

"What do you mean?" Angela asked.

"Well, he didn't think it was right for them to be raising Damon in the ways of Mexico, on account of he wasn't truly Mexican. Never could see any harm in it myself. Like I said, every one of them boys was a gentleman. 'Sides, Vernon wasn't living 'round here when they took the boy in."

"Were you?"

"Sure was. Nobody thought he was going to live. Everybody 'round here said she ought to let the boy die. Obviously somebody didn't want him for a reason. But Mrs. Rodriguez told 'em she had to listen to her heart. She was determined that boy would live. Had a way with herbs and prayer. Burned so many candles in the church that even at night it looked like day around there."

"And he survived," Angela said softly.

"Yep, and when he wasn't so scraggly anymore"—she slapped the counter—"Lord have mercy, was that boy handsome! And a pleasure to be around. Always took people aback the first time they heard him talk, though, on account of his Mexican accent, but he was a charmer. Just like his brothers. Course, then Ramon took an interest in Christine, and that didn't sit too well with Vernon."

"You knew about Ramon and Christine?" Angela asked, confused. She'd thought they'd kept their love a secret.

"I got eyes, ain't I? They never did nothing in public to let on that they had feelings for one another, but Lord, the way that young man looked at her—like she hung every single star in the sky. A woman could do no better than to have Ramon Rodriguez glance her way, I can tell you that. Course, Vernon never saw it like that. Couldn't see beyond the fact that they were of Mexican descent. Kept saying they didn't belong here. Surprised the livin' daylights outta me when we learned the family was stealing cattle. Made no sense."

"Because they were such good people," Angela offered.

" 'Cause they were richer than Midas."

Stunned, Angela leaned forward. Lee had failed to mention that. "They were wealthy?"

"Richest people in these here parts. But like I said, you wouldn't know it by the way they acted. It was the little things. Fine clothes, good horses, huge *hacienda*. Little over half of it burned that night. I expected Vernon to tear the rest down, but he never did. Reckon he figures it serves as a reminder of what can happen when you go against the law."

"Or what happens when someone takes the law into his own hands," Angela said quietly.

Within the confines of the small cell, Lee sat on a bunk, his back against the brick wall. Iron bars separated the narrow room into four compartments. The clanging of the door after he'd walked into the cell had reverberated between the walls, through his tightened chest. He was that much closer to paying for his crime.

A Texas Ranger, Sean Cartwright, sat in a chair outside Lee's cell. His back was also against the wall, his hardened gaze focused on the door that led into the sheriff's main office, a rifle resting across his lap. When the sheriff had brought in breakfast, Lee had seen the speed with which Cartwright could maneuver the rifle and aim it at the door. He thought the man was almost as skilled with weapons as he was.

"It makes no sense to me that while we traveled here, Montgomery did not bother to shackle me, but when I am behind bars, he sets you up to shoot me if I try to escape."

Cartwright gazed at Lee. "I ain't here to stop you from escaping, boy. I'm here to stop 'em from lynching you."

Lee sat up a little straighter. "Why put me here at all?"

" 'Cuz a wise man knows some rules you break, and some you're better off just bending. Captain's a smart man. He knows which is which. 'Sides, it's harder for those who might want to see you come to a bad end to get you out of here than it would be to get you out of the hotel. You ain't exactly popular in this state."

"You've been with Montgomery a long time?"

"Yep."

"Is he as skilled with a rifle as they say?"

"Better."

"When they hang me, if my neck does not snap, do you think he would . . . he would shoot me."

"Truth be told, I expect I'll see gunplay at a Bible meeting before I see you hang."

"But I'm sentenced—"

"This state owes your pa a debt. The governor knows it."

"You think he would grant a pardon?"

"If the captain asked for it."

Lee sank back against the wall. Would he ask for it? If he told him what had happened that fateful night, would he believe Lee, or would Juanita have to face the past as well? Would they understand his shooting a man from behind? Even he had regretted that cowardly act.

Cartwright chuckled low and shifted in his chair. "Did you see the look on that sheriff's face when we strolled in last night? When he caught sight of you, his jaw came unhinged."

"I thought Sheriff Evans looked afraid."

"Yes. Like a man who knew Judgment Day had walked through the door."

Weary from too many miles riding in the saddle, Kit walked into the hotel at Emilia. He'd been scouring the countryside for three days, asking questions, and searching for answers. Unfortunately he'd uncovered nothing of significance.

He noticed a man—with his head bent and his wide-brimmed hat hiding his features—sitting in a chair. Kit thought it odd that he was in the lobby at midnight. He considered investigating, but his desire for sleep was stronger than his interest in the stranger's presence. He went straight to the front desk. "My key."

The clerk retrieved it from a small cubbyhole, handed it to Kit, and tilted his head toward the front. "That man's been waiting two days to see you, Captain Montgomery."

"Who is he?"

"He wouldn't say. He just sits there like a turtle with his head hidden."

"Thank you."

With his curiosity aroused, Kit walked over to the fellow. "Excuse me. I hear you've been waiting for me to return."

The man snapped his head back, and his dark walnut-colored eyes grew round. "You are Kit Montgomery?"

"That's right."

Slowly he came to his feet. "You are the one who arrested Lee Raven?"

"Yes."

The man straightened his stance and met Kit's gaze squarely. "You made a grave mistake."

Kit arched a brow. "Indeed."

"*Sí. I* am Lee Raven."

Boredom was settling in with a vengeance. It made a man tired, made his mind wander. Lee moved to other end of his cot. Leaning his back against the bars of the adjoining cell was slightly less comfortable than leaning against the wall.

The faint moonlight poured through the narrow window above his head. He could almost see the stars. He wondered how Angela wished on a star—was it enough to be told one twinkled in the sky? Or did a person actually have to see it to wish upon it?

As hard as he tried, he couldn't stop thinking

about her. He was desperate to know if she remained in town or had returned to Fortune, but he refused to ask Cartwright. He didn't want anyone to know he still cared for Angela.

Memories of their time together made his chest tighten until it ached. Before Angela had stumbled into his life, he'd forgotten how wonderful it felt to smile and laugh. He'd stopped appreciating the beauty of the sunrise. He'd ceased to dream of a life that held the promise of love.

He'd become like an empty vessel filled with holes, unable to contain anything of substance. He'd found it easier to face the prospect of hanging when he had little to leave behind.

Now the nights were more lonely without her to warm his body and soothe his soul. He was grateful no one had brought her here. He didn't want her to hear how every sound echoed with emptiness or to touch the cool metal bars and envision his cage.

He didn't want her to remember him as a trapped animal. Terrified, alone, and completely at the mercy of others.

That aspect of this intolerable situation gnawed at him. He no longer had control of his life.

The far door opened. He looked around and shot off the cot. "Alejandro, what are you doing here?"

"I do not know that name," Alejandro said, as he averted his gaze and stepped into the cell that Montgomery had unlocked.

"What nonsense is this?" Lee asked.

Alejandro held his head high and thrust out his chest. "I am Lee Raven."

Lee settled for slamming his palm against his brother's cell since he couldn't reach his head. "Are you *loco?*"

Montgomery's mouth twitched. "Sean, it seems we have two Lee Ravens. You're responsible for both."

"Yes, sir, Captain."

"*Un momento!*" Alejandro cried, pointing at Lee. "You can let this one go."

"I don't think so."

Lee waited until Montgomery had quit the room before turning on his brother. "I cannot believe you did this."

"What did you expect me to do? I told you the woman would get you hanged."

Shaking his head, Lee dropped onto the cot. Alejandro sat as well and pressed his shoulder against the bars. "Perhaps if we keep saying I am Lee Raven, eventually they will believe us."

Lee glared at his brother. "I do not want them to believe you. Did you not take a good look at the man who brought you in here?"

"*Sí.* I almost swallowed my tongue when I saw him. He looks like you."

"No, Alejandro. I look like him. He is my"—he had yet to say the word out loud—"my father."

"Kit Montgomery is your father?" Alejandro asked, clearly stunned.

"*Sí,*" Lee answered.

"*The* Kit Montgomery? The man you admired from a distance?" Alejandro asked.

"*Sí*. The man whose adventures I longed to read about. Ironic, heh?" Lee shifted on the cot. "Not only that, but his family has an estate in England. Ravenleigh."

Alejandro's eyes widened. "That is your name all mixed up."

"*Sí*."

Alejandro slumped forward. "Then he will not believe me."

"Why are you not still in Mexico?"

Alejandro shrugged. "When night came and you were not home, I figured something was wrong. So I went searching for you."

"What about the others?"

"I told them to stay with Juanita."

The far door opened again. Montgomery walked in looking not only extremely tired, but irritated. At his side, Roberto looked as guilty as sin.

"It seems we have another one," Montgomery said, as he escorted Roberto into a cell. He slammed the door shut and scrutinized Lee. "How many more can I expect?"

Lee darted his glance between his brothers. "Jorge?"

"Oh, no," Roberto said. "Jorge said he had another plan."

"What plan?" Lee and Montgomery asked at the same time.

"He would only say that it was magnificent, but knowing Jorge, I figured whatever it was, it would not work."

"We can only hope," Montgomery said. "Sean, stay alert."

"Yes, sir."

Montgomery turned away.

"Montgomery?"

He stopped and glanced over his shoulder. Lee felt the heat suffuse his face, but he couldn't bring himself to call the man "Father." "Jorge is reckless, but harmless."

"Splendid. Let's hope he stays that way." Montgomery left the room.

Roberto pressed his face against the bars. "Lee, Montgomery looks like you."

"He's Lee's father," Alejandro told him.

Roberto's mouth dropped open, and he blinked before asking, "What is he like?"

"Fair. Honorable. He has promised me he will look into your claim that you own the land near Emilia. Alejandro, do you know if you had a deed?"

"If we ever had one, it would have burned in the fire."

"I was afraid that would be what happened, but there should be a record somewhere. Montgomery will find it."

"And then what?" Roberto asked.

"He will see that the land is given back to you."

"I do not understand, Lee," Alejandro began. "How did you come to get lost all those years ago?"

"I was playing with Angela."

"Angela?"

"Life is funny, is it not?"

"That first morning when you said her hair reminded you of something."

"It was a memory that taunted me but would not take hold. I think I must have been thinking of her."

"So finish the story," Roberto urged him.

"There is not much more to tell. Renegades stole me. Perhaps I got sick or was too much trouble. Whatever the reason, they decided not to keep me."

"Their loss was our gain," Alejandro said.

Standing on the other side of the door, listening intently, Kit thought his son did not sound like a man who would shoot another in the back without a good reason.

Bone weary, he strolled out of the sheriff's office into the night. Several minutes later he walked into the hotel and up the stairs to the second floor. He rapped softly on the door to Angela's room. "It's Kit."

She opened the door, her eyes swollen, but he doubted that it was from sleep. "I'm sorry to disturb you," he began.

"I wasn't sleeping. Did you want to come in?"

"No. I just wanted to let you know that I haven't been able to learn anything significant."

She slumped against the doorjamb, clearly disappointed.

"It gets worse. I have two of Damon's brothers in jail. Alejandro and Roberto."

"But you promised him—"

"I put them there for their own good. They were both claiming to be Lee Raven."

She smiled softly. "They love him, Kit. From the beginning I was confounded because I couldn't understand why they had so much admiration for a murdering thief."

"Do you know why Damon killed Floyd Shelby?"

Slowly she nodded. "I'll tell you what I've learned. I won't risk losing Damon again."

Hearing a gasp, Kit turned and froze at the sight of his wife standing in the hallway, with tears welling in her eyes and her slender hand pressed against her throat. "Ashton, what in God's name are you doing here?"

Chapter 20

Stretched out on the cot, one foot dangling on the floor, Lee jerked out of his light sleep at the sound of keys.

"Come on," Cartwright said, holding his rifle in the crook of his elbow as he swung the door open.

"Where are we going?" Lee asked.

"The hotel."

"What for?"

"Captain's orders."

"Why are you taking him?" Alejandro asked.

"Will you fellas relax?" Cartwright asked. "We just need to get this done before folks are moving through town."

"Get what done?" Roberto asked.

Sighing, Cartwright took Lee's arm. "Let's go."

Lee strode into the sheriff's office. "Where's Evans?"

"Comes in late, leaves early."

Lee stepped outside. Fog had rolled in and dawn lay beyond it. Cartwright tightened his grip and led Lee across the street, along the boardwalk, to the hotel. They went in through a back door and walked down a dark corridor. Cartwright opened a door. "In here."

Hesitantly, Lee entered the room. Cartwright followed him in, closed the door, brushed past him, and headed for the window.

"Just forget I'm here," he said as he eased the curtain aside and gazed out the window.

"Expecting trouble?" Lee asked.

"I always expect trouble." He glanced over his shoulder and nodded toward the tub of steaming water. "Get to it."

"I'm to bathe?"

Cartwright turned his attention back to the window. "Yep. Captain's orders."

Eagerly, Lee stripped out of his clothes, dropped them on the floor, and got into the tub. The heat of the water immediately seeped into his bones. Moaning low, he sank until the water lapped at his throat. He looked toward the bed. It was so clean that he wouldn't mind taking a *siesta* afterward, just a short one.

Three rapid knocks sounded at the door.

"It's all right, you can come in," Cartwright called out.

The hinges moaned. Lee's gut clenched as Angela glided into the room and closed the door. Although she was blind, even though she had caressed every inch of him—or perhaps it was *be-*

cause she had—he slid farther down and hoped Cartwright wouldn't notice his face burning bright red.

Her hair was piled on her head much as it had been the first night he saw her. She wore a shimmering dress of green that matched her eyes. She looked incredibly lovely, and for a while, she had been his.

Angela set a box on the bed. "Kit thought you might like to shave." She laid out towels and clean clothes. Holding a comb and scissors, she turned toward him.

Based on the accuracy with which she knelt beside the tub, he knew she'd been in this room before. "You arranged all this?"

"No, I just told them how to arrange things for my convenience. Would you like me to cut your hair?"

He looked past her to Cartwright. The man was staring intently out the window. Lee shrugged. "If you want."

She scooted behind him and repeatedly combed her fingers through his hair. Closing his eyes in sweet surrender, he hated to admit how soothing it felt, how much he had missed her touch.

"You're not going to question my ability to cut your hair?" she asked.

"I've learned, Angela Bainbridge, that you can do anything you set your mind to."

"It's gotten long," she said.

The comb's teeth scraped his scalp, over and over. Then he heard the snip of scissors.

"I always pictured it as dark," she mused. "Why didn't you tell me it was blond?"

"Because my family was Mexican. I always regretted that I did not favor them. I could not see the harm in not revealing everything."

She moved his hair aside and placed a kiss in the curve of his neck. "I love you, Lee."

"Are you trying to tempt me into breaking a vow? Is that what all this"—he swung his arm out in a wide arc, sending droplets spraying—"is about?"

"No, this royal treatment has nothing to do with us."

She began to work diligently, snipping away his locks. Leaning his head back, he wondered vaguely what it did have anything to do with, but decided that it didn't matter. Besides, he liked the way that her fingers fluttered over his hair.

"How short do you want it?" she asked.

"Doesn't matter." As long as she kept brushing his hair back, she could do it forever.

"How's this?" she asked, nudging his shoulder.

Lee opened his eyes with a start. Had he fallen asleep? He took the mirror she offered and studied his reflection. He grazed his knuckles along his earlobes. His hair fell to that point evenly on each side. The back skimmed the nape of his neck. "It looks good."

She smiled softly, and he wished he had more compliments to give her. "I like that dress."

Her cheeks blushed a becoming pink, obliterating her freckles. "Do you? My father bought me a few outfits to wear while we were in town."

"You should go home, Angela, to Fortune. There is nothing for you here."

"That's not true."

He looked back toward the window. Cartwright stood there like a statue. "Angela—"

"Dunk your head under the water, and I'll wash your hair."

The thought of her fingers circling his scalp was a temptation he could not resist. He slipped under the water, then came up, water dripping in his face. "You should not be here. You are an unmarried woman."

Taking the soap, she began lathering his hair. "In medieval England, the oldest daughter often washed gentlemen guests."

"This is not medieval England."

"No, I guess it isn't."

"You look tired."

Her fingers stilled. "I haven't been sleeping well."

She started rubbing his head again. He relaxed. "My hair is very dirty. We may have to wash it many times."

But she washed it only twice. When she was finished, she knelt beside the tub, took his hand, and began to scrape what looked like a very small board across his fingernails. "What are you doing?" he asked.

"Your nails are rough. I thought I would smooth them."

He leaned toward her, inhaling her flowering fragrance. "You do not like the way my hands feel?" he asked quietly, silkily.

Her face flushed, and she began to buff more quickly. "You know I like it."

"Where do you like my hands best?"

She stilled with her mouth slightly open, her flushed cheeks growing darker. "We're not alone in here, you know."

"He cannot hear me."

"Why are you doing this?"

Why indeed?

"To hurt me?" she asked. "Well, you're too late." She went to work.

"I am not the one who betrayed one of us."

"Aren't you? I'm supposed to accept and understand that you'd rather die for Juanita than live for me?"

"You do not understand."

"What I understand is that I lost you once. It's my fault that you're here."

"Angela, you were a child," he whispered harshly.

"You were my responsibility that afternoon. I was supposed to watch you. If I had stopped those men—"

"How many were there?"

She hesitated. "Five."

"You could have done nothing but what you did."

"I hid." Her disgust with her actions was evident in her voice.

"To have done anything else would have meant your death . . . or worse."

"But everything you've suffered is because I was too scared to do anything."

"You are not to blame," he ground out.

"Yes, I am, *Damon*. If you hang, I'll never forgive myself."

She flung his hand away from her. "Give me the other one."

"Do you plan to scrape it raw, as well?"

She sat up straighter. "Did I do that?"

Ignoring the stinging of his fingers in the water, he placed his other hand in hers. "No."

He studied her closely as she attended the task diligently. She looked more weary than he remembered her looking while they'd traveled to Mexico. Or perhaps he only paid more attention now. He was not choosing Juanita over her.

When she'd finished smoothing his nails, she held the mirror so he could shave. His gaze kept drifting to her and he nicked himself more than usual. After he scraped away the last of the lather, she skimmed her fingers along his cheek, her eyes wistful, and he wondered what she was thinking.

"I'll let you finish up now," she said as she rose to her feet.

"Angela?"

She stopped, her eyes honing in on him as though she could see him.

"I appreciate your help."

"You never call me '*querida*' anymore. That says everything, doesn't it?" Quietly she slipped out of the room.

Lee gazed at his reflection in the cheval glass. The black britches fit him snugly. The white shirt was soft against his skin, loose and billowy. Angela had done a fine job with his hair. Every time he thought of her, he felt as though he'd fallen into a vat of emptiness, with pain roaring around him. He'd loved her so deeply, so profoundly . . . and the truth was that he still did.

At the sound of footsteps, Lee shifted his attention to the doorway. Montgomery strode into the room as though he owned it and everyone in it.

Cartwright relaxed his stance. "He cleaned up real nice, Captain."

"So I see," Montgomery said.

"I'll be waiting in the hall iffen you need me."

"Thank you, Sean."

Montgomery waited until Cartwright had left the room before he approached Lee. "Your mother wishes to see you."

Lee felt as though someone had just thrust a rusty knife into his gut and twisted it. "My mother . . ." He sank onto the mattress. "It would be better if she didn't."

"I quite agree." Montgomery walked to the window and gazed out. "I had not planned to tell her that we'd found you . . . at least not until I was certain that you wouldn't hang."

Turning, he held Lee's gaze. "Your mother is frail. You were quite a handful. She always welcomed the way Angela would help her care for you when she came to visit. She feels as guilty as Angela does about your disappearance. I can't deny her the opportunity to see the man you've become."

He strode from the room. Lee stood and prepared himself for the hardest thing he'd ever done.

Kit took Ashton into his arms and pressed his lips against the top of her head. For over twenty years, he had loved her more than life itself. "I wish you would reconsider seeing him," Kit said softly.

She tilted her head back. "I want to see our son."

He touched his fingers to her cheek. "He is not the little boy you held and rocked to sleep."

"But once he was. And he's the one I gave birth to. I want to see him."

With a sigh of resignation, Kit stepped back and threaded his fingers through hers. "I've spent my life trying to grant your every wish. I don't suppose I can stop now. Just don't expect too much from him. I'm not quite certain he knows yet exactly who he is."

He led her into the room. At the doorway, she released his hand. "You wait here," she ordered softly.

Her health had never been good. Slender and pale, she appeared as fragile as a petal that would fall from a flower when touched. Therefore, he sometimes forgot exactly how strong she was.

Nodding, he leaned against the wall. As much as he wanted to protect her, he understood some things were best faced alone. He watched as she approached their son, standing by the window in a haze of sunlight.

Damon looked as though someone had just landed a solid punch to his gut.

When Ashton stepped closer and wrapped her arms around him, he did what Kit had never expected. He bent over slightly and enfolded his mother in his strong embrace. Kit could see the gamut of emotions playing across his face: recognition, disbelief, sorrow, joy.

Ashton leaned back and combed her fingers through her son's hair. "You look exactly as I imagined you would when you grew older. You look like your father."

"You look as I remember," Damon said in a strangled voice.

Ashton touched his cheek. "Your memory is faulty. My hair is more silver now and my face has many more wrinkles."

Damon smiled and the transformation almost knocked Kit off his feet. He became a mischievous lad who laughed often, ran before he learned to walk, and woke up before dawn because he feared missing out on some wondrous adventure. "I gave you rocks."

Ashton's smile radiated through the room. "I kept them in a jar on my dresser. I still have them." Tears welled in her eyes. "We thought you were dead."

Damon took her back into his arms, and Kit watched mother and son hold each other, no more reminiscing passing between them, only an occasional murmuring, comforting words spoken in Spanish that Kit didn't fathom. Little wonder Angela had thought Lee Raven was Mexican.

Without the gift of sight, she had possessed nothing to tell her otherwise, for when he spoke there was no evidence of the culture into which he'd been born, only the culture in which he'd been raised.

After a while, Ashton stepped from Damon's embrace and touched her fingers to his cheek. "I'll come back to visit."

Damon took her hand and brought her fingers to his lips. "It is best if you do not." His words were spoken with a tenderness that Kit never would have expected of him.

Ashton gave him a wavering smile. "Ask your father. I've never done what was best for me."

She walked gracefully from the room, her head held high. Kit followed her into the hallway. Turning, her face ravaged with grief and tears, she fell into his embrace. "I don't want him to hang," she whispered brokenly.

He stroked her back, feeling wholly inadequate. "I know."

She lifted her face. "Do something."

Words clogged his throat. He kissed her forehead and glanced at his second son, whose gaze darted between his parents and the nearby door that stood slightly ajar. "Take your mother to our room. See that she lies down."

"I'm sorry, Father," Spence said. "I tried to convince her not to come."

Spence had told him late last night that she'd wanted to come only to reassure herself that Angela was all right. He'd hoped to warn Kit that she was about, but their paths had never crossed.

"I know."

He waited until his son had escorted his mother from the dim hallway before walking back into the room where his older son waited. Damon had one shoulder pressed to the wall, his head bent.

"You call her 'sweetling,' " he said quietly as Kit approached.

"Yes."

Nodding, Damon lifted his head. "We lived in a house with stairs."

"Yes."

"I had a . . . a gray horse . . ."

"Merlin."

"I was a knight."

"Yes. Sir Ravenleigh. We used to go to Fortune each summer for a jousting tournament, a ritual we started the first year that Harry, Gray, and I came to Texas."

Damon held his gaze. "I cannot tell you why I killed Floyd Shelby. I can only tell you that I have thought about that moment a thousand times, and if I had it to do over . . . I would still kill him."

"By shooting him in the back?"

"Any way that I had to in order to get the job done."

Kit nodded. "Very well. I need to get you back to the jail."

Damon fell into step beside him as they left the room and walked out of the hotel. "I don't suppose you would consider releasing my brothers. They are harmless."

"I put them behind bars for their protection. I've made several inquiries and it seems Shelby succeeded at convincing everyone in town that your family was a pack of thieves."

"Rodriguez!"

Kit swung around at the angry voice bellowing from down the boardwalk. A short, stocky man strode up to them, his ruddy cheeks so red that Kit feared he'd have an apoplectic fit at any moment.

"Vernon Shelby," Damon said beneath his breath.

"Ought to be a law against a man diggin' his own grave and then not lyin' in it. I want my money, every penny you stole from me, you son of a bitch!"

Kit was amazed at how calm his son remained in the presence of this highly agitated man.

"I do not have it," Damon said in an even voice. "You stole our land. Land Houston granted our grandfather for his help in Texas's fight for independence."

"You don't honestly expect anyone to believe that, do you?" Shelby roared. "They're Mexicans! Who the hell do you think Sam Houston was fighting?"

"You would be wise not to open your mouth to speak, because when you do, you show your ignorance. Not all Mexicans fought with Santa Anna. Some wanted what a free Texas would provide. Three signed the Texas Declaration of Independence. Seven died defending the Alamo. They risked much for freedom, just as our grandfather did. What did you risk, Shelby, when you never touched Texas soil before 1880?"

"Boy, you've always had a smart mouth. You're gonna tell me where my money is, and you're gonna tell me who told you where to find it!" With arms flailing, the man lunged at Damon.

Kit grabbed him, threw him to the ground, and stood over him. He heard the cocking of a rifle and knew Sean was nearby. "I'm Captain Montgomery, Texas Rangers. You'll not strike this prisoner."

The man struggled to his feet. "I don't give a good goddamn who you are. I'm Vernon Shelby, and I have powerful friends in this state."

"So do I," Kit said in a silky voice. "Don't underestimate my influence."

Shelby jabbed his finger in the air at Damon. "Before you hang for murdering my son, you'll tell me what I want to know. By God, you will."

Kit watched him storm down the street. "I don't much like that man."

"Indeed," Damon said with an astonishingly accurate British accent. "Then you would have despised his son."

Chapter 21

The day had passed painstakingly slowly. Lee paced the small confines of his cell. Ten steps one way. About-face. Ten more steps. He must have pivoted a thousand times since Montgomery had returned him to this hell.

"You know, boy, that pacing is about to drive me plumb *loco*," Cartwright drawled.

"I'm not a boy," Lee snapped.

He plowed his hands through his hair. The shortened strands ruffling across his fingers reminded him of Angela. He did not want to think of her, the dark circles beneath her lovely eyes, her gaunt cheeks that made it look as though she was losing weight.

He started pacing again. "What is Montgomery up to?"

"Reckon he'll tell us when he's good and ready."

Lee came to an abrupt halt and glared at Roberto. "When was Jorge going to put his magnificent plan into action?"

Roberto shrugged and raised his hands.

Lee sank onto the cot. "I need to get out of here, to find out what Jorge is thinking."

The far door creaked on its hinges. Lee bolted to his feet and wrapped his hands around the bars. If it was Montgomery, maybe he could convince him to release him. Disappointment reeled through him as Spence walked into the room. Lee certainly had no desire to see this man. He dropped back onto the cot.

"I'll take a watch for a spell," Spence said as he sauntered toward the chair.

Cartwright stood and stretched. " 'Preciate it. How long you want?"

"Just come back when you're ready." Spence sat in the chair without making a sound as Cartwright closed the door in his wake.

Like a gentleman, Lee thought derisively.

"Well, brother, this is cozy, isn't it?" Spence asked.

Lee's stomach clenched. He still found it difficult to think of a family other than the Rodriguez family belonging to him. "I am not your brother."

"How I wish that statement were true. I've spent the last fifteen years living within the shadow cast by your disappearance, carrying the burden of being the eldest," Spence said. "I was the heir presumptive to Ravenleigh, our family's estate in England. Until we stumbled into you. Now I suppose that honor is yours."

"I don't want it."

"Whether or not you want it, British law will insist that you take it."

Lee unclenched his teeth. This man's arrogant presence made his jaws ache. "Why are you here?"

"Curiosity. I wanted to again look at the man who deepened the lines in my father's face and put the tears in my mother's eyes." He held Lee's gaze. "I love my parents—our parents. Your death is likely to destroy them."

"You should have thought of that before you conspired with Angela to betray me!"

Spence shot to his feet. "She was trying to save you, you bloody idiot! There were eleven of us. Do you honestly think you would have come away unscathed?"

"I prefer a bullet to a rope."

"What of your brothers here? Do they prefer a bullet to life?"

Lee darted a glance at his brothers before meeting Spence's stare. "I would not have let you kill them."

"With at least eleven rifles trained on the house, twice that many pistols loaded, and men who weren't afraid to use them, how in the bloody hell were you going to stop us?"

"I am very skilled with weapons."

"So are we," Spence said with deadly calm. "Now, tell me what would you have done?"

Lee backed up a step.

"To protect your sister and your youngest brother, what would you have done?" Spence asked.

Lee shook his head.

"To stop a single bullet from being fired into the house, what you would you have done?" Spence yelled.

"I would have surrendered!" Breathing heavily, Lee glared at the satisfied expression on Spence's face.

"Exactly," he said quietly. "Angela was afraid if we tried to take you at the house, your brothers would do something stupid. Considering the fact that you now are enjoying the company of two of them, I think her concerns were justified." He took a step closer. "You didn't see her when she made her decision to deliver you to us. I did. By God, she looked as though I'd plunged a rusty knife through her heart."

Lee's anger deflated, and his chest tightened until it ached. "She should not feel that way."

"Tell her that, not me."

"Where is she now?"

Spence shrugged. "It's a little after ten. She's probably in bed. If you don't give me any trouble for the remainder of the night, I'll send her over with breakfast in the morning."

Lee shook his head. "I do not want her to visit me in here."

"Understandable. Oh, by the way"—Spence reached inside his jacket—"Angela mentioned you were looking for a specific book, so while I was home, I looked around." He extended a dime novel toward Lee.

Holding his breath, unable to believe it, Lee took the offering and, in awe, trailed his fingers over the cover, over the words: *The Marshal Who Didn't Wear a Gun.* "I have looked everywhere for this book."

"And here you've owned a copy all along."

Lee lifted his gaze. "I don't understand."

"Father gave that to you years ago. Look inside."

Reverently, Lee folded back the cover and read the words. *"For my son Damon. May your journeys through life always lead you home. My love, Father."*

"Don't believe everything you read," Spence said.

Lee glanced up. "What?"

"Father has a tendency to laugh at the grandiose exploits they print about him."

Lee didn't care. He sat on the edge of the cot, still unable to believe that he was holding this book, that it was his. "Alejandro, Roberto, I am going to read to you."

As he began to read, he realized that he'd heard the story before, long ago.

Angela strolled along the boardwalk, missing the stalwart wooden Indian, longing for the cacophony of sounds that spilled out of her father's saloon. This town had a saloon, but she found no comfort in the din. Nothing was familiar, nothing calming. She concentrated on counting her steps. As long as she walked in a straight line, and pivoted at the end of the street, she should be able to find her way back to the hotel easily enough.

Not that she particularly wanted to return. She'd grown accustomed to sleeping with Lee, longed to be held by him again, to feel the strength in his arms, the warmth of his breath, the steady pounding of his heart beneath her palm while his scent wafted around her. Only he wasn't Lee; he was Damon.

She pressed a hand to her chest as the joy exploded within her, only to be shredded by the pain ripping through her. How could she have been so blind? She had fallen in love with a man four years younger than she was, a man who had been a boy whom she'd taken delight in, played with, and loved as an older sister loves a young sibling.

He had always seemed so familiar. Had her heart known all along?

And now, was her love that of a child for a child, or a woman for a man? Whichever it was, it was tearing her apart.

She had lost Damon once; she was losing him again. Her grief eclipsed what she'd felt before. She'd been a child then, but now she was a woman. She might lose him, but his family would not—neither family would lose him.

She would tell the authorities what she knew, and by God, she would make them believe it.

She would make them feel the agony she'd heard in Lee's voice when he awoke from the nightmare. Five years ago, he had been a boy, only fifteen, forced to choose between two evils—kill a man, or leave his sister to the man's brutally. How could anyone blame him for deciding to pull that trigger? But after talking at length with Kit, she'd come to understand his concern was the reason behind Lee shooting the man from behind. Obviously, she didn't know his entire story.

She understood his need to protect Juanita. Juanita would never recover from the incident by hiding away. She and Lee both had to face the past if they were to heal and have any chance at a satisfying future.

The boardwalk came to an end. She spun around and halted. She'd stopped counting her steps. How far had she strolled? It really didn't matter. Before she'd begun her walk, she'd run her fingers over the entrance to the hotel until she was certain she'd recognize the double doors with the glass embedded in them. She'd simply have to trail her fingers over each building as she passed, across windows and doors, until she reached the one she recognized.

Except for the far off music from the saloon, the town was incredibly quiet, like the eye of a hurricane waiting for the winds to be unleashed. Her heart began pounding. She wasn't lost. She skimmed her fingers across a smooth window, onto roughened wood. A stench, similar to that of spoiled eggs, assailed her. She stilled and cautiously inched her hand along the wood. It hit a barrier. Coarse, hairy skin that sent images screaming through her mind of rough handling, harsh breathing—

"Little lady, we got us some unfinished business."

His brothers had drifted off to sleep, but Lee continued to read about his father's exploits. His father. He thought it was only just beginning to sink in that Kit Montgomery was truly his father. He had thought Fate cruel, and perhaps it still was, but it had also given him a gift. Bits of faded memory that began to fill the emptiness that had been a part of him for so long.

Cartwright had returned to finish out the night watch. Spence had left, leaving Lee to wonder whether or not he might have turned out as polished and refined if he had not been playing a fifteen-year game of hide and seek. He'd never known his beginnings, but with the Rodriguez family he'd always felt as though he knew his roots. They'd taken hold the first time Maria Rodriguez had embraced him. They'd embedded themselves deeper into the fabric of their love many times after the first time Juan Rodriguez had called him "son," the first time Lee and Alejandro had gotten into a scuffle and Lee had won, bloodying Alejandro's nose in the process. He had expected the family to turn him away then. Instead, they'd only held him more tightly.

The far door banged open, and Lee came off the cot as Montgomery stormed into the room, Bainbridge limping in his wake.

"It seems we at last know your brother's magnificent plan," Montgomery said, as he thrust a slip of paper through the bars.

Lee quickly read the words. "I've got Raven's whore. Deliver him to the hanging tree or she dies." He shook his head. "Jorge would never call her that."

"Shelby then?" Montgomery asked.

Lee plowed his hand through his hair, searching the recesses of his memory . . . his gut tightened into a painful knot. "One of the men he hired to capture me thought Angela was my whore and attacked her. Shelby might have had the man do this so he could convince you to deliver me where he wants me."

"Where is this hanging tree?" Bainbridge asked.

Lee darted a glance at Alejandro, who blanched. "It is on our land, near what remains of our house. It is a giant oak. The one from which they hanged our father and brother. The one from which Shelby wishes to hang me."

Chapter 22

Lee paced the cell impatiently, every nerve ending on edge, his anger roiling out of him, shimmering around him. He desperately wanted to plow his fist into something, and had considered hitting the brick wall, but once he figured a way out of here, he would need his hand to hold a gun.

Leaving Bainbridge and Cartwright behind, Montgomery had left to search for the sheriff. Lee could not imagine that finding him would serve any purpose.

"How did they manage to get Angela? Were you not watching her?" he asked Bainbridge.

"I can only assume that she was taking one of her infamous midnight strolls."

"You really must break her of the habit of going out at night alone."

"She is more stubborn than her mother, and I wouldn't change either one of them, even if I had the power to do so."

"But you see what happens when she goes out at night."

"Yes, she ages me by ten years, but to cage her in . . . she would wither away and die like a flower hidden from the sun. Then my heart would break. As much as it hurts to give my daughters freedom, it would hurt more to lose them completely." Bainbridge held Lee's gaze. "You need to make your peace with Kit."

"He has a son."

"He has two. And you have two fathers. You won't betray those who raised you if you accept back into your life those who first loved you," Angela's father said in a low voice.

"No, but I'll carry them all to the gallows with me."

The door opened and Montgomery strode in, followed by Spence, whose hair stuck up on the side where sleep creases marred his face. Angela's mother also came into the room. Bainbridge had told Lee that she'd found the note on the floor scant inches from the door when someone's knocking had awakened her.

"We couldn't locate the sheriff," Montgomery said. "Can you draw us a map to the ranch?"

Lee glared at him. "No."

Bainbridge took a step toward him. "They are threatening to kill her!"

"Which is the reason you must let me out of here."

"So Shelby can kill you?" Montgomery asked.

"Better me than her. I am destined to hang anyway. At least let some good come from my death."

Montgomery averted his gaze, and Lee watched him swallow hard as though he fought to accept that his son was lost to him once again.

"Can't you round up a posse of men?" Angela's mother asked.

Montgomery shook his head. "I've made inquiries, Jessye. Shelby did a thorough job of convincing people of this town that the Rodriguez family was rotten to the core and deserved what they got." He looked ashamed as he admitted, "There were times when I almost believed it myself. I don't think they'll help us."

"Not even to save a young woman?" she asked.

"They'll believe we're on a fool's errand. Harry, Shelby told you he'd hired bounty hunters. Any idea how many?"

"Eight," Lee said quickly. "Eight were following us."

Bainbridge glanced around. "Those aren't bad odds against us."

"He'll probably have some of his ranch hands there as well as the sheriff. It is me he wants. So you take me there, exchange me for Angela, and then you go. Before the unpleasantness starts."

Montgomery quirked a brow. "Unpleasantness? Good God, lad, he's going—"

"I know what he is going to do!" Lee barked. "Talking about it will not change it. All it will do is delay us and give you less time to get Angela away. I do not want her near enough to hear . . ." He shook head. "I do not want her anywhere near there."

Montgomery gave a brisk nod. "Very well, then. I suppose we have no choice. We'll give Shelby what he wants."

With her ankles bound together and her hands tied behind her back with rough hemp that bit into her wrists, Angela sat huddled in a corner. Her fingers had grown numb. She could feel the heat of a lantern and considered trying to roll toward it, but her captor was nearby. Not the man who had taken her, but another, the man he worked for. Vernon Shelby.

He'd introduced himself with menacing glee, and when she'd spit at him, he'd hit her. Her cheek still smarted and she felt certain she would have a bruise, possibly a blackened eye.

They were using her to lure Lee, and she couldn't think of any way to stop them. She could only hope that her parents would realize that she'd never forgive herself if she was the one responsible for this man harming him. Why couldn't she ever find a way to save him?

She heard the strike of a match and the slow drawing in of breath. The sweet scent of a cigar filled the air.

"They should be arriving any minute now," Shelby said.

"You can't possibly think the Rangers will simply hand Raven over to you."

"Oh, they'll serve him to me on a silver platter. If they don't, I'll hang you in his place."

Escape seemed impossible. Insects that chirped merrily at night were fading into silence. Dawn, she was certain, was hovering. Her jaw tingled and she swallowed. She had to give the appearance of being strong, even though she felt ill. Why couldn't she enjoy her midnight strolls in peace? If she survived this predicament, if Lee survived, she'd never take another walk.

"Do you know why he killed your son?"

"I don't care why he killed him. I only care that he did, and now he's going to pay for his actions."

"You killed his father and brother—"

"They stole my cattle! A man has to protect what's his."

She heard determination in his voice, and something even more frightening. He believed his own lies. Arguing with him would be fruitless, striving to absolve Lee would do no good.

Her heart leapt into her throat as she heard a commotion beyond the walls. No, no, please don't let Lee have come, her mind screamed. Please.

A heavy lumbering tread echoed around her.

"Let me go, you great ape," a woman ordered.

Then came rapid steps and a thump, as though someone had been shoved aside and fallen. Rapid breathing.

"Found her sneaking around outside," the man said.

"I was not sneaking around," the woman insisted.

"Christine, what in the hell are you doing here?" Shelby asked. "Visiting that damn grave again?"

Christine Shelby.

"What are *you* doing here?" Christine asked. "And what are you doing with this woman?"

"Taking care of some unfinished business. Ezra, tie her up. Then get your boys situated. I don't want any mistakes this time."

"Tie me up? Are you insane?" Christine shrieked.

Angela listened to the woman's struggles and knew they would be in vain. Christine fell against her.

"Father, you can't do this!"

"Keep quiet or I'll gag you. Ezra, let's go."

Christine banged her head against the wall. "Damn it, damn it, damn it."

A familiar rose fragrance wafted toward Angela. She turned her head toward the woman. "Your perfume."

"We're prisoners in the burned out shell of a house and you have an interest in my perfume?"

"I've smelled it before."

"Not likely. My father has it specially made in France," she mumbled distractedly, her clothing rasping as she apparently twisted. "Damn it! He knotted them too tightly."

"*You* know Lee Raven."

She ceased her efforts. "I beg your pardon?"

Angela's heart thundered. "Lee left for a while and when he came back he was wearing your perfume on his clothes."

"Oh, my God. Are you the woman he kidnapped, the one who convinced him that revenge wasn't the answer?"

"I don't know that I convinced him of anything."

"Why does my father have you?"

"You don't know?" Angela asked.

"I don't know anything. I've been away. Lee had told me that it was time to let go of the past and lead our own lives. I just wanted to come back one last time—to say a final good-bye to Ramon. What *is* going on here?"

Angela sighed. "It's a long story." She explained as quickly as she could all that had happened since she'd betrayed Lee. "Now your father wants to exchange me for Lee."

"Damon will come," Christine said with resignation. "I mean Lee—"

"I know who he is. I just haven't been able to think of him as . . . 'Damon.' " She shifted around, her back aching, her neck stiff. "Can you turn so we can put our backs together? Maybe I can untie you. I've been struggling for so long that I've only managed to tightened the knots on my rope, but maybe yours won't be so hard to untie. My hands are a little numb, but I'm used to doing things by touch."

They shifted, scooted, and bumped against each other until Angela could touch Christine's hands.

"Can you tell anything?" Christine asked impatiently.

"There's three knots."

Christine released a sigh of frustration. "It'll take forever to get me untied."

"Then I'd better get started," Angela said. With so little mobility, she found the task difficult. And her fingers often refused to cooperate.

"Do you love him?" Christine asked softly. "Do you love Damon?"

Did she love Damon? She loved the boy he'd been. She loved Lee Raven. Could she honestly say that she loved Damon Rodriguez? Yes. But did she love Damon Montgomery? Did she even know him? Because if all went as she hoped, if all her efforts bore fruit, he would again become Damon Montgomery, heir presumptive to Raven-leigh. He would step back into the role he had been born to, travel a path that would take him away from her.

"Yes," she whispered. "I love him." Enough to let him go.

She tugged on the knots. "I can't get a good hold." She twisted for more leverage. Her foot hit something and she heard a pop. "What was that?"

"Oh, my God," Christine wailed. "The lantern!"

Stretched out on his stomach a good distance away, Lee studied the charred remains of the house that had sheltered him, where a family had nurtured and loved him. His chest tightened. If he was going to die, it was good that it would be here, where most of his pleasant memories resided. Even the nightmares couldn't erase them.

He and the others had left their horses and crawled here on their bellies, every man armed. Montgomery had released his brothers so they could accompany them. Bainbridge, Spence, Cartwright, and the other Ranger were here as well.

"There aren't many places that provide cover," Spence whispered.

"Probably a few men are in the barn, one or two are in what remains of the house, and some might be hiding behind a tree. The rest are probably on their bellies like us," Lee said. The house had not been completely destroyed because a heavy rain had begun to fall, as though nature mourned and wept over the brutality of man.

"If we wait until dawn to go in, our chances of survivin' are gonna be less than a hen's at a meetin' of coyotes," Cartwright said.

"You're quite right, Sean, we can't wait. We'll have to make our move now," Montgomery said.

"No one is making a move. You are taking me in, then you are taking Angela out."

"You don't honestly expect me to hand you over to that man?"

"You have no choice," Lee said, grateful his voice sounded flat, convincing. "Look around you. There is nowhere to hide. We have no idea how many men there are. We could try to sneak around, pick them off one by one—but it only takes one of us making a mistake, creating a noise, being spotted . . . Shelby will carry out his threat and kill Angela. It is not worth the risk. One death or many deaths. That is the way of it. You accept one death."

The respect that filled Montgomery's eyes was so strong that even the shadows of the night could not hide it. It unsettled Lee to know his words had touched this man.

"I must say, Juan Rodriguez did a splendid job of raising you," Montgomery said, holding his gaze.

"You provided him with a good foundation on which to build." It was the closest he could come to admitting what Kit Montgomery had given him, as much as he dared to reveal. If he gave in to the emotion with which his heart was thundering, he didn't know how he'd find the courage to let go of what he'd just obtained in order to face what awaited him. "Let's get the horses."

He turned away before his face exposed his emotions. A man did not need the memory of his son mourning for all that might have been—and all that never had been.

A woman screamed. Lee swung back around and fell flat to the ground. Another cry echoed from the house, its pitch different from the first. Two women? Shelby had two women inside the house?

He saw flames sprouting up behind a window. "There's a fire!" he yelled, before jumping to his feet and drawing his guns from his holster.

A terrorized shriek ripped through the air as a bullet whizzed past his head. Firing with a gun in each hand, he dove to the ground, rolled while bullets ricocheted around him spitting dirt into his face, lunged to his feet, and, with legs churning, raced like a madman to the house.

Something bit into his side as he neared the house. The flames were dancing wildly, climbing higher.

Clutching his guns, he tucked his arms in close and leapt through the window at the side of the house. Glass shattered around him as he landed on the floor. "Angela!"

"Lee!"

Ducking low, Lee began to make his way through the front room, his eyes burning from the thick and heavy smoke created by the twisting, writhing fire meticulously devouring what remained in its path. "Angela!"

"Lee! This way!"

"Stay where you are! Just keep calling to me!"

He worked his way through the house, dodging falling debris. Her voice faded in and out as she coughed and gagged.

He staggered into what had been his parent's bedroom and found her and Christine on their side, inching forward. Tears streamed along their blackened faces as they gasped for air. Tossing the guns aside, he drew his knife from its scabbard and sliced through Christine's bonds. "Get out!"

Nodding, she scrambled to her feet and dashed through the doorway. Lee turned to Angela. He sawed the knife through the thick rope at her feet. He rolled her onto her stomach and cut through the ropes securing her wrists. Fire licked at her skirt. "Lie still!" he ordered as he stood and began to stomp on the flames.

When the last died, he reached for her. An explosion ripped past his ear. He spun around.

Shelby stood in the doorway, gun drawn, eyes dancing as wildly as the flames. "Drop the knife or I'll kill her!"

Doing as ordered, Lee began to slowly move away from Angela. "Let her go, Shelby. She has nothing to do with this."

He ducked as debris fell. Shelby fired. Angela screamed. Lee jerked his gaze to her. She sat up, breathing heavily. He could see no blood.

The heat was growing unbearable, the wall of flames closing in. He turned his attention back to Shelby. "Let her go. She is nothing to you."

Shelby's smile grew. "But she's everything to you, isn't she, Rodriguez? Beg me. Drop to your knees and beg me like my son must have begged for mercy."

The bile rose in Lee's throat, his chest tightened. He'd never in his life begged for anything or anyone. He went down on his knees and lifted his gaze to Shelby. "I'm begging you, let her go." His voice grated like fine wood rubbed over sandpaper. "She is blind. Let me get her out of here, and I give you my word that I'll put the noose around my neck myself."

A gunshot tore through the air. As though incredibly surprised, Shelby looked down at the bright red splotch blossoming on his shirt. Then he crumpled to the ground.

Lee turned to Angela. Her hand shaking uncontrollably, she still held the gun. "Is he dead?" she rasped.

He pried the gun from her fingers and lifted her into his arms. With the flames nipping at him, Angela clinging to him, he rushed forward, burst outside, staggered forward, and dropped to his knees on the ground.

"Angela!" her father cried.

As gently as he could, Lee laid her on the ground. "Angela," he rasped.

"I'm all right." Tears welled in her eyes, and she pressed her trembling hand to her mouth. "I had to kill him."

"I know." He pressed a quick kiss to her forehead as her father struggled to the ground and took her in his arms.

Before anyone could stop him, he rushed back into the burning house.

Chapter 23

"That was the damnedest, stupidest thing I've ever seen!" Montgomery yelled. "What in the bloody hell did you think you were doing?"

Leaning against the hanging tree, Lee watched the sun bathe the earth in a brilliant hue of orange and gold. Apparently, Shelby's assassins, the best bounty hunters money could buy, had easily been subdued by Montgomery's group. A few of Shelby's hired guns were wounded, but no one had died, not even Shelby. Lee shook his head.

"I did not think there was enough blood for it to be a fatal wound. I know what it is to kill a man, to wonder every day if I could have done something differently. If I had left him, Angela would never have believed that she was not the one responsible for his death. Guilt is a terrible thing. It eats a man up from the inside out until nothing is left, until he becomes hollow and is only a shell of what he might have been. It would have destroyed her."

As though sensing that he had more to say, Montgomery held his silence. Lee dropped his gaze, studying the ground beneath his feet.

"That night when they came, my sister stood on the porch, her deep brown eyes big and round, her white nightgown in sharp contrast to the black night. She was twelve and Floyd Shelby took her. By the time I found them, he had already stolen her innocence, her childhood. But still I fought him. It felt so good to put my fist into his face. But I only hit him once.

"I had been shot. I was weak. And when he punched me in the side where I was wounded, my blood flowed—so damned much blood. He kept driving his fist into me. When I could not get up anymore, he went back to Juanita.

"He had removed his gun belt earlier. I saw his pistol beneath the tree. I wrapped my fingers around it, aimed at the back of his head, and squeezed the trigger." He lifted his gaze to Montgomery's and held it. "If I could have crawled, I would have for the satisfaction of looking in his eyes when I killed him. But I did not have the strength."

"And he almost died," Christine said quietly.

Montgomery turned and Lee glanced over his shoulder. Smiling softly, Christine stepped closer, rubbed his arm, and looked at Montgomery. "I found them. Floyd was dead. Damon was unconscious beneath the tree. And Juanita. Poor Juanita. If you ask her about that night, all she can tell you is that there were one thousand six hundred and forty-seven stars in the sky. She counted them while she lay there with the animal that my father called son."

She sighed and pressed her head against Lee's shoulder. "I helped Juanita nurse her brothers back to health, and then we hatched our crazy plan. We were so young, Captain Montgomery. Young, scared, and hurting. The only ones we trusted were each other. The sheriff had given my father carte blanche to do what he would. So as wrong as it might have been, we took the law into our own hands. We dug a grave for those who had died and one for Damon. Made markers. And decided that whatever money my father earned from this land, we would steal and put to good use to make up for all the bad that had been done. In their memory we've built a church, an orphanage, and two schools."

"You told Damon where the money was?" Montgomery asked.

She nodded. "My father, like his son, thought women have but one purpose in life. He had no qualms about discussing how much money he was placing in which bank while in my presence. Thinking that I didn't have the wherewithal to pay any attention to such matters. I would tell Damon, and he would take out the money to the penny. I think that's what made my father angriest. Lee Raven knew the amount down to the penny." She moved away from Damon and held out her hands. "If I have to go to prison for my part in our scheme, I will."

"No, you won't," Lee said. "It was my plan. I alone am responsible for what we did."

She rolled her eyes. "Damon—"

He held up a finger. "You have a son. He needs his mother to raise him, not an old spinster aunt."

"You have a son, Miss Shelby?" Montgomery asked.

Christine's face blossomed. "It's not Shelby, Captain. It's Rodriguez. Two weeks before my father attacked, Ramon and I got married with his family in attendance. He wanted me to tell my father, but I was afraid my father might . . . get angry. I seriously underestimated his wrath.

"When he regains consciousness, I think I'll break the news to him that he killed my husband, not my lover. And yes, Captain, I have a beautiful son with his father's dark eyes and hair. He lives with my mother's sister—although recently Damon convinced me that my son needed to be living with me. That's the reason I was here. To say good-bye to Ramon. I'm not sure where I'll go, but it's time I left the past behind. If I can find a lawman who isn't afraid of my father's reputation or influence and is willing to arrest him, I'm eager to testify against him in court."

"Mrs. Rodriguez, I arrested your father the minute he drew his first breath after Damon carried him out of the house."

*   *   *

Kneeling beside the grave, Angela slowly outlined the letters carved into the wooden marker. Damon.

What a strange set of events she'd set into play because of an innocent midnight stroll. She must have walked those streets of Fortune a thousand times with nothing of consequence happening. Yet somehow on that night that now seemed ages ago, fate had intervened and her path had crossed that of a man who had once been a boy whom she loved.

She had loved the child's smiles, his laughter, and his innocence.

She loved even more the man's smiles, laughter, and passion. Not only the passion he aroused in her with the touch of his lips or the skimming of his fingers, but his determination to repay the love of a family who had adopted him.

He didn't seem to realize that love collected no debts. That family extracted no payments. Because for a while, he had possessed neither love nor family. Because she had failed to protect him when he was a child.

Had she managed to save him now?

She heard the approach of his familiar footsteps, the beloved popping of his knees. Her heart constricted until it wept for what she might have had with Lee Raven, but would never have with Damon Montgomery.

She had found him, and in so doing, she had lost him.

"Angela, are you all right?"

She wasn't certain if she'd ever be all right

again. She desperately wanted his arms around her. She forced herself to nod. "How is Shelby?"

"He will live."

Tears welled in her eyes. "A part of me wishes he wouldn't, and another part is relieved. Even though I knew you'd killed Floyd Shelby, understood why . . . I didn't truly comprehend how difficult it must have been for a boy of fifteen . . . tonight, when your knife thudded to the floor, when I knew that you had completely surrendered to him, could feel his hatred, realized he was going to kill you . . . a part of me died. I remembered where I'd heard your guns fall earlier, close to me. My fingers were cold when I picked one up. I concentrated on the location of his voice . . . even though I knew I had no choice, I never expected it to be so damned hard to squeeze the trigger."

A sob broke free, and he drew her into his embrace, rocking her gently, whispering comforting words in Spanish.

"You told me once that you begged for nothing, for no one."

"But I would beg for you. I would die for you, Angela."

She tilted her face back. "I want you to live for me."

She heard him swallow hard before he pressed a kiss to her forehead. "I told Montgomery why I killed Floyd. I do not know if it will make a difference in my destiny . . ." With his thumb he wiped away a fallen tear. "But for you, *querida*, I will do anything. You have but to ask."

More tears surfaced. "Forgive me. Forgive me for losing you when you were a child."

He skimmed his knuckles across her cheek. "There is nothing to forgive."

"But what you've endured—"

"Angela," he interrupted softly. "Do you not remember our picnic? You told me then that Montgomery's son was named Damon, and I thought just for a fleeting moment, what if I had been that boy? And what if after I died, you found out?"

"Is that the reason you shared stories from your youth?" she asked, remembering the love he'd woven through the tales.

"I wanted you to know all my warm memories."

"But so much of your life has been filled with ugliness—"

"No, Angela. Most of it has consisted of beautiful moments that always shine more brightly than the darkest of days. For a while, I think I forgot. I got lost in the darkness, but then I stumbled across an angel whose smile lit up my heart. I love you, *querida*."

His mouth blanketed hers not with the urgency of the past, but with hope for the future. Slowly, leisurely, as though he had all the time in the world, he kissed her. She sank against him, relishing the sturdiness of his arms and the firm muscles that rippled as he deepened the kiss. She wanted to stay here forever, surrounded by his love.

But a warm wetness intruded as it soaked

through her dress. She pulled back. "What in the world is that?"

"I started bleeding again."

"You're wounded?" she asked, horrified. "Did I shoot you?" Had the bullet passed through him to get to Shelby?

"I do not know who shot me, but it was before I got to the house."

"You need to treat it."

"It is only a little thing."

"You have to tend it."

"I would rather tend to you," he said, and she heard the laughter in his voice.

"Lee—" She stopped and sat back on her heels. "I don't know what to call you."

"I think," he said quietly, "that Lee Raven rushed into the flames to rescue you. But Damon Montgomery carried you out."

They were putting their prisoners on their horses when Damon heard the rumble of wheels. A wagon bounced over the uneven ground. He narrowed his gaze trying to get a better look at the man and woman sitting on the bench seat. He could see a man in the back of the wagon and a small boy clutching the side.

"Who is it?" Montgomery asked.

"My family." With long strides, he started walking toward them. "Alejandro! Roberto! It's Jorge!"

Alejandro and Roberto hurried to catch up with him.

"What is he doing here?" Alejandro asked.

"Juanita is with him?" Roberto whispered.

Jorge brought the wagon to a halt. Eduardo helped Miguel clamber out and the boy hit the ground running. "Lee! Lee!"

Damon scooped him up and held him above his head. "Miguel, what are you doing here?"

"Jorge has a magnificent plan! I get to be Lee Raven!"

Shaking his head, Damon lowered him to the ground and crouched in front of him. "I don't think so, Miguel. I think you are Miguel Rodriguez, and that is who you should be."

As though he'd already forgotten Jorge's magnificent plan, he broke free of Damon's hold and rushed forward. "*Señorita!*"

Angela smiled sweetly and knelt in the grass. "Miguel."

He wound his arms around her neck, and she hugged him tightly.

"You did not say *adiós*," he chastised at her breach of etiquette.

Leaning back, she ruffled his hair. "I know. And I'm sorry."

"Is it your birthday yet?"

Her smile blossomed. "No, but maybe we can find another reason to have a *piñata*."

Damon's chest tightened with how incredibly lovely she looked sitting there with a child on her lap discussing all the different times when a *piñata* might be appropriate.

"I suppose we could have a *piñata* at a wedding," Alejandro murmured.

"*Sí*," he acknowledged. "We could." Damon turned on his heel and strode to the wagon. He smiled warmly at his sister and held up his arms. "Juanita."

Tears welled in her eyes, and she pressed a hand to her mouth. "I was afraid you would be dead."

He lifted her off the wagon, and rocked her gently while she wept.

"I was so afraid," she whispered.

"Shh. You do not have to be afraid."

"Angela told me how scared she had been of the dark, and I thought that perhaps she could teach me not to be frightened of the truth." Sniffling, she shuddered before leaning back and wiping the tears from her eyes. "I want to tell them."

He cradled her face. "You do not have to tell them, Juanita."

More tears surfaced. "I do not want you to hang."

"I seriously doubt he's going to hang, Miss Rodriguez," Montgomery said.

Gazing past him, she opened her mouth slightly. Damon stepped aside. "Juanita, this is my father." The word reverberated through him as he looked at Montgomery. It was the first time he'd acknowledged the man as such in his presence. The affirmation in his father's eyes made him wonder why he'd waited. "He is a just man, a fair man. You can trust him."

His father extended his hand toward Juanita.

"Take a walk with me, Miss Rodriguez, and I shall tell you the story of a little boy who became a man I'm proud and honored to call 'son.' "

Damon watched as she tentatively placed her hand within the larger one. His father smiled warmly before escorting her toward what remained of the house. This fire had completely destroyed it.

"He is your father?" Jorge asked.

Damon turned to his younger brother. "*Sí.*"

"How did that happen?"

"Jorge," Alejandro began, "I think it is time we talked to you about women."

Jorge's cheeks flamed red. "That part I know. But the rest of this—"

"Is a long story," Damon assured him. "But first we must talk to you about your magnificent plan. To tell Miguel he could be Lee Raven ... what were you thinking?"

"That was not my magnificent plan. It was Miguel's."

"Then what was *your* plan?" Alejandro asked.

Appearing embarrassed, Jorge twisted on the seat and pointed back. "It was Eduardo's plan."

Eduardo smiled. "I overheard Angela tell Juanita that a slow journey was better than no journey. So we decided to come home, slowly."

"How would that save Damon?" Roberto asked.

"We were going to chop down the hanging tree."

Alejandro shook his head. "There are other trees."

Eduardo's face registered disappointment. He was only fifteen, as old as Damon had been when he'd decided to become Lee Raven. He clapped his youngest brother on the back. "Eduardo, I think that *is* a magnificent plan."

Chapter 24

Damon was ready for the celebration to end. *Damon Montgomery.* He didn't know if he'd ever get used to the name or learn to respond to it. Both his families were with him in the small ballroom of the hotel.

Celebrating his unconditional pardon.

He had read stories of Kit Montgomery. Angela had told him Montgomery was influential.

Still, he'd had a difficult time breathing as, just that afternoon, he stood in the telegraph office and listened while the man behind the counter tapped out the steady staccato rhythm. Captain Christian Montgomery's request to the governor that an unconditional pardon be granted to Damon Montgomery, alias Damon Rodriguez, alias Lee Raven.

"We'll wait for a response," his father had told the clerk.

Damon had stood by the window, gazing out, wondering what he would do with the rest of his life, if he had one. When the tapping began less than an hour later, he'd closed his eyes and prepared himself to accept disappointment with honor. He thought only a refusal of the request could come that quickly. The tapping had stopped almost as soon as it had begun. He'd faced his father.

His father smiled broadly. "Granted."

Damon had stared at him. "That's it. That's all he had to say."

"It's all he needed to say."

"So it is over."

"For Lee Raven, yes. For Damon Montgomery, I hope it's just beginning."

So they'd come to the hotel where everyone had taken rooms, and everyone was waiting. Amid a round of cheers, toasts, and jubilation, Damon Montgomery was once again officially born.

His mother had wept as she held him close to her. Even his new sister, Mercy, whom he had just met, had cried. She strongly resembled her mother in both appearance and temperament.

Angela seldom left his side, but she was quiet and pensive, and he wondered if it was difficult for her to feel comfortable where there was so much noise. As much as he wanted to spend time with his family, he wanted to be alone with Angela.

Damon's gaze swept over the room. Juanita sat in a large stuffed chair in a distant corner, away from everyone, curled around Miguel, who sat on her lap asleep. She had explained to Damon that she wanted to be Miguel's mother, not his sister, to know the joy of motherhood. He had been with her when she'd tried to explain the truth to Miguel. The boy had accepted her words, but Damon didn't think the child truly understood all the implications. He was too young, too innocent, which was no doubt for the best.

But what would happen when he grew older and wanted to know of his father? What would she tell him then? And how would he feel when he learned his uncle had killed the man responsible for his existence?

Damon narrowed his eyes as he spotted Spence on the other side of the room—watching Juanita. He didn't like the speculative expression on his brother's face. He brought Angela's fingers to his lips and kissed them lightly. "Excuse me for a moment."

In long strides, he crossed the room to Spence. "Stop looking at Juanita like that."

Spence jerked back as though he'd been asleep and suddenly awakened. "Like what? Like I find her intriguing? Like I think she's beautiful?"

"Like you want to bed her."

Spence's face burned beet red. "Are you always so blunt?"

"She has no interest in men."

"Yes, I can see that."

"She has had a hard life."

"Yes, I can well imagine that having you for a brother was a constant torment."

"That is not what I meant."

"I know what you meant. You and I are not that different," Spence said quietly. "The veneer of civilization is quickly and easily stripped away when someone we love is threatened. On the off chance that you're not as smart as you appear, I think you should be aware that Father never would have let Shelby hang you. He might have gone along with your part of the plan that allowed us to exchange you for Angela so we could get her out of harm's way, but that noose never would have gone around your neck."

"He might have had no choice."

"No offense intended, but Father possesses wisdom and experience that you and I have yet to attain. That you were willing to die so readily impressed even me. But I assure you it never would have come to that." A corner of his mouth quirked up. "By the way, congratulations on the pardon."

"Even if it means you are forced to give up your inheritance?"

Spence shrugged as though shooing away a pesky fly. "It was mine by default. You were born to it. It's the English way. I have no quarrel with that. Ravenleigh. Lee Raven. Who would have thought?"

With a simple turn of his head, Spence dismissed him and returned to studying Juanita. "Introduce me to her."

"You haven't met her?"

"Not officially, no. Besides, you owe me."

"Oh, *sí*, for the book. *Gracias*."

"Not for the book. Once the excitement died down a bit, I rode to the county courthouse to check on deeds. I located the original land grant. No doubt about it. It's Rodriguez land."

Relief swamped Lee. Everything was finally falling into place. "I do owe you."

"Then introduce me to your sister."

For a full minute he debated the wisdom of the request. Juanita seemed so isolated, withdrawn. "I will probably regret this."

He crossed the room with Spence dogging his heels like a puppy who anticipated being tossed a bone. Juanita looked up and smiled shyly as he approached. She shifted in the chair and Miguel awakened. He smiled brightly. "Lee!"

Damon knelt in front of Juanita. "Uncle Damon, remember?"

"Oh, *sí*. I forgot."

He ruffled the boy's hair. "We will probably all forget for a while."

Juanita's eyes widened with alarm when Spence knelt beside Damon. Damon was more convinced than ever that this idea was a bad one. Spence poked him in the ribs with his elbow.

"Juanita, this is my new brother, Spence." He had expected Spence to do something stupid like try to take Juanita's hand. Instead, Spence just smiled warmly.

"It's a pleasure to meet you," he said with sincerity. "Who is this handsome lad?"

Juanita shifted her gaze to Damon, then to

Miguel, and finally to Spence. "He...he is...
my son."

"What a fortunate lad, to have such a lovely
mother. What is that behind your ear, Miguel?
Dirt?" Spence slipped his hand behind Miguel's
head and brought it forward holding a coin.

"A peso!" Miguel laughed and slapped his
hand over his ear.

"What a funny place to keep your money,"
Spence said as he handed Miguel the coin. "Best
to keep it in your pocket, I think."

"Do you know another trick?" Miguel asked.

"I know many tricks. If your mother will allow
you to come with me, I'll show you how to make
cookies disappear."

"Can I?" Miguel asked Juanita. "Can I go with
him?"

Juanita looked at Damon and he gave her a
quick nod of assurance.

"Sí," Juanita said quietly. "You can go."

Miguel scrambled off her lap and slipped his
hand into Spence's as he stood. Spence winked at
Juanita. "I won't keep him long."

Damon watched them walk toward the table
laden with refreshments.

"He seems nice," Juanita said softly.

"I think he is a good man." He took her hand.
"Do not be so afraid, Juanita. Most men are not
like Floyd Shelby."

She nodded. "I know. It is just hard sometimes
to remember that." She gave him a tiny smile.
"You are going away."

"Not for a while yet. But even when I go away, I'll never stop being your brother."

Damon Montgomery, with the woman he loved at his side, stepped onto the boardwalk outside the hotel.

He heard a movement and turned. Standing in a corner, Christine smiled at him. "It's been a long journey, Damon."

"*Sí*. We are celebrating inside. You should join us."

"I think I will."

"I can't thank you enough for telling Kit everything," Angela said softly.

"We should have gone to the authorities long ago, but since the sheriff is one of my father's lapdogs, everything seemed hopeless. We assumed the murder of Ramon and his parents would go unavenged. We were so young."

"What will you do now?" Angela asked.

"I have a small home near one of the schools. I'll probably teach." Reaching out, she touched Damon's cheek. "I brought someone I'd like you to meet."

Tightening his hold on Angela's hand, Damon nodded. He followed Christine to the end of the boardwalk where a buggy was parked. "Between the buildings, a little boy is tossing a ball to a young woman," Damon explained to Angela.

"Mary is his governess," Christine said.

"What does he look like?" Angela asked.

"Black hair and dark brown eyes," Damon said. "He is my brother's son."

"Raymond," Christine called out.

Damon watched with an ache in his chest as the boy smiled and ran to his mother.

"Raymond, I want you to meet Mr. Montgomery."

"Howdy." The boy beamed up at him.

Damon crouched, aware of his knees popping and his heart bursting. "You can call me Uncle Damon."

"Are you my uncle?"

"*Sí*. You have many more uncles, and we all have many stories to tell you about your father."

"Mama says he was a good man."

"He was the best of us," Damon acknowledged quietly.

Damon stood on the boardwalk outside the hotel, staring at the moon. The celebration had finally ended, with everyone retiring to his or her room. He knew he should go to bed as well, but he'd needed a few moments of solitude to sort through events, to contemplate the serpentine path he'd traveled to arrive at his present destination.

He could only remember fragments of his life before he'd been abducted. He'd been happy. The events that had led him to the Rodriguez family were vague. He didn't dwell on them because he was convinced they were better forgotten. He preferred to acknowledge that he'd been fortunate to know the love of two good families.

He spotted a silhouette wandering through the darkness, a familiar shadow. His father approached, stepped onto the boardwalk, leaned against the railing, and looked at the moon. "Couldn't sleep," he said simply.

"Neither could I," Damon admitted.

"I like the Rodriguez family," he said.

"They are good people, but I have been searching the recesses of my mind for long-ago memories, memories before I became Damon Rodriguez, and I can find so little," he said quietly.

"You were a good boy, a joy to me and your mother. And you are again. Your life will change considerably when you inherit Ravenleigh."

Ravenleigh. How had the name become so jumbled in his child's mind?

"My life has changed before. I can adjust. I have much to learn before I will be ready to become the earl, however."

"We have lots of time to teach you. I think your mother is rather looking forward to having you here for a while. Well, I'd best be off to bed. She doesn't go to sleep until I turn in, and she needs her rest." He moved toward the door.

"Father?"

His father stilled, and Damon felt the expectancy shimmering on the air between them. From the moment he'd realized who Montgomery thought he was, Damon had avoided addressing him, had failed to recognize his place in Damon's life. "I remember a silver star . . ."

"I cut it from the bottom of a tin can. Not an uncommon practice among law enforcement officials who needed a symbol of their authority. I believe you wanted to be a sheriff."

"I wanted to be like you."

He heard his father swallow hard. "It's better to be your own man. I think you've succeeded at that."

"When I was boy and you had to leave, I was afraid that you wouldn't come back," he rasped.

"I always came back, didn't I?"

"Do you remember what you'd do when you returned?"

His father's arms were suddenly around him, and Damon clung to him as he had when he was a child and his father had returned home after being gone so long. "I love you, Damon."

"I love you more." He spoke the refrain he had repeated so often in his childhood.

He felt a tremor ripple through his father. "Dear God, but it's good to have you back, Damon."

He was lost, so lost, stumbling in the darkness, searching for home . . . warmth, security, love . . . but they remained beyond reach. Perhaps he didn't deserve them.

Shaking, cold . . . blood, too damned much blood. Screams, cries . . . tears. An explosion. The loss of all his dreams.

He swirled through the haze until he saw them, waiting for him, arms outstretched, eager to welcome him home. But he couldn't go home, not now—not after what he had become.

Then she was there. His angel, holding out her hand, beckoning him forward. He slid his hand into hers.

Damon awoke with a start. Something was

wrong. He wasn't bathed in sweat. He wasn't breathing harshly. He touched his cheeks. No tears. Yet he was sad.

He scrambled out of bed, snatched his britches from a nearby chair, and put them on. He crossed the room and walked into the hallway. It was quiet, so quiet.

He crept down the corridor to the room where Angela slept. Gingerly, he turned the knob, grateful it was unlocked. Tiptoeing into the room, he closed the door behind him. Like a shadow, he glided to the bed.

Angela lay on her back, her hair fanned out across the pillow, the moonlight dancing over her face. He'd almost lost her. First because of his pride, then because of his past. But she was his future. He knew that as surely as he knew his name.

He unfastened his britches, shucked them off, slid beneath the sheets, and drew her against his body. She sighed and burrowed into him. He rained kisses over her face. A thousand little kisses, then larger kisses until he wanted more. With his tongue, he tasted her. So sweet.

"Damon?" she asked groggily.

"*Sí.*"

Moaning low, she undulated her hips against his. Passion ignited within him.

"What are you doing here?" she asked.

If she didn't know, then he needed to work harder at being a lover. He lowered his mouth to hers, kissing her slowly, gently, as though she'd been spun from moonbeams, delicate and fragile.

He wanted to focus all his energies, all his talents on the woman who had stolen his heart . . . shortly after he had stolen her. With deft hands, he made short work of removing her nightgown until she lay beneath him, her flesh against his.

She sighed softly as he trailed his hot mouth over her body, licking, suckling, teasing. She ran her hands over his broad shoulders, along his strong back as long as she could reach them—until he was skimming his lips over her thigh, along her calf. First one leg and then the other. "*Querida*, you did not answer my question."

"What question?" she mumbled.

"When we were by the river that last morning, I asked you a question. You did not give me your answer."

"Question . . ."

"Will you marry me?"

She gasped and her eyes flew open. "We need to talk."

Hers was not exactly the response he'd been hoping for. She'd been unusually quiet most of the afternoon and evening. He knew she was happy about the turn of events, but something was bothering her. He knew her too well not to recognize that fact. "I am a man of many talents. I can kiss you and listen at the same time." He nibbled on her earlobe.

"I can't . . . I can't talk when you're doing that."

He smiled. "Then don't speak, just moan . . . ow!" He grabbed her wrist. "Why do you yank my hair like that?"

"Because I want your undivided attention."

Obviously fully awake now, she shoved him aside, sat up, and swung her legs over the side of the bed. She clasped her hands together in her lap.

Trepidation sliced through him. Something was very wrong. He eased off the bed and crouched in front of her. "What's troubling you, *querida*?"

"Do you know how old you are?" she asked.

He shrugged, a movement totally wasted on her. "Twenty."

"Do you know how old I am?"

"Why are you giving me mathematical problems when we could be making love?"

"I'm twenty-four. Four years older than you!"

"*Sí*. I can do the calculation."

"Oh, Damon!" She bolted off the bed and waved her hand through the air. "A woman is usually younger than a man."

Damon slowly unfolded his body. "Is that the law?"

She came to an abrupt halt and faced him. "No, but that's the way it usually is. Your mother is younger than your father. My mother is younger than my father. It's the natural order of things."

"I don't understand what you are saying."

"I can't marry you."

"Angela, I love you."

"You can't."

He watched tears surface. "But I do," he said.

Despair filled her eyes. "We should have never fallen in love. Oh, Damon, you're only twenty years old! You're so young. You haven't had time to sow wild oats or know what you want from life."

"Are you more bothered by the fact that I am twenty than by the fact that you are older?"

She sighed. "Yes."

He took her hand. "Come here."

She resisted. "Damon—"

"Come here. Now I want to talk." He led her back to the bed. "Sit."

He knelt in front of her, took both her hands in his, and pressed them against his face. "Angela, look at me."

"Damon—"

"Look at me." She slowly traced her fingers over his features. "Mine is not the face of a man who has only known twenty years of life. I have seen more, experienced more than most men do in eighty. I am really a very old man."

She gave him a tremulous smile. "Damon, I don't think you realize how your life is about to change. As the heir to Ravenleigh, you could marry any woman you wanted."

"I plan to marry the *only* woman I want."

She squeezed her eyes shut.

"Don't you love me?" he asked quietly.

She opened her eyes, pools of sadness that he couldn't understand. "With all my heart."

"Do you remember when I told you about the angel who would visit me when I was a boy?" he asked tenderly.

She nodded and a tear rolled down her cheek.

He framed her face between his large hands.

"She was you, Angela. You were my angel when I was a boy, and now that I am a man." He eased her down onto the bed. He kissed her temple, each cheek, and the tip of her nose before settling his mouth against her lips. She was incredibly precious, and he wanted her to realize that she would be forever.

Too many nights had passed without her sharing his bed, and the temptation to sate his own hunger was strong, but his desire to pleasure her was more powerful.

While he deepened the kiss, he grazed his fingers along the length of her body. She curled against him much as she had the first time she'd slept in his arms, as though he provided solace.

He planned to give her everything—the warm hues of dawn and the calming shades of a sunset. He'd take care to always mention colors and fill her world with the rainbow of his love.

Holding her hip, he pressed her more solidly against his hardness and groaned low as the pleasure speared him. How could she possibly think he would consider giving her up because of his youth?

As far as he was concerned, he'd been fortunate to find her as early in life as he had. The many years stretching before them held exhilarating promise.

And the nights. They would have more nights than they could count, each one ending as this one was beginning . . .

Easing her onto her back, he trailed his mouth along her neck and dipped his tongue into the hollow at the base of her throat. She dug her fingers into his shoulders, as though she needed a tether, but he wanted her to fly.

He circled his tongue around her nipple, relishing her gasp and the shudder that rippled through her.

She outlined the muscles of his back, touched his side, and stilled. "Your wound—"

"—is nothing," he assured her. Although he'd bled profusely, the bullet had only creased his flesh, and a doctor had closed the gash with a few stitches.

He returned his attention to her soft, pliant breast. Suckling gently, he listened as she moaned. She rubbed her foot up and down his calf while she slipped her hand between their bodies and stroked him, stirring the banked embers of his desire into a roaring blaze.

Cradling her face, he ordered, "Say my name."

She skimmed her fingertips along the grooves of his face. "Damon."

He lowered his mouth, kissing her voraciously as he joined his body to hers, taking pleasure, granting pleasure. He'd never possessed her with such absolute freedom because always before the shadows of his past had hovered around them.

But his lady had bathed them in the light of her love until they no longer existed.

Increasing the tempo of his movements, he tightened his hold on her and buried his face in the abundant thickness of her hair. He was aware of her body growing taut beneath his, her short gasps, her fingers digging into his buttocks—

Her back arched as she cried out his name. "Damon!"

He gave in to his own raging needs, one last thrust spilling his seed into her. With his limbs quaking, he smiled with pure male satisfaction and nuzzled her neck.

Lifting himself, he lovingly gazed down at her. "Don't ever doubt that we were meant to be together."

"I want you to be certain," she said drowsily.

"If you could look into my eyes, you would know that I love you, Angela, with all my heart and all my soul, and I always have."

Epilogue

The moon glistened over the waves as they rolled on to the shore. Standing barefoot in the Galveston sand, Damon Montgomery contemplated the twelve months that had passed since he'd first acknowledged his name and his original family.

It was with a great deal of satisfaction that Damon had testified at the trial of Vernon Shelby. More satisfying was the verdict of guilty. Less satisfying was the sentence: twenty-seven years for each murder.

Damon tried to find contentment in the knowledge that Shelby would die within prison walls and that the years would pass slowly, giving him a chance to reflect on all he'd instigated that fateful night.

Angela, Damon, and his brothers had visited

the schools, church, and orphanage that Christine had built with the money that they'd taken from Shelby's accounts.

Juanita had declined the invitation to go with them. They had rebuilt the *hacienda*, and she wanted to remain there, working to make it "home," but Damon feared she was simply withdrawing more from the world around her. Miguel had begun to call her "Mama," and she only seemed happy within the house when Miguel was with her.

Sheriff Evans had been summarily removed from office. Roberto Rodriguez was hired to replace him, a quiet man with a steady temperament. Damon knew he would serve the town well and expected to read of his adventures someday in a dime novel.

Within the church built in memory of his family, Damon had taken Angela as his wife. Eight months later, she'd given birth to a son: John Christian Harrison Montgomery. At this moment, Johnny was in a nearby cottage being spoiled by two sets of grandparents and too many uncles and aunts to count.

Spence Montgomery was attending the university where Damon had once planned to study. Damon was about to embark on what he knew would be the first of many journeys that would take him and his family to Ravenleigh, where he would begin learning the intricacies of managing the estate Spence had thought he would one day inherit.

So many twisted strands of their lives were woven together that Damon wondered if it was fate's perverse way of building strong bonds between families.

"Are you going to stay out here all night?" Angela asked quietly behind him.

Reaching back, he tugged her forward, wrapped his arms around her, and settled his chin on the top of her head. "How is it that you can always find me?"

"Not always, Damon."

"Always, Angel. Perhaps not as quickly as you'd like, but you do manage always to find me."

He blanketed her mouth with his own, drawing her closely against his body. She clutched his shirt as he drank deeply, briefly sating an unquenchable thirst that would return the moment she left him. He inhaled her sweet scent, heard her soft whimper. As long as she drew breath, he knew that Damon Montgomery would always find his way home.